ROCK

the

BODYGUARD

NATALIE DEBRABANDERE

DEDICATION

For A.

ACKNOWLEDGMENTS

To all my readers:

Thank you for reading and reviewing in all the good places.

I appreciate you greatly!

CHAPTER 1

Angelina Cristoforetti, founder and CEO of Dagger Inc., a close protection firm based in Lewiston, looked up from her cup of coffee at the sound of a motorbike rumbling into the parking lot of the busy beach café. There was no need to check her watch as it beeped on the hour. Tristan Briggs, one of only two female operatives on her books, had yet to be two seconds late for any of their appointments. Angie watched her get off the sports bike, a beast of a thing that looked as if she would growl at you if you dared to stare too long, and stow her helmet on the side of the saddle. Briggs was in her standard uniform. Faded blue jeans, lace-up combat boots, and a leather jacket over a simple t-shirt which concealed the compact 357 Sig in the holster on her belt. As she made her way toward the terrace, she seemed oblivious of the many admiring glances that she received along the way from both men and women alike. Angie knew it was only a false impression. By the time she arrived at their table, Briggs would have memorized all their faces, and probably be able to tell her what each person was having for their lunch.

"Hello, Tris," Angelina greeted her.

Piercing green eyes met her brown ones and held intently.

"Angie." Tristan took the seat across from her. "Good to see you."

"You too. How are you?"

"Fine, thanks."

Tristan rarely elaborated beyond a single word when asked this kind of personal question, and Angelina had learned not to push for more unless it really mattered. She observed her now, as the former cop ordered herself a coffee; black, no sugar, and passed a hand over her shaved head. The jet-black stubble was thick enough to shade her skull, but not to grasp or hold. The bold hairstyle certainly suited her face, which was angular and lean with a strong jaw line, and often in sharp contrast with her attitude. Lately, elusive did not even begin to describe it.

"So," Tristan prompted as soon as her coffee was delivered and the waitress safely out of earshot. "You've got a new job for me?"

"Straight to the point, as ever," Angelina remarked.

"Might as well," Tristan shrugged. "Since you're paying for my time."

Angelina did not allow herself to be rushed. Briggs worked for her, indeed, and not the other way around. She watched her and the stuff that she probably thought she could hide. Casual acquaintances may not have noticed anything, or even dared to look, but Angie knew the woman. She knew her story. She could spot subtle signs of tension in her gaze and in the set of her shoulders. It was not hard for her to recognize that Tristan Briggs was not a woman at peace.

"Sure you're okay?" she asked in a lowered voice.

"Yes." Tristan's eyes flashed in warning. "Just not keen on forced R&R, that's all."

"Well, sorry about that," Angie smirked. "But as you know, by law, I have to give you some vacation time whether you like it or not. So, how was it?"

"Beyond boring."

"Did you do anything?"

Briggs regarded her with a mix of reluctant and suspicious frowning, as if she had just been tasked with explaining the meaning of life, the universe, and everything else.

"I went to the gym," she offered.

"Right," Angie sighed. "Forget I asked."

She would not inquire about the AA situation, and whether Briggs still attended weekly meetings. Eighteen months ago, this had been an express condition of her employment with Dagger. Angie had insisted on it despite Tristan's fury at the time, not to satisfy company policy but for Briggs' own safety. They never discussed the events of the night in question, which had led to the requirement. Bringing a potential breach of contract under the spotlight was not worth it at this point either. Briggs may be struggling a little, but at least she did have her drinking under control. How she stayed sober did not matter in the end, so long as she was.

"I need to work, Angie," she murmured, her eyes fixed onto the ocean in the distance.

It was as close as she might come to admitting a weakness, Angie knew, and even this short sentence clearly cost her. Angie was not interested in making her beg. She needed her in the job as well.

"I do have something for you," she nodded.

"Great," Tristan breathed in relief. "What is it?"

"Alys Huxley."

"Who?"

"Oh, for goodness' sake! Really?" Angie rolled her eyes impatiently. "What planet do you live on? *The* Alys Huxley? Come on!"

3

Briggs shrugged, a sexy grin tugging at the corners of her mouth. Now that they were discussing an upcoming job, instead of vacation that she never wanted in the first place, she appeared a lot more relaxed.

"The name rings a bell... Are you talking about the British reporter who covered the retreat of US troops from Afghanistan last year?"

"No, that's Hurley. Alys *Huxley* is an American singer."

"Wait a minute... You don't mean the Disney girl, do you?"

"She did perform a Disney movie theme song. It was several years ago but yes, that's exactly who I mean."

Right on cue, Briggs' fragile relaxation vanished in the blink of an eye, as well as her smile.

"Are you kidding?" she snapped.

"Of course not," Angelina said calmly. "Why would I?"

"Come on, Angie! My previous two assignments were close protection jobs for high-ranking diplomats at the US embassy in Iraq."

"Yes, and you aced them both. So?"

"Don't play games with me," Tristan growled. "You know damn well that I'm looking to take on the same sort of job. Front-line stuff. Meaningful. Not babysitting for a bubblegum pop star!"

Pissed-off looked good on Tristan Briggs, though Angelina refrained from commenting on it. She also did not mention the obvious to her. That she seemed to enjoy frontline kind of stuff, as she called it, the jobs which could turn deadly at any moment, a little too much for it to be healthy.

"I do realize it's not your usual fare, Tristan," she simply acknowledged. "But I think you'll be perfect for her, and I want you to take this assignment."

"Why? Is Huxley moving to Baghdad or something?"

"She's had a string of bad luck with close protection officers in recent times." Angie offered, ignoring the sarcastic question. "Her last bodyguard was caught attempting to sell nude photos of her to the tabloids."

"Son of a bitch." Briggs snarled. "How old is that kid?"

"Twenty-eight." Angie snorted at her surprised look. "Like I said to you, Tris, she's no longer a kid or a Disney girl. And if you paid even the slightest bit of attention to popular culture, you would know that."

Rubbing her face with both hands, Tristan heaved another aggravated sigh.

"Okay. So, what's the threat to her?"

"Nothing specific. This one's just regular duty."

The term was bound to raise a few hackles, and it certainly did.

"What will my job be on the regular then?" Briggs sneered. "Chaperone lunches with her pop star girlfriends? Be her escort on shopping trips to Beverly Hills?"

"Yes, and whatever else she requires."

"Angie, listen—"

"No, you listen to me, Tristan." It was Angie's turn to snap in irritation. "Huxley's manager wants Dagger onboard with this because none of the other firms could satisfy. This assignment is an open door for more business to come our way. I will not turn it down or fail at it like the others. As for you, you just told me that you needed to work, right? *Right*?" Angelina insisted when no answer came.

"Right," Tristan agreed through gritted teeth.

Catching her darkening expression, Angelina took a settling breath and she rested a gentle hand over her arm.

"Look. Huxley requested a female bodyguard this time, and you're the best operative I've got. I'm asking you to take on this assignment as a personal favor to me. Please."

Briggs shot her a deep penetrating glance.

"What else are you not telling me, Angie?"

"Nothing at all."

"Is the business, Dagger, in trouble?"

"You mean financially?" Angie shrugged at her quick nod of assent. "Of course not. But all the same, I'm not going to miss an opportunity to shine where others couldn't. I want to secure Dagger at the top of the supply chain. I want to be everybody's first choice. This could be our chance."

"Competition," Briggs groaned. "That's what it's all about."

"In part, yes. I won't lie. But a woman's safety is at stake as well."

"Didn't you say there was no threat to her?"

"She's a pop star with a capital S, Tris. Adored by millions all over the world. People faint in her presence." Briggs grunted, prompting Angie to chuckle. "Yeah, it happens. Her fans tattoo her name on their bodies, spend thousands of dollars on music and merchandise, and wait for hours or sometimes days in front of hotels she's staying at, just to catch a two-second glimpse of her. I don't need to explain what this level of obsession might lead to in a person who's not too well-balanced, do I?"

"No, you don't." Briggs exhaled.

"So, will you take the job?"

"Yes. For you."

"Thank you." Angie squeezed her arm in appreciation and relief, feeling the hard bicep contract in reaction. "It's only for three months initially. Once you've broken the ice with Huxley, we'll find you a replacement."

"Fine. Anything else I need to know?"

"It's a residential job, they want you on site at all times."

"Of course they do." Briggs shot a quick glance upwards, as if searching for patience in the cloudless sky.

"I've messaged you all the other details."

"Okay, I'll study the file."

"Huxley's manager, Bradley Wright, is expecting you at her residence at 12:00 noon tomorrow."

"Copy that."

"Keep me posted on how it goes, okay?"

"As per usual, yes. I will." Never keen on idle chit chat once official business had been taken care of, Briggs met her eyes with a simple, "Are we done?"

"Yep, we are." Angie threw her a smile and a friendly wink as she stood up. "What are your plans for your final afternoon of forced vacation? Anything fun?"

The question was only meant as a tease, an easy conclusion to the meeting. She blurted it out without thinking, and instantly regretted it when the color drained out of Briggs' face. The ex-cop gripped the side of the table and she visibly swayed. Angie shot to her feet in alarm.

"Tristan!" Worried at the highly unusual reaction, she laced a supportive arm around her waist. "Are you—"

"Fine! I'm fine," Briggs snapped. "Let go, dammit."

"Sorry," Angie apologized and immediately released her. "I was just... I didn't mean..."

"I know," Tristan cut her sharply. "You're alright, Ange."

"What about you?"

Briggs shot her a stormy look, looking as if she might walk off without another word. Angie must have appeared dismayed and concerned enough for her to reconsider.

"I'm spending the rest of the day with Katie Sullivan," she offered with a sigh and in a much lower voice. "She needs some work done on the house. It's two years today since Jake..."

Angie did not need her to finish that sentence; she knew. Two years since Briggs' police partner was brutally murdered in the line of duty, leaving his wife to fend for herself and their two-year-old child. *Do you still blame yourself for his death, Tristan?* Angie knew the answer to that one as well. It was written all over Tristan's face, obvious from her sudden pallor and the bruised expression in her limpid green eyes. The signs of pain and emotional struggle were there one second and gone the next though, replaced by iron control and the simmering heat of unresolved anger.

"Gotta go," Briggs said.

"Take care of yourself, Tris," Angie murmured.

"Yeah."

CHAPTER 2

A mile down the road, Tristan was reminded that allowing her mind to wander while riding her Kawasaki Ninja at top speed was a recipe for disaster. She roared into a tight bend at more than twice the speed limit and failed to spot a line of loose gravel across the middle. Her back tire struggled for grip, the bike fish-tailed wildly under her, and she barely avoided a major crash. *Focus on the road, you idiot!* Easing off the throttle, she cracked her visor open and took a deep breath of salty ocean air. She was annoyed. First of all, there was the job. Babysitting a capricious pop star may appeal to some of her colleagues in the private security business, but it was absolutely not her thing. Tristan was used to high-stakes jobs by now. She much preferred the sort of assignment which engaged all her skills and attention, and left her with no time, or energy, to think about herself or reflect on the past. Working in the Middle East in a dangerous area had been ideal for that. *Oh well...* She weaved in between lines of heavy traffic through the city center. At least, Angie had been honest about the reason for this new assignment. Tristan did not mind as much taking one for the team if it was for her.

Angie had offered her a job at a time in her life when not many others would have taken the risk. Tristan owed her, and gladly so. She reminded herself as well that she had yet to meet Alys Huxley in person. With luck, the singer would not be an entitled, annoying, insipid vanilla princess, the kind of character traits which Tristan associated with a typical pop star. Even if she were... A job was a job. She had to admit, to herself at least, that her irritation had more to do with her show of emotion. She hated to appear vulnerable in front of anyone. With Angie, the only person who knew the truth of how low Tristan had once hit, she hated it even more. *Let it go...* She did; and spent the rest of her free afternoon and evening with her partner's widow in Old-Lewiston. It had been Jake's lifelong dream to own a traditional fisherman's house in that coveted part of the city. By a cruel twist of fate, he only had a week to enjoy living in it with his wife and young son before he was savagely killed. The leader of a state-wide organized drug gang cut his throat with a razor blade – *After* he sawed off all his fingers. According to the Medical Examiner's report, the torture would have taken a long time to be performed. In the end, it was not a quick or easy death for Jake.

"Tris?"

Tristan turned from staring at his framed photo on the wall when Katie came back into the living room and spoke her name softly.

"Hey, Kate," she smiled. "All good with young Jake?"

"Yes, the boy was asleep before his head even touched the pillow."

"I wish I could do that."

"Yes, me too!" Katie laughed and pulled her into a familiar hug. "Thank you, Tris."

"No problem." Tristan held her close. "Your yard was due a good tidy-up, and the back fence needed fixing. Now you can let Jake loose on the lawn to play safely."

"Yes, but I don't mean just that. You spent your entire week off here, babysitting for me and doing maintenance jobs around the house. I'm grateful for all your help, but—"

"It's okay," Tristan interrupted. She had not mentioned that to Angie but yes, she'd had a busy week. Katie was on her own with Jake, with a full-time job and no one around to help. Tristan was the closest thing she had to family. "I know I don't have to, but I enjoy spending time with Jake and doing stuff for you. I'm back on the job tomorrow, so I won't get as many opportunities to come round."

"Not abroad again, is it?" Katie prompted with a worried glance.

"No, it's right here. Client's a famous singer."

"Can you say who, or is it confidential?"

"Alys Huxley. Just don't repeat it."

"Oh, okay." Katie relaxed, which had been Tristan's aim in sharing the information. Hopefully, a job with a pop star would sound a lot less scary to her than if Tristan announced that she was off to Baghdad. Still, Katie asked for confirmation in a quiet voice. "You'll be careful, won't you?"

"Yes. Always am, Kate."

"I know." Now Katie flashed a quick smile, and gave her a tight squeeze before letting go. "Tristan…"

"Yes?"

"I need to tell you something."

"What's wrong?" Tristan inquired, instantly anticipating a problem.

"Nothing, don't worry. It's good news, actually."

11

"Okay, go ahead." Katie eyed her intently and in silence for a moment or two. Biting on her lip, she appeared both nervous and excited. "What is it?" Tristan prompted, now with a chuckle. "You look like a kid on Christmas morning."

"Well, not quite, but... Tris, I've met someone."

Why this should come as a shock, Tristan had no idea. Katie was a beautiful, intelligent, caring woman. She was still young, and deserved all the best that life had to offer. This included a loving relationship, for sure.

"Tristan? Are you okay?"

Wordlessly, Tristan nodded. It might just be the realization that even Jake's wife was getting ready to move on with her life. And Tristan still felt so stuck...

"Hey," Katie insisted, her blue eyes warm as they held her own. "Talk to me."

"Yeah." Tristan shook herself. "You met someone. Uh... A guy?"

"Yes," Katie smiled. "That's how I roll."

"Of course." Tristan rolled her eyes at her own self and they both laughed. "Sorry, Kate, I'm being dumb."

"No, you're not."

"What's his name? How did you meet him?"

"His name is Mark Lee; he's a physiotherapist. Two months ago, he started working at the hospital every Friday. That's how I met him, through an appointment. You know my back always gives me trouble, right?"

"Yeah."

"And, as a nurse, I qualify for free physio sessions."

"Right. Yes, I know. So, you guys started dating?"

"Not yet," Katie replied, her smile a little flushed. "I wanted to run it by you first."

"Oh, Katie!" Tristan exclaimed in surprise and a huge dose of reluctance. "You don't have to ask for my permission to date someone!"

"No, I know, and that's not what I'm doing. Sorry, I didn't phrase that very well. I just wanted to tell you first. Mark lost his wife two years ago when their daughter was born. He's been on his own ever since, like me. He's kind. Patient and gentle. You'd like him."

"Yes, I'm glad he's nice. But really, this is not my—"

"Tristan," Katie snapped, her eyes suddenly filling up with tears. "You were Jake's partner. He spent more time with you on the job than he did with me!"

"Hell." Tristan stiffened. "Kate… You know that's the way it goes with cops."

"Yes, and it's fine, of course. I'm not saying it isn't." Katie went on. "But you've got to understand; now, you are the only connection that I've got left to my husband! God knows I haven't wanted to be close to anyone since I lost him. For a long time, even just the thought of it made me sick. But it's different with Mark." She swallowed hard. "Telling you about him… To me, it's like a way to settle it with Jake."

Tristan stared in stunned silence.

"I'm sorry." Katie let her go with a sharp sigh. She covered her mouth with her hands and turned her back to her. "I know it sounds like the rantings of a crazy woman. Please, forget I said anything. You're right, it's not your—"

"No, no." Tristan put her arms back around her very gently, slowly coaxing her to face her. She could feel her trembling, and her rapid breathing.

"I'm sorry," Katie repeated in a murmur. "This is unfair to you."

No. What is unfair is that Jake died because of me. Protecting me! But Tristan did not say it. She had never told anyone that, not even Katie. *Especially not Katie.* The thought of unloading on her, of using her partner's wife to lessen the pain of her own guilt, felt obscene to her.

"It's not unfair. I understand," she assured her in a soothing voice. "Jake talked about you all the time, you know?"

"Tell me again," Katie demanded, her voice muffled against the side of her shoulder.

"My wife," Tristan replied. "Plenty of guys on the force used less than affectionate terms for their partners, as if they resented being attached to them. Showing off, you know?"

"Yeah, the macho types," Katie groaned.

"For sure." Tristan stroked the tense muscles in her back. "But Jake always said, *'My wife'*, with the biggest smile. He was so in love with you, Kate. More than anything in the world, he wanted you to be safe and happy."

"And I wanted the same for him. God, I miss him so damn much!"

"Yes, me too." Tristan closed her eyes and she gave Katie what she wanted. Fortunately, it was easy. And she did not have to lie about it. "He would be happy for you right now."

"Are you sure?"

"Hundred percent. *'Grab that gentle guy and run, woman!'*. That's what your husband would say if he could."

Katie chuckled and she relaxed a fraction.

"I can hear his voice when you say that."

"There you go."

"Oh, Tristan… Thank you!"

"You don't need to thank me," Tristan murmured as Katie snuggled close against her chest.

14

••

She ended up at a venue simply known as The Club. Close to midnight, and Tristan knew that she should probably go home, but she was too wired to sleep. Since alcohol was not an option for oblivion these days, it left her with only one thing, and thank goodness she had it. The women-only club would be difficult to find if one did not know of its location, tucked in the sprawling basement of an old warehouse without any sign on the outside. The beefy female bouncer at the back door took her twenty and let her in with zero sign of recognition. Anonymity was fiercely respected here. Tristan took the stairs quickly down to the main room and stepped into a world of alluring shadows and pulsing music. Hot bodies swirled under hazy strobe lights on the dance floor. Couples huddled in dark corners, lost in the enjoyment of each other and oblivious to the rest of the world. Off to the sides were scene rooms; adult play rooms which attracted the BDSM crowd. Tristan walked past, not interested in stopping to watch tonight, although she sometimes did. She reached the second bar area, ordered herself a non-alcoholic beer, tried to imagine that it was the real thing, and observed the stripper currently on stage. She'd seen this performer before and knew that she was good. Tristan leaned against the side of the counter and allowed the atmosphere to wash over her. It was hot in here, in more ways than one. A moment later, she felt a light presence behind her. A flutter of breath against her ear. A woman whispered;

"Hi. It's good to see you again."

Tristan did not turn to look at her. It didn't matter, in the semi-darkness, what the woman looked like. They knew each other in a world of shadows and desire. Here, it was enough.

15

"Hi," she murmured.

Smooth lips kissed the side of her neck just below her ear, making her shiver.

"Enjoying the show?" the woman asked.

"Very much," Tristan said.

"Good. Keep watching."

The newcomer stood behind her to massage her shoulders, making her sigh as she expertly dissolved a bunch of tight knots. Then, practiced fingers slipped under the hem of her t-shirt and caressed the hard muscles in her stomach. Wasting no time, the woman popped the buttons on her jeans open. Tristan did not wear anything underneath. The fingers of one hand stroked her lower abdomen while the others reached upwards to cup each of her breasts, in turn, twisting gently then harder at her nipples. Tristan suppressed a groan and she stiffened. She never liked it too easy, and this was good. Her body responded instinctively to blunt stimulation and without conscious direction from her. She did not move to touch her partner in return; she never did, and it would not be welcome anyway. But she was instantly aroused. Hot, hard, and ready to go.

CHAPTER
3

Her legs trembled as a hot hand found her boldly and precisely, cupping her with just the right amount of pressure to make her pulse, but not enough to send her tumbling right over the edge. Tristan was close though. Blood pooled between her legs and her vision blurred. She gripped the edge of the bar for control. *Not yet!* As her partner allowed her a brief respite, she turned her head aside in silent invitation. The response was immediate and thrilling. The woman took her mouth with a rough, demanding kiss, as raw and primal as the hard beats that pounded through the floor and flowed into their bodies. Tristan let go of the bar. She allowed herself to lean back fully into her partner's embrace. So not her style, to not be the woman in total control... But it was okay to give in to this sort of need in the dark. The woman held her tightly against her, realizing without needing to be told that Tristan needed that as much as the sexual touch. It was not their first encounter. She was a professional who worked at the club, and it was strictly that between them. Just business, of the sexual kind. No names had been exchanged and there would be no chat afterwards. It was the only way that Tristan could let go.

She knew others would be watching. Public sex was no big deal here. Through a haze of arousal, under deliberately dim lights, they were just ghosts in the shadows. Tristan, usually so private and in control, did not give a hot damn about being on display. Mounting pressure made her spasm, commanding her focus and destroying her resolve to wait. She wanted it all, and she needed it right now.

"Please," she whispered, and closed her eyes.

With two rapid strokes and a well-placed push against her center core, Tristan came undone. Hard, yet without a whimper. Her lack of outward reaction belied the fierceness of the orgasm that tore through her, and she rippled with it for almost half a minute afterwards. Only when it became obvious that she had regained the use of her legs, did her partner release her fully and step to the side of her.

"Thank you," Tristan murmured.

"You're welcome. I have enjoyed it too."

Tristan had no illusion that she was anything special to this woman, even though she fucked her so warmly and attentively. Just another stranger in need of release, and no questions asked. Part of her did hope that the pleasure was not completely one-sided. She pressed two-hundred dollars in the stranger's hand and met her gaze briefly. Confident blue eyes stared back at her, glinting in genuine satisfaction.

"Take care of yourself, okay?"

"You too," the woman smiled. "Until next time."

••

The next day, Tristan left the Kawasaki at home and drove her Dagger Inc.-issued Range Rover to Huxley's sprawling mansion.

She arrived early, intentionally, and drove around the property to get an idea of how difficult it might be for someone to enter the premises. The house was surrounded by a six-foot high wall of solid brick. There were no trees or vegetation close by to hide behind. Anyone attempting to climb over the wall would have to do so in plain view. *Good.* Street lights in strategic places would not make it that much easier at night, although of course there'd be less traffic. On the whole, Tristan would be happier to see a few rolls of barbed wire on top of that wall, or an electric fence. And where the hell were the security cameras? The first and only one that she spotted was by the front entrance gate, mounted on the side of the intercom and within easy reach, even from inside the car. She stuck her hand out to cover the lens as she pressed the intercom button. Just a little test to see how they would deal with it.

"Yo!" a deep male voice answered after a few seconds. She could hear music pumping in the background. Some kind of rap song going on. "Who's there?"

"I'm here to see Mr. Wright," she said, deliberately ignoring the question.

"Say again?" the guy prompted through a burst of static.

"I'm here for Bradley Wright," she repeated.

"You have an appointment?"

"Yes."

Tristan was genuinely shocked when no other question was asked and the gate began to roll open. *Jesus Christ!* Were she an armed intruder intent on causing harm, she'd be laughing at the ease of it all. But as Alys Huxley's new chief of personal security, she was not amused. Tristan waited until the gate closed behind her, noticing how slow the process was. Anybody would be able to sneak in on the wheels of an expected guest.

"What a joke this place is," she muttered.

Having studied the file that Angie had sent her, she'd been pleased at the aura of professionalism and quality that seemed attached to the Alys Huxley brand. Now, she wondered if that only applied to the entertainment side of the business. Some things would have to change here, and *Pronto*. For now, Tristan parked her car in front of the modern two-story Mediterranean villa. The house was set back among tall cedar trees from a perfectly manicured lawn. She noticed artfully-designed beds of colorful flowers. *Attention to detail on all the wrong things.*

"Hey!"

A huge guy with bright red hair and tattooed sleeves over his muscled arms bounded down the steps toward her. He was wearing jeans and a black t-shirt with the word SECURITY on the front. Tristan did a quick double-take at his flip-flops. Unless he was an expert at barefoot running, he'd be useless in a chase. From the massive bulk of him, she figured that running probably did not feature too high on his training schedule. Still, she'd give him the benefit of the doubt.

"Hi," she smiled. "How's it going?"

"Sound. Was that you at the gate?"

"Huh-uh."

"I didn't catch your name, dude."

Dude? Well, it wouldn't be the first time that someone had got it wrong. She took off her dark Oakleys to give him a better chance.

"That's because I didn't give you my name. And you didn't see my face on the camera either. Yet, you let me in and all the way up here." She watched annoyance and distrust flicker in his blue eyes. "That word on your t-shirt: it's there for a reason, or is it just a fashion thing?"

She kept a friendly tone, still smiling despite the rebuke. He stared, visibly stunned at her audacity. But then he squared his voluminous shoulders and took what he must assume was an intimidating step forward. The flip-flops worked against him on that.

"Alright," he growled. "You got two seconds to tell me who you are and what you want."

Tristan bit back on a laughing retort. *Or what?* She wanted to ask but thought it wiser not to. She'd made her point. Better let him off the hook before she made a real enemy of the guy.

"My name is Tristan Briggs. I'm with Dagger."

"Well, you're not on the list of guests for today. And what's Dagger anyway? Dancing agency?"

Tristan did chuckle at that. With her crew cut, well-muscled frame, and gender-neutral clothes, it kinda made sense that she was often mistaken for a guy. But a dancer? Yeah, that was a first for sure.

"Close protection," she enlightened him. "I have a meeting with Bradley Wright today at twelve o'clock. Can you take me to him?"

He regarded her suspiciously and reached for his phone.

"Let me check." *Better late than never.* Tristan shot a pointed glance at her watch, which earned her a dark frown. Then he just turned his back on her, which again made her roll her eyes inwardly. "Hey, Brad? Yeah, I've got a Kristan Briggs looking for you. She is? Well, not on *my* list!"

He sounded even more irritated at being left out of the loop, and she suppressed a sigh. As well as an untrained security guy, it was obvious that they also had a communications issue on this team. The behind-the-scenes organization of the Huxley business seemed to be in a bit of a mess.

21

"Okay, follow me," he grunted.

"Thanks. By the way, you got the gender right this time, but it's Tristan with a *T*."

"Okay, got it." His eyes dropped to her hips and lingered over her chest on the way back up. Apparently satisfied at the overall shape of things, he had the good grace to look sheepish. "Hey, sorry about that."

"No worries."

"You train, uh?"

"Sure. It's part of the job, right?"

"You bet."

"What's your name?"

"Erik Huxley; I'm Alys's cousin. I'm her driver and I keep an eye on things on the side."

That explained it then. Family members being put in charge of a job that they were not trained for, just because of blood ties. This one looked the part, to his credit. Unfortunately, bulk did not automatically equate with skills. Tristan followed Erik to the back of the house and to an office where another guy sat behind a desk.

"Ah, Ms. Briggs." This one was lean and wiry as he stood up to greet her, dressed in leather pants and a fitted purple shirt to match the silk scarf around his neck. His long black hair was tied in a loose ponytail. Tristan took in the heavy gold chain around his neck, shiny cowboy boots, and his quick, inquisitive black eyes as they searched her face. "I'm Bradley Wright, how do you do?"

The distinguished British accent was a surprise, although he did look a bit like Mick Jagger, with a sprinkle of Elton John and a dash of Willy Nelson. A dizzying combination. Tristan shook the hand that he offered.

"Nice to meet you, Mr. Wright." She noted the way that he briefly held on to her fingers as she let go. Power move? Or just a lack of sensory acuity?

She would reserve judgment for the time being.

"Have a seat, please," he invited. "Erik, I need you for this too."

"Could have told me you were bringing in someone new today," the big guy complained.

"Didn't I?"

"Nope!"

With an overly dramatic sigh, Wright gestured to the pile of paperwork and three open laptops on his desk.

"Well. You know how busy I am with all the rest of it at the moment, and organizing the next world tour. Ms. Briggs is here to replace the, uh... The gentleman who was looking after Alys before."

"That asshole pervert, you mean?" Erik grunted.

"Mmm..." Wright winced and pressed an index finger to each side of his temples, as if these words hurt. Tristan did not say anything. She just studied him impassively as he picked up a beeping phone and frowned at the screen. "These people cannot survive two seconds without me, I swear! Be with you in just a minute, Ms. Briggs."

Her gut feeling alerted her that he was making her wait on purpose, a ridiculous controlling move which would confirm the handshake thing she had noticed earlier. This was a far cry from her last job, where every briefing had run efficiently and without ego, and where everyone excelled at their duties. Right now, the picture was clear: Huxley's security guy was insecure. And her agent, addicted to whatever sense of power he derived from his position.

"I have an important meeting in twenty minutes, so let's get this done and dusted now, shall we?" Wright announced when he put down his phone.

He made it sound as if arranging protection for his famous client was a waste of precious time. The longer Tristan remained in the office, the less she liked the guy and the more she wanted to put him in his place.

"Let's do it," she agreed with a level of enthusiasm that she absolutely did not feel.

"Right. So, due to the heightened level of threat which Alys is currently facing, we need to—"

"Whoa, hold on a minute," Tristan interrupted as the words sank in. "That's news to me. What heightened level of threat are you talking about exactly?"

CHAPTER 4

"Because the guy is a prick, Angie," Tristan fumed when she got on the phone to her liaison after the briefing. "He's known about the threat for a while but decided to keep it to himself because, quote: *'I didn't want to upset her'*. As if being kidnapped or hurt because she has no idea of the danger that she's in wouldn't upset the woman more!"

"Gosh… That's insane!"

"Yeah, it is. Fucking irresponsible."

"How long has this been going on behind the scenes?"

"From the time that Wright hired the guy who tried to take pictures of Huxley in the shower. By the way, I found out that it was her first experience with close protection at the time. Before that, she never had a personal bodyguard."

"Really? I find that hard to believe."

"Well, she did have security at events, concerts, etc., but it was all arranged via third party. Then, recently, she took a career break to reinvent herself. There was no need for extra protection when she stopped touring and giving interviews, and more or less just faded into anonymity."

"Alys Huxley couldn't fade into anonymity even if she fell into a black hole, Tristan," Angie remarked, sounding amused at the idea. "She's that kind of person."

"Well, I'm just reporting what they said to me. Now she's back from her sabbatical. And her new, edgier persona, seems to attract a much more mature and rowdier crowd."

"You sound really pissed-off, Tris. Are you okay?"

Tristan was livid, actually. If there was one thing she hated, it was mediocrity. And being left in the dark about important things. Lack of accurate information could lead to making all the wrong decisions, and these could get someone killed. *Not on my watch. Not again.*

"I'm just fine," she replied. "But you know, Angie, this stuff should have been contained in the file that you gave me."

"Hey," Angie came back in a serious tone. "I'm as baffled and irritated as you are, trust me. I told Wright about the golden rule of personal protection. He said he understood, and I had no reason to doubt him."

"I don't think being honest with his team ranks high on this guy's list of priorities," Tristan snorted. "He comes across as full of himself and a right control freak."

With the phone to her ear, she walked briskly past a tennis court and on toward the swimming pool area. Wright had ended the briefing by telling her that Huxley was in her private studio, at the bottom of the yard, shooting a video for her new album. And some backyard this all was... To Tristan, it looked like the grounds of an exclusive resort. Wright had quickly lost interest in her once he filled her in on the situation. She knew that he'd enjoyed seeing her confusion as he began to explain, and she was glad to be rid of him for the time being. *Narcissistic asshole...*

"So, what's the threat?" Angie asked.

"Creepy love letters. Apparently, that's nothing unusual for a star, and Huxley has always received her share of this kind of attention; outpourings of love from her fans around the world, unwanted gifts, marriage requests from guys on death row, etc. But this is different."

"How?"

"Content and frequency. The messages started out mellow enough, but gradually turned angrier, darker, and pornographic. Two months ago, they went from sporadic to a lot more regular as well. A new letter comes through every Tuesday now."

"Via regular mail?"

"No, attached to a blank email sent to her website."

"O-kay…" Angie said pensively, drawing out the syllables. "Is that what made Wright decide to come clean, then? When he realized this could be serious?"

"No, not even that," Tristan huffed. "The admin guy who handles Huxley's fan mail grew concerned with the tone of the letters, and he went directly to her. Based on this, I don't know why that idiot Wright still has a job on her team. I'd have fired him immediately."

"He's been Huxley's agent for more than two decades."

"I know, but it wouldn't stop me. There's no excuse for this kind of incompetence. He put her life at risk."

"I hear you, Tristan," Angie said quietly, probably catching on her frustration. "I take it the police have been informed now too… Yes?"

"Only recently. But yes, they know about the letters."

Tristan glanced over her shoulder, aware of Erik following her at a distance. Not sure if he thought he was being stealthy or just mindful of her privacy while she was on the phone. He was the goofy type, so probably neither.

"How does Huxley feel about the situation?" Angie asked.

"From what I heard, she's unconcerned. Quick to dismiss it as just another weird person who fixated on her. I suppose she's used to extreme behavior from some of her fans, but still, that's putting it mildly with this one."

"Give me a flavor of the letters, please."

"It's brutal stuff, Angie. Lately, the guy's been describing in graphic details all the ways that he wants to fuck her and make it hurt."

"Shit," Angie said flatly. "Sounds serious, indeed."

"Yeah."

"Are we sure that it's a guy, though?"

She was on the ball and paying attention. Tristan felt better for having someone like her in her corner, to talk things through if and when she needed to.

"No," she admitted. "We're not sure of that and I shouldn't assume anything about this subject. You're right; men don't hold the monopoly on insanity."

"Haven't you spoken to Huxley yet?"

Tristan growled in renewed irritation at the question.

"No, not yet. I'm on my way to see her now. The woman is harder to pin down than a sniper's bullet. And I also don't think that she's very interested in meeting me."

Angie laughed easily this time.

"Well, at least the first part is good, isn't it? You don't want her to be an easy target."

"True. But I do want her to cooperate with me."

"I'm sure she'll be fine with you, Tristan. After all, she's the one who requested a female bodyguard this time. She may seem dismissive of the threat, but when you get her on a one-to-one, it might be a very different story."

"Yeah, I hope so," Tristan sighed. "I'll keep you posted."

"Okay. Good luck, Tris."

Erik, who had definitely been watching, caught up with her on the final approach to the studio. He looked all excited for a reason that she could not fathom.

"Yes?" Tristan prompted with an impatient eyebrow raised.

"Uh, yeah. Nothing," he grinned. "Just, you don't mind if I tag along, do ya? Since we're going to be partners now?"

The word brought her up short and a vivid image of Jake's smiling face flashed across her mind. *See you later, partner.* These had been his last words to her. The next time she saw him, it was inside the abandoned warehouse where the gang had taken him. They left his dead body strapped onto a metal chair, both wrists tethered to the arm rests with zip ties. He must have struggled so hard to break free that the plastic was embedded deep in his flesh. Tristan remembered feeling weirdly detached as she took in the scene. The sharp metallic tang of blood lingered in the air. Not surprisingly, she could smell the violence and fear as well. Jake's mutilated fingers lay in a pool of slowly congealing blood around the chair. His head was down but she could see that they'd cut his throat in the end. She could imagine the frenzy of the torture as it went on. Jake's screams. He would have known he was going to be killed, realized he'd never see his wife and kid again.

"Hey, you okay?" Erik asked. "You've gone all white."

Tristan blinked the nightmare images out of her mind.

"Fine," she said, and cleared her throat. Part of her wanted to tell him that her partner was dead, and that she worked alone. But it wasn't his fault, and she liked to keep this stuff private. So, she ignored the comment and just went on briskly. "A number of improvements are required around the property, Erik."

29

"Sure! What do you need?"

"I want security cameras installed on top of the perimeter wall, and an electric fence added to it. The entrance gate camera needs to be repositioned as well."

"Oh, you think so?"

"Yeah. Out of reach. And you," Tristan shot him a warning look. "You need to start taking your job a lot more seriously. You let me swing in here even though I wasn't on your list, without seeing me or my vehicle. What if I turned out to be the person behind the letters? What would happen if I showed up at the house with five armed guys in the back of the car?"

To his credit, he did not scramble for excuses. Just stopped smiling and looked genuinely apologetic.

"I guess you got a point, uh…"

"How long have you been in the job?"

"For security stuff, only about six months. But really, I'm a driver."

"Trained and qualified?"

"Hundred percent. I aced the state police course on speed and evasive techniques last year."

Tristan was pleasantly surprised at the news.

"Aced the course, did you?" she challenged a little bit. "Is that your own assessment of your performance?"

"Nope." His grin made a speedy return. "It was the opinion of the training officer at the time. I am legit a fantastic getaway driver."

"In flip-flops?" This time she smiled, and he laughed.

"Not in flip-flops when I'm driving, I promise."

"Alright, then. I look forward to seeing what you can do behind the wheel. For now, though, I need to meet with Alys."

"I'll take you right to her."

He pulled open the side door to a large rectangular building and let her walk inside ahead of him. The vibe in there was just like at The Club. Dark, hot, music pumping. A narrow hallway led to a much bigger space, the size of a small hangar, set up like a movie set.

"Great job, people!" a woman carrying a clipboard shouted loud enough to be heard in Canada. "Let's take five before we shoot the chorus."

Tristan looked around, trying to spot Huxley in the middle of the small but noisy crowd. Technicians, camera operators, and dancers showing a lot of skin, all congregated around the edges of the set. Some of the dancers started stretching or reached for a drink. Others sat down in a make-up chair. Meanwhile, a guy in bright pink overalls climbed a ladder to install a giant disco ball on the ceiling.

"So, where is she?"

"Come with me," Erik invited. He led her to a room marked *Private,* and told her to wait as he went to investigate the singer's whereabouts. "I won't be long."

"Yeah, alright."

Tristan clamped down on her impatience as she remained standing in the middle of the plush lounge, noticing the silence. The walls were clearly sound-proofed in here. It was nice. She observed a mixing deck in the corner and a walled-off partition on the side, with a couple of microphones on stands. Obviously, a recording booth. Mounted on the wall opposite was a row of electric guitars. Walking closer to it, she noticed that they all bore signatures. *Eric Clapton; Joan Jett; Stevie Nicks.* Each guitar on that wall would be worth a small fortune.

"Well, well...." A husky voice sounded behind her. "If this isn't G.I. Jane herself, come to the rescue."

31

The raspy timbre held a sure touch of irony, if not pleasure. It was also rich and vibrant, laced with something inexplicably sexy which had a startling effect on Tristan. The voice made her spine tingle and she closed her eyes briefly in reaction. Turning around, she would not have been surprised to find Aretha Franklyn, or Joan Jett herself. Instead, she discovered a tall blond woman, with an exquisite figure and fire in her icy blue eyes. As Tristan stared, exceptionally taken aback at her appearance, her expression turned sour.

"Yes, it's *Her*," the woman quipped acerbically. "Not going to faint on me, are you?"

CHAPTER 5

The photographs in the official file were obviously way out of date. They made Huxley appear like an innocuous pop icon, a lot younger, and so demure... But everything about this woman screamed Rock Star. Tough and in control.

"Ms. Huxley?"

"One and only, my friend." The answer came on the wings of a filthy chuckle.

Huxley looked powerful in black stilettos, dark-red leather leggings, and a fitted tuxedo jacket – also black, and deliberately open to reveal that she went bra-less underneath. Her eyes were heavily made-up in a style that Tristan was not particularly fond of usually. But the smoky-grey and gold tones brought out the fierceness in Huxley's blue eyes. Red lipstick. Shoulder-length blond hair messed up perfectly to achieve that *'Just Fucked'* look. And enough badass attitude radiating out of her slender frame to set the whole building on fire. *Holy smoke...* Tristan quickly got over her brief moment of surprise. She was not exactly star-truck, and certainly in no danger of fainting. But she did find it quite a bit harder than expected to take her eyes off the woman.

33

That arresting voice was something else, too. Attractively rough, enigmatically mellow, and beyond sensual. Tristan would be lying if she tried to deny that it did not grab her and slide under her skin. Careful to return her expression to neutral, she held out her hand to the singer.

"Hi, I'm Tristan Briggs. Your new chief of security."

Huxley's handshake was all business, firm and self-assured. There was no attempt to control the exchange, although she did step way up close for a lingering stare. If Wright had dared to invade her personal space in similar fashion, Tristan might have snarled in warning. Not now. They were almost eye to eye, and she found herself tumbling straight into the woman's gaze with devastating ease.

"Have you been briefed?" Huxley asked.

Damned if the sharpness of her tone did not make Tristan want to salute.

"I had an initial chat with your manager," she confirmed, staying still. "But you're the one I really need to talk to."

"The corner of your mouth just twitched. Why?"

Tristan liked a straight shooter, and she allowed her grin to show.

"You sounded more like a police captain than a pop singer when you asked me if I'd been briefed," she revealed.

"Did that surprise you?"

"A little bit, yes. In a nice way."

"Well, I'm no pop star… Briggs. May I call you that?"

"Yes, Ms. Huxley, you may."

"What if I prefer G.I. Jane?" The singer shot her a coy glance over her shoulder as she moved to the brown leather sofa in the middle of the studio.

"I'm no G.I.," Tristan answered diplomatically.

34

"Apparently not. But with your looks, you could feature in my next video. No need to even audition."

She obviously did not expect an answer, which was a relief because, despite the fleeting compliment, Tristan would struggle to come up with anything other than an emphatic, *'Hell, NO!'*. And there was no need to come across as rude or dismissive. She watched Huxley cross her legs and drape an elegant arm over the back of the couch, a possibly calculated gesture that caused the tux jacket to split open invitingly. Aware that the singer was testing her, watching for a reaction, Tristan did not give her one. Huxley's next words were not so nice. "You know, I really don't want you here. *Briggs*."

Even with the emphasis on her name, Tristan knew not to take the remark personally. It was not the first time she'd heard this sort of thing. In an ideal world, no one should require an armed guard standing by 24/7 to guarantee their safety or that of their loved ones. She'd hate to be the one in need of protection, and understood Huxley's reluctance.

"I realize that, yes," she nodded calmly. "I'm sorry you had an unpleasant experience with your previous bodyguard, but I'll work to make this as painless and unobtrusive for you as I can, Ms. Huxley."

A knock on the door cut through the heavy silence which ensued.

"Yes," Huxley muttered impatiently.

The woman who seemed in charge of things earlier popped her head in.

"We're ready for you on set, Alys."

"Yeah, I'll be right there, Joan."

"She with us?" Joan asked with a glance toward Tristan.

"No," Huxley sneered. "That's my new bodyguard."

Could she sound any more deprecating, referring to her as *'That'*? Tristan noticed, but again, the remark more or less went in one ear and out the other. Meanwhile, Joan studied her as if she were a piece of furniture, before leaving the room without a smile or another word.

"Is she on your team?" Tristan inquired.

"Joan Beck is the director for this video we're shooting."

"Have all the performers and the rest of the film crew been vetted?"

Huxley stared defiantly.

"They're all regulars who've done plenty of jobs for me in the past. Needless to say, I trust them."

Needless to say, as well, Tristan would make it her business to confirm that they could be. She could easily acquire a list of names from Erik or Wright, and send it to Angie for background checks. Deciding that it was not worth arguing with Huxley on their first encounter, she did not mention her intentions to her. The singer had started off friendly enough, but she'd also made her position clear when it came to Tristan's presence in her life. And now, her demeanor was getting chillier by the second.

"No problem, Ms. Huxley," Tristan nodded. "I'll just need a copy of your daily schedule. And if you'd keep me in the loop as to any last-minute changes, I'd appreciate that too."

"I have an official schedule," Huxley replied. "You can ask Erik for a copy."

"Okay, thank you."

"But I'll warn you, Briggs: expect the unexpected. I make no difference between my professional and private life, and it's all very fluid with me. I go with the flow. Those who accuse me of being too impulsive and fickle have no frigging idea of how the mind of an artist works!"

Tristan was trained to notice and interpret micro-changes in a person's face, from the tightening of someone's lips to a subtle shift in the color of their skin or the size of their pupils. Whoever had told Huxley that she was too fickle had obviously hurt her feelings. She probably thought that she had it under control, but for a second, her composure slipped, and Tristan saw behind the facade. She answered gently.

"Thanks for the warning."

"Yeah, so you'll just have to keep up," Huxley insisted, as if surprised at her easy acquiescence. "If that's a problem for you, Briggs, I really don't care."

""No problem at all, Ms. Huxley. I'm very good at keeping up and fading into the background." *Even with high-maintenance and difficult clients.* "Most of the time, you won't even know I'm there."

"Fine."

"This being said…"

Huxley stopped abruptly at the door, so close to her again that Tristan could see tiny individual bits of glitter in her make-up.

"This being said, what?" she snapped.

Even like this, angry and reluctant, her magnetism never dimmed. Tristan felt it deep in her chest. Undeniable attraction. She could count on the fingers of one hand the number of times when she'd experienced this kind of charisma. It was appealing, for sure. And rare.

"If you don't try to lose or confuse me on purpose, it will be easier for me to do my job." She gave a light shrug, as Huxley pinned her with fiery eyes. "My goal isn't to interfere with your lifestyle, but to keep you safe. So that you can carry on enjoying it for a long time to come."

Huxley stared back in pure challenge.

"You don't think the two are mutually exclusive?"

"What? Security and going with the flow?"

"Yes, of course!"

Tristan held back on a rough and ready reply, the kind that was sure to destroy the already thin ice that she seemed to be on with Huxley. Without standards to maintain, her personal ones and Dagger Inc.'s, she might have asked her how steel shackles might affect the woman's flow, since her insane admirer planned to give her some. How about just plain being murdered? Would that do wonders for her sense of creative fluidity? Tristan kept a tight lid on her sarcasm. Ethics aside, she also detected a subtle plea in the singer's voice, as if Huxley might be unconsciously asking her for reassurance. She held her gaze for a brief moment, searching for confirmation. It was obvious and not surprising in the least that the personality which Alys Huxley presented to the world was a construct of her own choosing. But how deep did it go? Tristan had seen under the mask once already... This time, she could not penetrate it.

"Ms. Huxley, just trust me, please," she murmured. "And I promise we'll make it work."

It was the sort of answer which would make Angie proud, no doubt. Heartfelt in a way that surprised even Tristan herself. Sadly, it seemed totally lost on Huxley. For some strange reason, the singer actually looked even more annoyed.

"Yeah, Briggs," she bristled. "How very slick of you."

"I'm just being honest." Tristan insisted. "You may not be used to this kind of thing, but what you see is what you get with me."

With a final glance that said she was not buying any of her bullshit, Huxley pivoted on her heels and headed back to the set.

Tristan followed at a safe distance, feeling relieved that the confrontation was over. Well… At least, for the time being. No doubt Huxley would find a way to challenge her another time. Perhaps just standing in front of her in a similar outfit would do the trick, actually. Tristan had managed not to look, but she had been painfully aware of the singer's naked breasts the entire time they were talking. She had a feeling that Huxley knew it too, and had enjoyed toying with her a bit. Tristan was not sure how to feel about that.

"Okay, everyone!" Director Joan yelled to gather everyone's attention. "Dancers: on your marks. Alys: looking hard and glam in equal measures, my darling."

"On point, then." Huxley answered arrogantly.

Tristan faded into the background, as promised, to observe the players and proceedings. From the sidelines, she tasted the razor-sharp edge of professionalism that she'd already come to associate with the Huxley brand. At least one thing in the client file had been correct. Seeing this up close and personal, Tristan was able to confirm that it was all down to her. Huxley's vibe, vibrant and strong, was obviously contagious. As she watched her take center stage, interacting easily with the crew and her dancers, Tristan smiled a little without being aware of it. Even with no previous experience of this kind of world, she could tell that she was in the presence of greatness here. Everyone really did appear on top of their game.

"ACTION!" Joan shouted, and the music started pumping.

The song was edgy, nothing pop about it. Huxley's vocals were impeccable. Her speaking voice was unusual; it might not be everyone's cup of tea. But when she sang, it made sense. She displayed a fantastic range, starting out in haunting lower tones before layering up into a shiver-inducing roar for the chorus.

Tristan watched a handsome, olive-skinned male dancer, hover suggestively around the singer. Huxley wailed perfectly to the background track about dark desires and forbidden pleasures. The lights, the outfits, and choreography, were all designed to tease and mesmerize. As a female dancer joined in, the display started to resemble something that Tristan might witness at The Club on a Friday night. Huxley crooned about being untamable. At the same time, she fisted a hand in the guy's hair and yanked him roughly in between her legs. The gesture was arousing, and Tristan was not immune.

"CUT!" Joan chose that moment to shout. "Kyle, darling, you need to be looking the other way."

"Oh yeah, sorry…"

"That's okay," Huxley smiled. "I was going off-script."

"Keep going, we love it when you do that," Joan approved. "Background dancers, stay on track! Kyle and Rose, you follow Alys. We're rolling. Aaaand… Action!"

The interaction between Huxley and her two dancers grew progressively bolder and steamier, with both of them following the singer's lead and keeping up just fine. Near the end, the male dancer between her legs was for real caressing her dangerously close to target. Huxley flashed a lazy grin and lifted a leather-clad leg to rest the sharp heel of her stiletto over his shoulder. The dancer reached under her open tux jacket.

"Yeah, you guys, super hot, laaaavely!" Joan commented in a tone that made Tristan wonder what other kind of videos she directed in her spare time.

Huxley made suggestive gestures at the camera while the operator circled smoothly around the trio, capturing close-ups from all angles. She seemed totally connected to her partners but also strategically detached at the same time, and almost bored.

Everything about the scene conveyed the idea that she was a Queen being worshipped, accepting her dues from lesser lovers. It suited the song, the suggestive lyrics, her voice... *And the woman, too.* It occurred to Tristan that she had her work cut out as a bodyguard.

"Let's end on a high," Joan encouraged.

Alys chuckled, grinned, and grabbed the female dancer for a deep, open-mouthed kiss.

CHAPTER
6

Alys spent the next three hours after the shoot holed up inside her recording studio, editing raw cuts of the video. With her for the first part of it, she had Joan; Andrew, her artistic director; and Rose, who was not only a talented dancer and red-hot kiss when required, but also a dear and trusted friend.

"One word, Alys," Andrew grinned eventually.

"What's that, darling?"

"FIRE!" he exclaimed.

"I agree," Joan approved. "Awesome work right there."

"Rose?" Alys prompted. She'd been pacing as they worked, supervising and directing her official directors. Rose, who sat on the back table with her legs dangling, smiled and grabbed her to ruffle her hair as Alys stopped in front of her.

"Absolutely! This video is so you, babe... I love it."

After they left, Alys stayed behind another ninety minutes, tweaking and splicing minute changes until she, too, was totally satisfied with the result. She never relied on anyone else to get it right on her behalf, and did not expect even the people that she employed to be as obsessed and dedicated as she naturally was.

Her manic workaholic ways made people call her a freak more than once... But as Rose often said, *'A damn cute and loveable one!'* It was ten p.m. by the time Alys decided to call it a wrap, not too late by her own standards. Happy with the day's achievements, she walked smiling into the hallway... And immediately froze at the unusual sight which greeted her. *Dammit... Forgot about her!* Her new bodyguard sat on a solitary armchair pushed against the wall, with her head tilted slightly back and her eyes closed. Since she had not been spotted yet, Alys took the opportunity to stare all she liked. Briggs did her blue-jeans justice, the material stretching nicely over hard-muscled legs. Nike running shoes that looked as if they had seen a good few miles on her feet. And a simple checked shirt over a black t-shirt. She wore it loose and open with the sleeves rolled up to her elbows, probably just to cover the weapon that she carried on her belt. Even obviously at rest like this, she managed to look focused and attentive. Alys lingered on her face. Silently, she observed the strong line of her jaw, naturally long and lush black lashes, and full red lips. She recalled Briggs' earlier promise to her. *'Most of the time, you won't even notice that I'm there...'* Alys reflected that she might prove a difficult one to ignore, actually. She sighed a little too sharply, betraying her presence, and Briggs opened her eyes. She seemed instantly alert, green eyes impossibly clear and intense as they focused on her.

"Good evening, Ms. Huxley."

Suppressing a shiver, Alys held her gaze unapologetically, as if she'd not just been caught scrutinizing every inch of her.

"Briggs." She nodded once. "Already falling asleep on the job, I see?"

A flicker of amusement registered in those vivid eyes.

"Not quite. I was just tuned in, Ms. Huxley."

"Oh, is that what you call it." Alys snorted, unwilling to let the woman see that she appreciated her answer. "What are you then? Some kind of Ninja?"

"Some kind," Briggs smiled, standing up. "Are you ready to go?"

"Yes, it's time for home."

Briggs led the way to the exit door and held it open for her. She seemed relaxed but alert on their way up the path that led back to the house. It was dark out now, although lights along the way provided ample illumination. The night was still, warm and fragrant, and Alys felt strangely at peace. When they passed the pool area and Briggs just kept going, though, her irritation flared up.

"You're not going to set up camp outside my bedroom, are you?"

"No, I was not planning on it…"

"Good."

"But I haven't had a chance to assess the inside of the house yet, so I might just—"

"No." Alys was leading the way on the narrow path at this point. She whirled around aggressively, forcing Briggs to take a step back in order to avoid a collision. Granted, she did not look intimidated. How could she; when she was taller, stronger, and armed? She was just being polite, obviously, giving her some space. Even so, Alys took pleasure in causing her reaction. It was childish, she realized. But she enjoyed knowing that she could surprise this seemingly unflappable woman. "There is no need for you to follow me home," she stated. "The house is safe, and Erik lives there, too. Thank you for your dedication to your job. Goodnight."

"Um… Ms. Huxley?"

Alys might have completely ignored her if Briggs had not spoken so quietly and gently. She turned to find her standing in the same spot with a sheepish smile. It looked good on her lips; Alys could not help notice that too.

"Yes?" she prompted, sharply, to hide her true feelings.

"Before you go, could you just point me in the direction of my quarters, please?"

Alys resisted hitting her with another G.I. Jane tease at the term. Where did Briggs think that she had landed here? An army bootcamp?

"Erik was supposed to get you settled in," she said. "I take it that didn't happen?"

"No."

"Typical! Come on, I'll take you there now."

"In his defense, I insisted on going straight to see you when I arrived," Briggs added, falling into step with her.

"I understand. And I appreciate you mentioning it. But Erik is good at *'forgetting'* the things that he deems as not worthy of his time. As my cousin, he probably thinks that he can get away with it."

If Briggs had an opinion about the family situation, she was wise and intelligent enough not to express it. Alys flashed her a curious glance as they approached the annex.

"You don't mind living on site?"

"I don't think about it. It's part of the job."

"That's not what I asked you. Don't give me the runaround, Briggs. We need to trust each other and make this work between us, remember?"

Alys was appropriately sarcastic as she served her a re-hash of her own lecture. Both tone and words were obviously not lost on Briggs, and she favored her with a cute grin.

"To be honest, Ms. Huxley, living on site can be a bitch."

"Aha!" Alys chuckled in satisfaction. "Now you're talking like a real human being. Good!"

"But like I said," Briggs added, falling back on what seemed like natural reserve. "It comes with the territory. I'm pretty good at adapting to new circumstances."

"Are you ex-military, then?"

"No, I was never in the armed forces."

"You sound a lot like a soldier from time to time. And your hair… What's up with the crew cut?" Alys did not add that it really suited her. With her intense green eyes and lean features, Briggs could make a fortune as a model.

"I practice martial arts," she offered.

"I see. So, you have to have short hair to be a Ninja?"

"There's no rule that says that. But if it's too short to grab, that's one less thing an opponent can use against you to gain the advantage. One less vulnerability to worry about when you are fighting."

It was a stunning answer; not one Alys would have thought of first. And it certainly gave her more insight into the mindset of her bodyguard. *Talk about dedication, for sure…* Briggs looked like a woman who wouldn't even know the meaning of the word *'vulnerable'*. Although, as Alys knew, it was often the quiet ones who carried the heaviest load on the inside. How about Briggs? What secrets or painful wound did she hide under her stoic exterior? Alys was an excellent judge of character. It never took her long to dissect people, both inside and out. She got a sense that Briggs may not be so easily cracked, though. It made her all the more intriguing.

"Here you are," she announced as they reached the guest-house.

The studio apartment was pretty small, but well-appointed and efficiently laid-out. Main room with a sofa, coffee table, and TV; kitchen area at the back. Separate bedroom with ensuite and French windows leading onto a nice patio outside. Briggs barely glanced at her new digs before nodding.

"Perfect, thanks."

"There's food for you in the—" Alys stopped as she opened the fridge and found it empty. The cupboards were equally bare. Another thing Erik *'forgot'* to take care of. "Ah, well. I guess not, after all."

"It's okay," Briggs said, her mind obviously still very much on the job. "Ms. Huxley, I'd like to walk you to your home and make sure that you're okay before I sort myself out. Please?"

••

Tristan was surprised when the singer agreed to her request, and even more so when she invited her to her private apartment. She mentally assessed vulnerabilities on their way through the first part of the house, not the least of which was the front entrance door: it was unlocked when they arrived, and Huxley waltzed in as if it were the norm.

"You do have a brand-new security system in this house," Tristan stated, spotting the panel on the side.

"Yes, but we've not been using it much."

"Okay. Why not?"

"No idea!" Huxley shrugged a touch impatiently. "This has been my home for many years and we never had a problem. It feels safe, that's all I can tell you."

Tristan understood the illusion of safety brought on by easy familiarity. It invariably led to complacency and serious trouble.

The urge to give Huxley a bit of a reality check was there, but it was early days with her still, so Tristan phrased her answer to be positive and encouraging instead of a rebuke.

"There are things we can do to make your home even safer for you, Ms. Huxley. Easy ones like educating your team, adding extra cameras, or using the systems already in place. I'll set up your house alarm for you and show you and Erik how to use it, okay?"

"Okay," Huxley muttered, as if Tristan had just suggested a lengthy stay at the local jail.

"Great, thank you."

Tristan followed her to the first floor, and a sprawling suite with large glass panels along one entire side. In the distance, the lights of Lewiston were visible. Come daylight, the view across the ocean would be fantastic from up here too. She bit on her lip, feeling a chill running down her spine.

"I know what you're thinking, Briggs."

"Yes?" Tristan turned to face her new client.

"Yeah. How hard would it be for someone with a good telephoto lens to spy on me if they wanted to. Right?"

"That's part of what I was thinking," Tristan nodded.

"Well, I can reassure you on that, at least. Privacy matters to me a great deal." Huxley raised her hands in front of her, palms out to emphasize the point. "A fucking great deal! This location is secure."

"Now it's your turn to use tactical terms," Tristan observed.

She flashed a friendly smile but Huxley did not return it. Instead, her blue eyes darkened as if Tristan had insulted her. It was amazing how quickly her moods seemed to change. Hard to establish a baseline with her. Complex and complicated seemed to be the thing with Huxley.

"I'm not as naïve as you may think," she snapped.

"I wasn't thinking that at all, Ms. Huxley," Tristan answered calmly. *Sincerely.*

"Tell me what was on your mind then, to make you look so grim when you stared out the window." The singer groaned in frustration. "Goddammit! If there's one thing I cannot stand, it's people telling me lies in order to spare my feelings. I don't need that kind of protection. Give it to me straight, Briggs."

Tristan was careful not to grin because Huxley was likely to take it the wrong way. But yeah… she wanted to. There was the baseline: pure fire and grit expressed in that ballsy statement. In reaction, Tristan felt herself moving effortlessly into alignment. In the blink of an eye, her previous reluctance vanished. Never mind wanting to go back to the Middle East for some real action; Huxley was the opposite of bland and mundane. Her personality sparkled harder than the glitter on her eyelids, and all Tristan wanted in that instant was to keep her gorgeous flame burning. She would give her best to Huxley. Keep her safe until the cops found and arrested her stalker. Or die trying. Tristan Briggs was crystal clear about that.

CHAPTER
7

"Tell me," Huxley insisted. "I want to know."

Tristan nodded. A few moments earlier, she'd not been sure that she even liked the woman... And of course, it was not a prerequisite for the job. Being as neutral as possible actually helped to remain focused. Feelings or opinion aside though, Huxley had just won her respect. Tristan would not lie to her.

"It is grim," she admitted. "Looking out through the glass, I was wondering how hard it would be for a good sniper to take you out with a bullet from a mile away."

Huxley visibly paled under her makeup. For the first time, she seemed a lot less assured.

"That thought never occurred to me," she murmured.

"That's okay," Tristan said gently. "That's why I'm here, Ms. Huxley. To think of these things for you and prevent them from happening. Just so you know, I'm very good at my job."

Huxley stared harder than at any point before, and she was pretty good at staring too. Then, she pressed a button on the wall and the glass turned dark. Tristan breathed easier, for sure. The singer's next sentence was a surprise, considering...

"I make a mean tofu scramble, you know?"

"I didn't, but I believe you," Tristan smiled.

"I'll be right back. Don't go anywhere."

She left the room without a backward glance, the attitude of a woman who was well used to issuing commands and having them followed. Erik was probably the only exception to the rule, and it would be interesting to see how Bradley Wright behaved around his gifted boss. Tristan was especially curious about that relationship because what she had experienced of the man so far did not seem good enough for Huxley. She roamed through the spacious apartment as she waited for her to come back, taking note of weaknesses and absorbing the landscape of her private home. Bright spaces, sharp and clean lines. Any pictures Huxley had on the walls were abstract pieces, nothing personal. Tristan wondered if she was one of these artists who liked to keep their awards out of sight, either in the guest bathroom or locked in a bank safe. She was in the hallway, just about to enter the kitchen, when it occurred to her that she was being watched.

"Ms. Huxley?"

No answer, and no one there. Instantly alert and suspicious, Tristan rested a cool hand on her weapon and she moved closer to the wall. She caught a shadow on the other side, heard a strange huffing noise. *What the hell is this?* She moved forward, ready for action and to take someone out if she had to. Just then, her intruder revealed himself.

"Ah..." Tristan grinned at the sight of the cutest golden lab puppy, eyeing her shyly from behind the door. He vanished for a moment when he realized he'd been spotted, but then curiosity won and he slowly popped his head back around again. Tristan squatted down and beckoned him forward. "Hey, buddy! Come here, boy. Come!"

Reassured at her welcoming stance, the puppy trotted over on unsteady legs. Only a few weeks old, he was bright-eyed and rosy-tongued, wonderfully inquisitive. Tristan sat on the kitchen floor and gave him a helping hand when he tripped over himself and fell over.

"You're a clumsy little guy, aren't you? Haven't figured out how to use your legs yet, uh?"

Her new pal climbed all over her with obvious enthusiasm, licked her on the nose, and settled between her crossed legs with his belly up, inviting a cuddle which Tristan was only too happy to give. Behind her, a woman laughed.

"So, is this the way to take down my tough bodyguard? By unleashing a plump puppy on her? Cute, Briggs. A bit worrying, but cute."

Tristan looked and almost got taken down for real, actually. Huxley had changed into a pair of baggy grey sweats, socks, and an oversized hoody with the phrase, 'LICK ME, I AM A ROCK GODDESS', emblazoned across the top. She'd also removed her makeup and taken off all her jewelry. Not that she needed any of that stuff; she was as gorgeous now as before, just slightly less formidable. Her voice still gave her an edge, and her laughter, like warm caramel, hit the spot exactly right with Tristan. As Huxley bent over to scratch the puppy's belly, and her breasts brushed against her arm, she struggled not to react. Fortunately, her own voice returned before she could make a complete fool of herself.

"I'm not easy to take down," she assured. "But I am a dog lover. What's his name?"

"Officially, Sex Pistol."

"Oh, my gosh!" Tristan laughed. "This cute puppy?"

"Life's too short to be boring," Huxley smiled, lingering.

"Well, that's true. So, what do you call him unofficially?"

"Most of the time, Baby or Pup." Leaving him to chew on Tristan's fingers, Huxley walked to the fridge. "What would you like with your scramble? I'm having onion, spinach, tomato, and mushrooms. Sprinkle of chili and turmeric, 'cos it's good for you. You okay with that, Briggs?"

"Uh…" Tristan stood up, still holding the playful puppy in her arms. "You don't have to cook for me, Ms. Huxley."

"I know I don't have to. What? You don't like tofu?"

"Tofu's fine, but—"

"Worried I can't cook?" Huxley shot her a challenging look as she carried a bunch of stuff to the main counter.

"No, it's not that," Tristan said.

"What is it then, Briggs?"

"You seemed less than happy to have me onboard earlier, and now you want to cook me a meal? That's a little confusing, I guess."

Huxley grabbed a large wok and wielded it like a weapon above her head. Or perhaps Tristan was paranoid, and that's just what cooking with a flourish actually meant.

"Has it occurred to you that I may want to get to know the woman who'll be responsible for my safety?" Huxley asked.

"Ah, okay." Tristan nodded. "Shoot."

"Relax, Briggs, this isn't an interview."

"Do I look stressed?"

"No, you certainly don't." Huxley snorted. "Actually, there were a couple of times today when I wondered if you even had a pulse."

Were you watching me? If she did, Tristan had not noticed.

"I guess I'm just good at not sweating the small stuff," she shrugged.

"I'm sure you are. What did you do before bodyguarding?"

"I was a police officer."

"Huh-uh." Huxley was watching her now, definitely, even as she deftly chopped and sliced and got everything together for their meal. "What kind?"

"The Drugs and Organized Crime Task Force."

"Doesn't sound like the sort of job one just falls into. What made you want to leave?"

She was correct. Tristan had worked her guts out to make it on the DOCTF team. Now, she gave Huxley the official version about her departure. It was a big white lie, but a useful one.

"I was ready for something new. The CEO of Dagger Inc. is a good friend, and she was hiring at the time. For me, it was an easy decision to make."

"Who's the most important person you looked after?"

"You are."

"Me?"

Tristan smiled at the way that her eyes widened.

"Sure. Does that surprise you?"

"Well, I am beyond famous, that's a fact." Huxley shrugged and she reached for the cooking oil. "But really, I'm just a singer and a songwriter."

"Just, eh?" Tristan prompted, amused. "You say that as if it weren't much of a big deal."

"Well. Yes and no." The vegetables flew into the smoking wok, which briefly caught fire as a result. In Tristan's arms, Sex Pistol stared in utter fascination, with the occasional wriggle and whimper of excitement. Huxley brought the giant flame under control, before it could singe her superstar eyebrows, and carried on with the conversation. "It's not like I save lives or build star-ships, is it?"

"No, it isn't." Tristan reflected. "But you still make millions of people feel good with your music. You give them joy. I think that's probably just as important."

Huxley performed that clever trick with the wok instead of using a spatula to stir its contents, sending everything swinging high up in the air a couple of times before catching it back, and causing her puppy to whine in wonder. She flashed him a tender smile which turned ironic when she moved it to Tristan.

"Like I said before, you're a smooth talker, Briggs. Answer my question."

"I told you the truth. You are the most important client, simply due to the fact that you are my current one. No one else matters, it's as simple as that."

"Whaddaya think, Sex Pistol?" Huxley inquired in that hot mellow voice of hers. "Think the woman should be a politician? Because *I* sure do. Grab the ketchup, Briggs."

••

You could tell a lot about a person by how they treated a puppy, and Alys liked the fact that Tristan Briggs obviously turned to mush the second she laid eyes on Sex Pistol. She did not reveal that only a select few were ever invited into her private home. Close friends, like Rose. A lover, once or twice. But Erik rarely set foot in her inner sanctum, even though he was family; and Brad had only been up once. Indeed, Alys was fiercely protective of her privacy. She'd been burned before, learned the hard way not to trust too easily. So, why on earth she had felt the urge to bring her new bodyguard home, let alone cook her a meal, was a mystery. Sure, she wanted to know her; and she liked to treat her people right. No doubt the ex-cop could fend for herself, hey...

But all the same, dumping anyone at the guesthouse this late in the evening, without food, because Erik once again could not be bothered to do a simple thing she'd instructed, did not sit well with Alys.

"Is it okay?" she asked as they sat down to eat.

"It's fantastic," Briggs grinned around a mouthful. "Thank you."

Alys stole a few glances at her during the meal, trying to get a fix on the woman. Briggs seemed incredibly focused but also relaxed at the same time. Alys knew what it was. No matter the trade or line of work, this was the confident attitude of a person who'd earned every bit of her competence with tears, sweat, and perhaps, in Briggs's case, blood. Really, a genuine professional. This kind of excellence was sexy to Alys, and definitely another reason for Briggs' presence in her kitchen right now.

"What you said about a sniper taking me out earlier," she mused. "Do you really think that's a possibility?"

Briggs seemed to consider her response carefully; one more attractive quality about her. She came across as intelligent and trustworthy, although Alys would reserve judgement about the latter. Nothing personal, just the way she went about people and relationships.

"I've yet to read through all the letters," Briggs said. "And speak to the police. But I don't think your stalker has reached the stage to want to do that yet."

"Not *yet*? You mean it's only a matter of time?"

"Unfortunately, people like that do not magically improve overnight. This man, or woman, is writing violent fantasies with you in mind. It makes sense that they'll get worse over time. It's called decompensating."

"Right." Alys shivered involuntarily.

"That being said," Briggs added as she noticed, "the answer to your question is no, Ms. Huxley. Nothing bad will happen to you. I guarantee it."

"When you say it like that," Alys said with a dark chuckle, "I can almost believe it's true."

The bodyguard arched a quizzical eyebrow but remained silent. Alys held her gaze from across the breakfast bar.

"You know, receiving weird fan mail is nothing new in my business. I know it's a strange world we live in, but it's kind of expected."

"Strange world indeed," Briggs muttered. "Is that why your manager kept the letters from you at the beginning?"

"Yes. Brad is good at dealing with stuff."

"What kind of stuff?"

"Oh… Admin, generally. If I had to worry about every little thing that goes on behind the scenes, I wouldn't have any time to create. So, Brad handles the background noise and frees me up to focus on my thing." Again, Briggs stared impassively, but her silence spoke volumes. "I can tell you're not impressed."

"Not impressed is putting it mildly, actually. I don't mean to sound rude, Ms. Huxley, but didn't you just say to me that you hate it when people lie to you?"

"It's a fine line, for sure."

"One that I don't get," Briggs snapped.

CHAPTER 8

Suddenly, she sounded way sharper. Quite possibly, on her way to majorly pissed-off, and Alys was amazed at the rapidity of the change. *Not so at ease and in control, after all...* When Briggs leaned forward on her elbows, her open shirt stretching over her broad shoulders, there was an air of real danger about her. It seemed like the good kind, though, the sort which Alys appreciated in women. *I wonder what she looks like with her shirt off.* Triggered, obviously unaware of the heated thoughts that raced across her client's mind, Briggs carried on driving her point home. "In the weeks it took for your manager to get his act together, anything could have happened to you!"

"Just chill, okay?" Alys shrugged, intentionally provocative in her reply. "Nothing happened."

"No, although more by luck than judgment. You know, at first, I thought Wright must be totally incompetent. But now that I realize the directive came from you..."

"Yes?" Alys challenged when she stopped in the middle of her sentence. "Go on. Now that you realize it was me, what? You think I'm the incompetent one on this team?"

Probably aware that she was about to cross a sensitive line, and perhaps realizing that she was being led to do it, Briggs took a second, as well as a deep settling breath. When she spoke again, her voice was strangely flat.

"Secrets aren't conducive to good results, Ms. Huxley," she murmured. "At best, they compromise relationships. At worst, they cost people their life."

She lost someone... The realization hit Alys in the chest like a strike of lightning. She saw the truth in Briggs' eyes; a mix of pain, regret, and burning anger. Alys Huxley was not normally shy in conversation. When she wanted to know something, she pushed until she found out. And now, she burnt to ask... But for once in her life, she did not dare.

••

Tristan stopped downstairs on her way out to obtain a copy of the official schedule. Huxley did not keep one at home, she said, except in her head. Hard copy not fluid enough for her, Tristan supposed. She was feeling tense after their conversation, and not in the mood for any bullshit. Unfortunately, she had to speak to Erik before she could call it a day.

"Yo, Briggs!" He was naked when he opened the door to his apartment, with only a towel around his butt and a silly grin on his face. "The schedule? Yeah, sure. Come in. I'll get it for you."

It was clear that he wasn't alone, and Tristan was not happy about that either. Short of patience and understanding, she put it to him bluntly when he came back with the list.

"That woman in there? She's your girlfriend?"

"Shhh..." He glanced over his shoulder, obviously keen on not being overheard. "She, uh... She's a friend. You know."

"Do you?"

"What?"

"How well do you know her?" She stared hard at him when he hesitated. "Is that a difficult question?"

"No, Briggs, it's just weird as hell," he replied, falling on the defensive. "What does it matter to you who spends time in my bed?"

"Because, Erik, I am in charge of security around here now, and your bed happens to be in my client's house. You could say I have a need to know."

"Is that right?" he snorted, clearly not taking her seriously.

"Okay, never mind. I'll find out for myse—"

"Whoa!" He leaped in front of her to stop her storming into the bedroom, which she was about to do without any hesitation whatsoever. "Take it easy, okay? Man! Jennifer's not a security issue."

"Who is she, then?"

"A trainer at my gym. Doesn't give a damn who my famous cousin is, trust me."

Tristan glanced aside and she spotted the woman, wrapped up in a bed sheet, leaning against the doorframe at the entrance to the bedroom. She seemed a bit puzzled at Tristan's sudden appearance in the apartment, but still raised a hand in hello.

"Hey there…"

"Hi," Tristan nodded, unsmiling.

"Alys's new bodyguard," Erik informed his partner.

"Ah, okay." Definitely nonplussed, the woman flashed him a teasing smile. "But it's too late for official duties. Come back to bed, baby."

"See? It's me she's after." Erik chuckled. "Oh, damn. I need to show you the guesthouse…"

"Too late, your cousin took care of it."

"She did? Woops!" He laughed. "Guess I'll hear about it in the morning, eh? 'Night, Briggs."

Tristan had a raging headache by the time she made it back to her digs. But at least, she wasn't starving anymore, courtesy of Huxley's delicious cooking, and there was a 6-pack of Evian in the kitchen. Armed with a 2L-bottle, she threw her rucksack onto the bed and unpacked essentials: clothing and toiletries, running gear, back-up weapon and ammo. Pleased to discover a small hotel-style safe in the bedroom, she secured the extra Glock out of sight. A hot shower helped to remove some of the tension in her shoulders, and she climbed into bed with her laptop. Time for study. She normally trusted whatever client file Dagger Inc. provided her with. And when it came to diplomats or CEOs, the info was usually more accurate than anything she might find on Google. In Huxley's case, it had already proved a little flawed... Even if not, it would be helpful to know what the Internet had to say about her. As Tristan quickly found out, the answer was: *A LOT*. Information covered logical topics like new tour dates and location, where to buy tickets or download music, and serious interviews with the likes of Apple Music or Rolling Stone Mag. The most ridiculous and random stuff was trending out there too. A Twitter poll about Alys Huxley's Top 5 Best Hairstyles made Tristan laugh, and she absently rubbed the side of her own shaved temple. The headache was receding somewhat. People also discussed any hidden tattoos the singer might have on her, whether or not she was a genuine vegan, her fitness routine, favorite makeup, places to hang out, and who she may or may not be dating. Tristan took notes of her preferred spots, at least according to the website. She would check with Huxley and find other places for her to enjoy if the information proved correct.

Next, she moved on to heated rumors about her love life, and was surprised to find out that Huxley used to be married. To a guy, a famous Hollywood actor. It was only for a year, which hinted at a big mistake. From the information that she gathered about it, Tristan concluded that this may have been felt on both sides. The amicable divorce happened around the time Huxley went dark, supposedly to reinvent herself. Since returning as a more grown-up, bolder version of herself, she'd been officially single, although many photos posted online showed her kissing or in the arms of male and female *'friends'*. Tristan wondered to what degree Huxley controlled this sort of thing. From the tone of her own personal website, it was clear that she cultivated the image of a rebel rock star. No doubt that being seen as a bit of a renegade in her relationships would enhance that perception. The singer had just told her how much she valued her privacy. And Tristan had also witnessed her dedication to her work and brand. It made her wonder if these so-called *'stolen moments'* were only captured because Huxley wanted them to be. *So many questions...* With a sigh, Tristan switched off the laptop and she closed her eyes. Right on cue, her phone beeped.

'You up?' Angie texted.

Tristan called her back. She lay on the pillows, thinking this may well be the most comfy bed she'd ever slept in, and no need for a Twitter poll. For sure, it beat a single cot in the basement of the US embassy in Iraq.

"So, how's it going?" Angie inquired immediately.

"Ah… Could be worse," Tristan chuckled, stretching.

"Not sure how to take this, Tris… But I'm going to assume that it's good news."

Tristan refrained from saying *'Not bad'*, and she proceeded to fill her in.

"Huxley and her team don't seem very concerned despite being aware of the threat. I'd say she's been lucky until now and probably needs a reality check. Of course, I don't want anything to happen to her…"

"Of course not."

"It's infuriating. I don't think it's quite sunk in for her yet."

"But she's happy to have you onboard, right? She's going to work with you."

"I'd say resigned, more than happy. And I hope so."

"Okay. Well, it's only been one day, so well done you. How are you feeling?"

"Me?" Tristan frowned at the ceiling.

"Yeah, you. I know you weren't keen on this assignment."

Tristan rubbed her eyes as the headache pounded anew. Granted, it did not hurt as much if she recalled Huxley's sweet smile, and her tender expression when she held her puppy in her arms. A brand-new dimension opened up with the woman when she took off her makeup and put away the rock chick attitude. It was not just an act with her, sure; but she also seemed to be so much more under the surface. Tristan suspected that she did not let many see that side of her. It made her unusually curious. And attracted, she realized that. *Oh, man…* She closed her eyes.

"Are you still with me?" Angie insisted.

"Yes," Tristan groaned.

"So, talk to me. Is everything alright with you?"

"Yes, fine. But I may have been a bit intense with Huxley tonight."

"Dammit, Tris! Intense like an official complaint? Or a lawsuit landing on my desk? How serious are we talking here?"

"Relax, Angie. It's none of that."

"What do you mean, then?"

Tristan winced, regretting the beginning of an admission. The problem was not being intense as such, but getting personal. She had allowed her feelings to come up, and let Huxley see too much. She regretted that, for sure.

"Never mind," she sighed. "I was just very honest about the level of threat that she may be facing. To answer your question, I feel fine about the assignment. Huxley needs help, that's pretty clear. And I'm the best for the job. I'm happy to be looking after her."

"Perfect." Angie sounded a lot more satisfied. "Don't let the showbiz aspect of it get to you, okay?"

"Yeah, no worries."

"And let me know if you need anything, resource-wise."

"Will do."

Tristan hung up thinking that she was well-armored against the showbiz aspect of things... For at least one reason that she did not want to consider any further, the woman herself might prove harder to deal with.

••

Huxley's first scheduled outing two nights later was to a venue in downtown Lewiston, for what was described on paper as '*An intimate Live performance.*' Tristan got the details from Wright.

"Starting at 9 p.m., it will be a 45-minute performance with 15 minutes of Q&A at the end. Questions are being posted online and will be read out by the presenter. No direct chit-chat with the audience. Small crowd. Only a hundred people, no tickets on the door. And the show will be recorded, so a camera crew will be present. We know them well. Worked with these guys plenty of times before."

"How about extra security at the venue? During the show and for arrival and departure?"

"Yes, we'll have that too."

"Can you give me their contact info?"

"Of course."

The man sounded mildly disgusted when he had to interact with her, and downright condescending at times. But Tristan did not mind that, so long as he gave her the information required. She was pleased to discover that Wright was actually switched-on and precise when it came to organizational details. She got Angie to check out the other security company, which turned out to be a reputable one, and would provide adequate cover on the night. She also rode her bike to the venue one day, to recce the area. It was fine. Even Erik did not need to be instructed to wash and prep the vehicle, another Range Rover almost identical to the ones owned by Dagger Inc.

"Too heavy for my taste, but fun to throw around a bit," he told her.

"Where will you be during the concert?" she asked.

"Watching it, of course!" He shrugged as if it were obvious.

Knowing him, Tristan was not too surprised at the answer. And, *of course,* she had to set him straight.

"Whenever we go somewhere, I want you to stay with the vehicle at all times."

"What? In it?"

"Yes. In it, behind the wheel, and in contact with me. First, to make sure that no one messes with the car while the rest of us are at the venue. And also, if I need you quickly, you have to be able to respond immediately."

"Understood, Boss." He gave her a quick salute.

"I need you to take this seriously, Erik."

"I am!" He punched her playfully on the shoulder. "When you've known me a while, you'll realize that. I just like to smile at the same time. Life's too short to be grumpy, Briggs."

CHAPTER
9

After inviting her home on that first night, admittedly because she was curious about her, Huxley pretty much just ignored the new member of her team. Tristan did not mind that either. With improved security hardware and protocols around the property, she did not have to watch her client so closely when she was at home. For a couple of days, the singer seemed content to spend hours in her studio, work out in her private gym, or lounge by the side of the pool with Sex Pistol. She was polite when Tristan checked in with her, but did not encourage further conversation. Fair enough. Tristan was respectful of her private space and she remained out of sight as much as possible. The evening of the event, she dressed in her standard Go-Time outfit: blue jeans, running shoes in case she had to move fast, and a fitted jacket over a tight t-shirt to cover her weapon. Ready early, as was her custom, she waited outside the house with Erik for Huxley to come out. He was the first to see her.

"Hey, Al. Looking lush with a capital *L.*, girl!"

Tristan looked up from checking her phone. She planned a more professional hello, but even with that, the words failed her.

She'd grown used to seeing Huxley in a pair of baggy shorts, unlaced trainers, and a t-shirt. Tristan knew that tonight would be different, but she was still unprepared for the result. Huxley wore a black, backless dress, with a vertiginous slit down her left thigh. Lots of jewelry on show; large rings on every other finger, bracelets, a skull necklace, and a cuff-like, gold bangle, around her left ankle. On her feet were the kind of shoes that Tristan might wear if she deliberately decided to kill herself walking down the stairs. Her skin looked tanned and smooth. Make-up, perfectly applied. And she'd messed-up her hair again, giving her that wild and sexy look.

"Hell, yeah," Huxley approved of Erik's greeting in a rich and husky chuckle. "The Rock Goddess has arrived!"

••

Alys had been deliberately ignoring her new bodyguard because she did not enjoy being reminded of the reason for her constant presence. And something else, too... Now, it would be harder to pretend that she did not exist when they were sharing the same car to the venue. She could always invoke the need to get into the zone ahead of her performance, retreat behind a pair of dark glasses, and keep silent the whole way. But that would only be fooling herself. Ignoring Briggs also took a little too much effort. Upon stepping outside, Alys immediately struggled to take her eyes off her. The woman was handsome, dark, and dangerous in equal measures. Alys suppressed a shiver when their eyes met, something which only happened *after* Briggs took in every inch of her. She was very quick and polite with it, but she certainly did look, and Alys noticed her stern expression shift in reaction. It was only for an instant, but incredibly revealing all the same.

So many emotions were there for her to observe in that split second of not being so on guard: the layer of sadness which Alys had seen before, and reluctance, perhaps associated with it. But beyond that, she also detected heat, intensity, hunger... Damn, it looked a lot like desire. Alys promptly forgot where she was and almost missed a step in reaction to it all. For sure, it had nothing to do with her Jimmy Choos.

"Good evening, Ms. Huxley."

Briggs caught her elbow lightly yet no less commandingly, restoring her balance and establishing herself as her support for the night with astonishing ease. It hinted at lots of practice, and Alys was dismayed to feel a hint of jealousy at the thought. *Man, you're crazy.* Either that, or she needed to get laid as a matter of urgency.

"Briggs," she nodded. "Dressed up for the occasion, I see?"

"I did, actually." The answer came in that attractive mix of serious and amused. "Dressed for the job. Nobody's going to be looking at me tonight anyway."

Alys did not acknowledge the comment, which may or may not have been a subtle compliment, and she held back on one of her own. *You're wrong.* Briggs was sure to turn heads, no matter who the main attraction might be.

"Let's go," she declared.

Brad had gone ahead to the venue, so it was only the two of them in the back of the Rover. As Briggs climbed in next to her, Alys pushed the privacy button. Eric did not like it when she did that, cutting him off from the main cabin with a pane of opaque glass in between them, but hey; *Tough.*

"Everything okay, Ms. Huxley?" Briggs inquired.

"Everything's fine," Alys confirmed. "I just like some peace and quiet ahead of battle."

"Is that how you view this event?"

"Not in a negative way. Just show-time."

"I do know what you mean," Briggs said. "I call it my Go-Time."

"Are you nervous?"

"No. Are you?"

"Not in the least."

They shared a smile, and Alys allowed herself to lean a little closer.

"So. When we get there, it's going to be mayhem, okay?"

"Yes, I'm sure it will be. No problem."

"Just warning you, Briggs. My fans are hardcore, as intense as I am and sometimes more. I know this sort of thing can be a shock to the system if you're not used to it."

Steady green eyes turned to her, Briggs' expression quietly assessing. But Alys was only half-teasing. Women asking her to autograph their naked boobs in order to have her hand-writing tattooed on their flesh was on the tame side when it came to her admirers. Briggs returned her attention forward.

"I was in Iraq once, driving a client to the US embassy," she recalled. "Our driver took a wrong turn and we ended up in the middle of a street market. Had to stop and turn around. It took a while. Suddenly, the car was surrounded by armed Taliban."

Alys stared at her strong face in profile.

"How did you get out of it?" she prompted.

"We couldn't have," Briggs chuckled. "But we got lucky on that occasion, and they decided to let us go. I think I'll be alright facing music fans at a concert."

"Excellent. So, we're all set then."

"Yes. Extra security will be waiting outside. We'll just rush you in when we get there and—"

"No," Alys said softly.

"I'm sorry?" Briggs appeared momentarily confused.

Alys suspected that she was used to being the one in charge and issuing orders. Well. *Welcome to my world.*

"We won't just *'Rush me in'*, Briggs," she let her know. "This isn't UPS. I'm not some package to be handled. I'll take my time outside and say hi to my fans before going in. Some of them will have been waiting all day for this, you know?"

Briggs made a visible effort not to simply blurt out what she had in mind, which was all to her credit. Alys also quite liked to see her struggling a little.

"I understand it's part of the job," Briggs stated.

"Correct. I'm glad you do."

Alys had to believe that the gesture was intentional when her bodyguard rested her shoulder lightly against hers. Briggs did not strike her as the sort of person who acted inadvertently. And the move sure got her attention.

"Ms. Huxley, I'm not here to make your life harder."

"You said that to me before, yes."

"That's because I mean it."

She may not be a singer but her voice was well-modulated, expressive and warm. Alys allowed their shoulders to continue to touch, taking advantage of the moment.

"The other thing you said was about my music giving joy to people, and it's true as well. But it's not just that. People enjoy the Huxley experience. The looks, the voice, the attitude… The branded product is me. So, I have to give them access."

"Have to?"

"Sorry, wrong words. I want to!" Alys corrected. "Singing is my whole life. I am in love with it, and performing. Tonight, a ticket will set you back a hundred bucks. It's not cheap."

"No," Briggs agreed. "Especially not in these times."

"Too right! And without my fans, there would be no rock star Alys Huxley either. I love them too, just as much, and I want to give back to them."

"Of course, I understand."

"I hate having barriers between us. We're all people at the end of the day, aren't we? We should be able to connect freely. The idea that I won't be able to because of some creepy asshole drives me nuts!" Emotion crept into her voice and she clenched her fists. "Sorry, Briggs. I didn't mean for all that to come out."

"It's okay." The bodyguard flashed a bright and reassuring smile. "I like to hear it, and to see you like that."

"Like what?"

"All fired-up."

"You like it, uh?" Alys arched a dubious eyebrow in almost challenge. "How come?"

In the expectant pause that followed, she was almost afraid of what Briggs might answer. In all honesty, Alys realized now that she really wanted the woman to *'Like'* her... In that way. The sudden flash of insight blindsided her something crazy. *Oh my God!* She had known Briggs all of three days. Not even three full ones! *Well, we had dinner. Surely that counts for something too?* The little voice in her head reminded her of Rose, who always took such a measured and kind approach to situations when Alys generally tended to drive herself too hard and into the ground. *Be patient with yourself. You're so relentless. You know, you're doing better than 99% of people on this planet, Al! It's okay to slow down and take care of yourself from time to time.* Well... Alys had no idea. She only knew two speeds: a hundred miles an hour, or faster. And now, the gentle voice was attempting to find excuses for her silly ideas. She could not let it. *Can I?* Briggs smiled again.

"I like your attitude because it fires me up too," she said in answer. "Feeling your passion and dedication is a blast. I find it hugely motivating."

The admission was nothing too crazy, yet the way that she lingered afterwards, eyes locked onto Alys's and with that sexy smile tugging at the corners of her lips, was beyond alluring. It made Alys want to grab her by the scruff of the neck and kiss her until they both ran out of oxygen. She wondered if the thought carried through to Briggs. It was so intense that she would not have been surprised if it did. *Don't be stupid, Alys!* It took all her willpower not to stare at the woman's mouth, sensuous and full, and to draw back from her.

"Well," she snorted, hiding her feelings behind a joke. "We sound like a sports team ahead of a big game, don't we?"

"Yeah, something like that," Briggs chuckled in agreement. As the Rover slowed down, she leaned over to hit the partition button on Alys's side. Reaching across, her arm almost brushed against her breasts. The fact that it did not was, quite obviously, once again not an accident. This time, it felt like confirmation that Briggs was aware of her. Perhaps, *'In that way'*. And being careful with it. Alys did not share it with her, but she liked that very much too. As the glass panel went down, Briggs issued instructions to Erik. "Park on the street after you let us out. And remember what I told you. Okay?"

"Gotcha, Briggs," he answered, and shot her a wink in the rearview mirror. "Have fun, Alys. Set the house on fire!"

"Thanks, darling. I'm planning on it."

A red carpet had been laid out for her, and Alys took a deep breath. She was never nervous ahead of a performance, but she always felt butterflies in her stomach at this stage. Now that she could see the fans lined up, and hear them chanting her name...

She grinned in excitement, anticipation, and pure joy. It was the usual mix of emotions, and she welcomed them all. Alys relished the rush and absolutely thrived on it. Yet, tonight, there was also an unpleasant sliver of apprehension at the back of her mind. *Don't worry about it. Just focus on the job.* She quickly regained control, but it was as if Briggs were in her head this time. Warm fingers squeezed her wrist, the pressure gentle yet sure and firm. Confident. Her bodyguard spoke against her ear in a voice that only she could hear.

"I'll be right with you the whole time, Ms. Huxley. Even if you lose sight of me, don't worry: I won't lose sight of you."

Alys would not have thought of herself as the type to need this kind of reassurance… But it definitely steadied her, and she allowed herself to look Briggs in the eye for a second, and give her a grateful smile.

"Thanks. Let's do this thing."

CHAPTER
10

Granted, this crowd could not be compared to a band of Taliban armed with AK-47s. And Tristan only told Huxley the story to reiterate that she was in good hands, anyway. But yeah; her fans were quite something. As soon as the singer stepped out of the car, name-chanting turned into excited screaming. Tristan was fascinated to see the transformation in her client as well. She had noticed her slight hesitation before going out, and realized it had nothing to do with performance anxiety. In that instant, Huxley appeared strangely vulnerable. Even more concerning perhaps was the urge that Tristan felt to enfold her in her arms and kiss the fear away. She was not in the habit of kissing clients, to be sure. Then again, temptation was easy to avoid when they were all usually men... Anyway. Huxley recovered without the need for mouth-to-mouth. By the time she set one foot on the ground, she had morphed into character. Bye-bye, Alys; and Hello, Rock Goddess! Her fans obviously lapped it up as she approached the security barrier on the side of the club entrance.

"Alys! *ALYS!!*" A middle-aged guy screamed to try to catch her attention. "Marry me, please! Please, please, MARRY ME!"

Thanks to Huxley's heads-up about her plans, Tristan knew that she would hang around a bit and entertain. She clocked four officers, big strapping guys dressed identically in jeans and black t-shirts labelled as STAFF. They kept close to the barrier, facing the crowd, flanking Huxley on both sides. Tristan was happy with this tactic. She wanted the people to see these guys and take notice of their size and power. She would handle the close protection side of it.

"Ah, I'm not the marrying kind, darling," Huxley declared with a chuckle. She patted the guy on the cheek, which seemed for all the world to send him into a kind of trance. She moved on then, addressing other people like friends. "Hey, nice to see you again! How're you doing? I like the hair, babe. Selfie with me, handsome? Of course!"

Her unique voice cut spectacularly through the noise as she addressed her people. She was calm, slow, and deliberate, while in front of her, total chaos reigned. Phones were being thrust in her direction, selfie sticks brandished over other people's heads, flowers handed out or literally thrown her way. Tristan spotted a young girl pressed against the front of the barrier. Tiny, not more than twelve or thirteen. Her eyes shone full of emotion as she watched her idol make her way slowly toward her. Just at that point, one of the security guards prevented a big guy from trampling all over her in his attempt to get close to the front.

"Hey, what the—" he started to protest.

"Don't be an asshole," the guard said, and pushed him off.

Tristan did not linger watching that, since the situation was under control, but she certainly approved of the guard's move. Huxley could well have gone past the kid without seeing her, just due to her size and the sheer number of people. But she was obviously an old hand at this, and paying attention.

"Hi there!" She stopped in front of her and got down to eye level. "What's your name?"

"Jessie." The girl radiated a toothy smile bright enough to power the entire street.

"Duck under that barrier, Jessie," Huxley instructed. "Come on over to my side."

No doubt a photo with a young fan would look good on the cover of a tabloid magazine. But preventing the girl from being crushed by a heaving mass of people was more important, and Tristan appreciated the fact that it was Huxley's only intention in bringing her forward. She would have done it herself if not. The girl's official Huxley t-shirt was promptly autographed, and her phone passed on to Tristan.

"Briggs. Take a picture, will ya?"

Tristan's eyebrows rocketed upwards, prompting Huxley to wink in amused challenge. Since it would be safer to oblige than to argue with her about the importance of remaining uninvolved and focused on her job at all times, Tristan grabbed the phone and quickly snapped a couple of shots of the badass rocker and her young friend, who were sticking their tongues out at her and laughing. Fair to say that the kid would remember this day for the rest of her life. Tristan noticed that her head barely reached the top of the outrageous slit in Huxley's dress... Despite her best intentions, her attention was drawn to her figure again. She did well not to linger on the smooth expanse of naked flesh.

"We should move on, Ms. Huxley," she stated.

"Thank you all for coming!" Huxley addressed the crowd in her trademark husky voice. "Love you, beautiful people! See you later!"

Once safely inside the studio, Wright caught up with her.

"You're on in 20." he announced. "Feeling good?"

"I feel great," Huxley nodded. "Time to rock and roll!"

As the concert was about to start, Tristan positioned herself on the left side of the stage, as close to her as possible while still remaining out of line of the cameras. She had a good view of the audience from that spot as well. The four security guys lined up along the bottom of the stage. Tristan was satisfied with this set-up. If anybody tried to rush on stage and get to Huxley, they should be able to stop them. And if their attempt failed, Tristan would take care of it. She was pleased that everyone here tonight had gone through an airport-style metal detector at the entrance, and had their belongings checked. This was all as safe as could be. Reaching for her phone, she gave Erik a quick call.

"Just checking in, man. How's it going?"

"Nice and boring, Briggs. Nice and boring."

"Good. That's the best kind of news in my world."

"Haha!" He laughed. "I got a good spot to park in."

"Excellent. I'll let you know when we're ready to go."

In the meantime, Tristan prepared to settle and keep a close eye on the proceedings. Huxley was delivering a stripped-down performance tonight, with only herself and a guitarist from her regular band to accompany her. As advertised, this was going to be an intimate experience for her fans. And not just for them… Tristan soon realized that this evening could totally wreck her concentration if she was not careful. She had her eyes on the audience, scanning their faces for any sign of trouble. But when Huxley decided to kick things off with a long drawn-out and sultry, *"Hey-yeah-hey-eh…'* it made her look sharply back. *Phew…* Tristan had never heard anything quite so captivating. Huxley was naturally gifted with an incredible voice, but singing both Live and Solo brought an even greater dimension to it. *I wonder why she even bothers to bring on a band at other times…*

Tristan was so taken aback by that astonishing introduction to one of Huxley's best singles that she did not notice Bradley Wright standing next to her until he huffed in irritation. She did well not to jump. *Dammit, Tris!*

"Good evening, Wright." She re-focused instantly.

"Everything ok with security?" he asked.

"Couldn't be better, yes."

"Good." He shot her a downright suspicious glance. "Keep it that way."

He left on that, apparently just happy with being unfriendly and issuing unnecessary orders. The more Tristan witnessed of him, though, the more she could tell that he did an excellent job for Huxley behind the scenes. Since this was the most important thing, she would forgive him a few eccentricities.

"Thank you so much!" Huxley ended a dirty blues number to thunderous applause. "Y'all are the best!"

In between songs, she entertained with personal comments, cheeky flirting with the front row, and lots of laughter with the rest of the audience. Tristan remained alert and ready the whole time, but it was clear that everyone in the studio was deep under Huxley's charm, and here for the right reasons: entertainment and fun. The show went quickly. Soon, Huxley launched into her last song of the night. Halfway through, she stopped singing and encouraged the audience to finish for her while she sat back and made a show of enjoying herself.

"Beautiful!" she crooned. "You guys are the best!"

After the arranged Q&A, she treated everyone to two more songs from her new album for a remarkable Encore. Wright was back next to her by then and Tristan caught his impatient mutter under his breath.

"She's forever screwing with my schedule."

He was smiling as he complained, clearly also not immune to his client's special brand of charisma.

"Thank you for coming everybody! Goodnight!"

Huxley came off-stage on that, eyes fever-bright and totally high on the experience. She literally seemed infused with extra light. When she smiled, blue eyes locking on to hers, Tristan reflected that it would be hard, actually, not to fall a little bit in love with this incredibly woman. Perhaps, even for her.

••

"Uh, Briggs...?" Erik called just as Tristan was reaching for her phone to request a pickup. He sounded unsure and even a little spooked, which put her on alert.

"What's up, Erik?" she snapped.

"Some guy just dropped a note on my windshield!"

In front of her, just outside her waiting room door, Huxley was chatting with a group of people. Wright; her guitarist; the studio exec; the evening presenter. And a handful of reporters as well. She was glowing, her energy high. Tristan spoke low enough to stay under the radar, but she kept her tone sharp, so that Erik would pay attention.

"Where is that guy now?"

"Dunno, he legged it down the street."

"He touched the car?"

"Yeah, like I said... Lifted the wiper blade right in front of my face and slid a piece of paper under it."

"Did you get a good look at him?"

"No. He was all in black, hood up and dark glasses."

"You got gloves to wear?"

"Uh... No?"

"Never mind. You can retrieve the note off the windshield, but be careful not to touch it with your fingers."

"Ah, for fingerprints, yeah?"

"Yes."

"Why didn't you say, Briggs? I'm not that dumb! Hold on a sec."

Tristan kept her patience as she listened to sounds of traffic increase when he got out of the car. Two seconds later, she heard the door slam shut and Erik was back on the phone.

"Got it."

"So, is that a message?"

"Yeah…" Erik exhaled sharply in reaction. "Shit! Hey, that's creepy!"

"Tell me what it says," she hissed.

"*'I'M WATCHING YOU'*. All in caps."

Goddammit. Tristan instinctively pressed her hand over the weapon under her jacket and she narrowed her eyes at the rest of the assembled group. No member of the public was allowed backstage, but it made little difference. A little less pushing and shoving, maybe, but everyone appeared as excited. Some carried official photos and marker pens, obviously ready to demand an autograph. A bottle of champagne appeared out of nowhere and a woman yelled as the cork was popped. About to get rowdy in here, and certainly too crowded. *Time to get Huxley out…*

"Erik, I need you to come back here for pick-up," Tristan instructed.

"Okay."

"Wait fifteen minutes, then leave. Make sure no one follows you home."

"What about Alys?" He sounded puzzled.

"I'll take care of her, just do what I said."

"Alright, Briggs." She could almost hear him shrug. "You the boss."

Tristan pocketed her phone and eased her way to Huxley's side through a throng of her admirers. One or two looked at her funny but no one dared to get in her way. Few ever tried when she switched-on to full bodyguard mode.

"Ms. Huxley, we need to go."

Huxley barely spared her a glance before ostensibly turning her back to continue sipping her champagne and holding court. Tristan was used to being given the cold shoulder, as this clearly was. Attitude was fine, but it wouldn't change the outcome.

"Ms. Huxley." She did not raise her voice but gently clasped the singer's elbow.

"What is it, Briggs?" Huxley tossed impatiently.

"We need to leave. Now." The message was clear enough to spark a flicker of recognition in the singer's clear blue eyes, and Tristan felt her tense. "It's okay. Just follow me, please."

CHAPTER 11

Tristan took her hand, which was no big deal in her line of work. She had led plenty of clients of all shapes, sizes, and gender, by the hand many times before. Best way she knew of ensuring that they remained connected to her, and safe, during an extraction. But Huxley immediately laced her fingers through hers, the way she would hold onto a lover's hand. Her fingers were warm; her grip, the perfect mix of gentle and firm. The response was both incredibly familiar but also unexpected, and Tristan heated all over in reaction. Irritated at her own biological response, she ignored the sure rush of arousal, and caught Wright's eye across the hallway.

"Leaving," she mouthed silently for his information.

He had been briefed and knew to carry on as usual. Tristan led Huxley through a side door and quickly down a short flight of stairs. Left, through another door, and into a deserted parking space. She moved confidently, having memorized the layout of the building ahead of time. In less than thirty seconds, they had left the noise and groupies behind and were alone again. Tristan breathed a little easier then, but her relief was not shared.

"What the hell's going on?" Huxley huffed in frustration as her heels echoed across emptiness. "Way to go to kill the mood, uh?"

Tristan did not answer the obvious: *'Rather the mood than the woman.'*

"Sorry about that," she conceded. "But someone left a note on the Rover to say that he was watching you. We have to go."

"What?" Huxley came to an abrupt stop, forcing her to do the same.

"Yes, he's fine." Tristan squeezed her hand in reassurance. "And you're in no immediate danger. I just think it's best not to hang around here for too long."

Huxley stared, unmoving and hard.

"It's that guy, isn't it? The one sending me the letters."

"It could be, yes. But don't worry," Tristan added when she noticed her eyes go flat. "Erik will wait in front of the studio to give everyone the impression that you'll be out any minute."

"Where are we going?"

"Home, just not the way that everyone thinks."

Huxley was quick to recover as they started moving again, and soon treated her to a flirtatious chuckle, the likes of which she seemed so fond of dispensing on stage.

"You're slick, Briggs," she observed. "I said it before... And now you can't deny it, can you?"

Tristan met her eyes and found her smirking.

"I never said I couldn't be. But this is just decent planning and being a professional. That's why you pay me the big bucks, Ms. Huxley."

"I've no idea how much you get paid." Huxley snorted and she pulled on her hand. "Wait. I have to take these off if you insist on racing around like Jason Bourne."

Tristan kept her steady as she pulled off her heels, and her own jaw tightly clenched for control. It occurred to her that her fans would give a lot to see Huxley right now. Barefoot, in that fabulous dress, still a little hyper from the show. *Still holding my hand like...* Tristan did not allow herself to think of what it was like.

"Does your Highness require a piggy back, Rock Goddess?" she asked instead, eager to break the sudden tight knot in her stomach.

"Shut up!" Huxley laughed, and that did the trick.

They reached the fire exit, where Tristan made her wait as she checked the alleyway on the other side. All quiet and empty, as expected.

"Okay, we can go," she invited.

Huxley stepped out and looked around suspiciously.

"Are you going to call an Uber?"

"No." Tristan smiled and pointed to a regular Ford Ranger truck parked on the side. "This is our ride."

●●

So, her serious bodyguard had a sense of humor after all. Briggs was not afraid to tease her a little bit – *Even better.* Alys enjoyed a good roasting, even if not many people were up to the task of giving it to her these days. She was, after all, *THE* Alys Huxley! The hype tended to make folks shy.

"I don't know how to take all this," she blurted out as her escort jumped behind the wheel. "I'm not sure how to feel about it."

Briggs glanced at her, her gaze warm and sympathetic.

"A client of mine once said it was surreal."

"Yes, that's a good word. Surreal. What happened to that client?"

"The guy who threatened her was arrested and she's now being looked after by the Secret Service."

"High-up political person?"

"Yes."

"You're not going to tell me who?"

"Nope," Briggs smiled.

"You don't kiss and tell," Alys reflected. "I like that about a woman. So, what now?"

"We'll pass the note on to the police, see if they can lift any prints. CCTV on the street might give us a few more clues as to the identity of this guy. Now we know that your stalker is male. That's progress."

"Yeah." Alys groaned. "Slow progress…"

"For the time being," Briggs reminded her in a gentle voice. "Ms. Huxley?"

"Mm?"

"Buckle up, please."

Alys rolled her eyes for effect and mused privately that if she had to be micro-managed, having a woman who looked like Briggs doing it wasn't so bad, at least.

"I don't feel scared," she added.

"Good. There's no point, but staying alert is helpful."

And she certainly was… Alys observed her easy grip on the steering wheel as she drove with one hand, her free one resting on the gear lever. Strong hands… Graceful fingers. Holding onto her had been unexpectedly comfortable earlier, like a no-brainer. Reflecting on that, and thinking of how these attractive fingers might feel caressing her bare legs, was dangerous territory. Alys did not go any further down that road.

"Are you going to drive past the venue?" she asked.

"Yes, I'd like to take a look. Just duck down a little when we do, okay?"

Alys hid herself behind her shoulder as Briggs cruised past the studio on the far-sided lane of the street. She saw the Rover parked in front of the red carpet, where Erik had been instructed to wait, and rows of eager fans behind the security barriers, all waiting for a glimpse of her.

"I hate to disappoint them."

"I know… I'm sorry."

Briggs was sincere with that comment, which was nice.

"We should stake out the place," Alys suggested. "See if we can spot him in the crowd. Creepy should stand out, don't you think?"

"Not with you inside the car, Ms. Huxley."

"You could let me out then. I'll get a taxi."

Briggs turned her head fast enough toward her to give herself a nasty whiplash. Alys smiled apologetically.

"Sorry. Only kidding."

"Right. Of course, you are."

"So, you planned all this ahead of time?" Alys prompted as they drove on. "Extra vehicle and a hidden escape route, in case something bad happened?"

"It pays to always have a backup plan for public events of this kind, yes. It's standard procedure, close-protection 101."

"Where did you learn this stuff? Bodyguarding school?"

"There are courses you can take. As a cop, I was…" Briggs' tension was noticeable in the way that she suddenly gripped the wheel with both hands, tight enough to make her knuckles turn white. She swallowed hard before finishing abruptly. "I just took all the courses available."

And I bet you aced them all... Alys did not comment on that. Just like the other night in her kitchen, Briggs' reaction was both intense and telling. And once again, she knew not to ask her any more. Briggs' energy had shifted to a metaphorical *'BACK OFF'* vibe. Whatever happened to make her so sensitive to the topic of her previous career was obviously still off-limits.

"Alright," Alys simply nodded. "Thank you for getting me out of there."

"Sure." Briggs relaxed. "You're welcome, Ms. Huxley."

In the ensuing silence, it occurred to Alys that she was now off-schedule and also off-grid, pretty much. Not performing or on her way to a concert; not stuck at home or in the studio; not doing an interview or a promo event. At this precise moment, no one knew where she was or how to get hold of her. No demands, no responsibilities... As Briggs accelerated smoothly on their way out of Lewiston, it was thrilling to realize that the night was all hers. For once in her life, Alys Huxley was AWOL. And indeed, totally free. Her heart swelled in reaction.

"Let's do something crazy!" she exclaimed.

"Yeah, let's not," Briggs muttered, frowning as she stared at the road ahead.

"Hey, I'm serious."

"Yes. So am I."

"Briggs, listen to me." Alys laid an insistent hand over her thigh and was instantly rewarded by the feel of hard muscles contracting under her palm. She may have been wrong but it felt as if Briggs shivered. Alys kept her hand in place, not dwelling on the sense of power that the reaction gave her but enjoying it all the same. "What's the point of having a getaway car if you don't make good use of it, right?"

"I'm sorry?"

"Let's go to the beach."

"What? It's after one o'clock in the morning."

"Damn! Too late for ice cream, you think?"

Briggs did turn to shoot her a confused look at this point.

"You are serious, aren't you?"

"Hundred percent."

"Ms. Huxley, I don't—"

"Hold on." Alys leaned closer. "Do you know how often I get to do the kind of stuff that everybody else takes for granted? Like popping out to Starbucks or hitting the beach late at night, just because it's hot and I feel like it?"

"Probably not very often," Briggs reflected.

"That's right. Lately, make that never. I do love my life, but sometimes I wish that I could just be a regular girl with a regular existence. I'm very good at— What is it?" Alys invited when she noticed Briggs' quick and private smile.

"Just thinking of what Angie said to me once."

"Angie, yes. Your boss. What did she say?"

"That you couldn't fade into anonymity even if you fell into a black hole."

"Gosh, what a depressing description!"

"I'm sorry, Ms. Huxley. She didn't mean it as an insult."

"Yeah, I know." Alys shrugged and heaved a heavy sigh as she moved away slightly, her mood darkening. "Don't be sorry. It may be depressing but it's accurate. It is what it is."

She pulled the rings off her fingers, unclasped her necklace and bracelets, and threw the whole lot in her clutch bag. Briggs' phone, in a holder on the dash, went off as she started to take her make-up off with wet wipes.

"Erik." she replied instantly. "Sit-rep, please."

"Uh... Say again?"

91

Alys shook her head in fresh irritation. Even she knew what a situation report was, dammit! Briggs did not seem to mind having to re-phrase the question, and she also didn't waste time enlightening him.

"Just fill me in," she requested. "Where are you now?"

Sharp and to the point, as always. Efficiency, skills, all-round excellence... For sure, these were attractive qualities in people. But for some reason, with this particular woman, Alys got even more of a kick out of it than usual. She'd been furious at the thought of requiring another bodyguard, but now... *I wonder what it is about her that makes it so painless.* Perhaps it was simply the fact that Briggs was female and attractive. Relaxed yet tough, and quick to smile as well. Alys had noted how expressive her green eyes could be, although Briggs obviously kept herself on a tight leash. Her reserve did not appear only professional. What would a woman like Tristan Briggs, apparently so accomplished and in control, be like when she allowed herself to let go? And actually... *What would it feel like to be the one to take that control away from her?* Alys bit on her lip and she suppressed a shiver. Meanwhile, Erik was talking.

"I waited fifteen, like you said," he confirmed. "Then I left crying fans in the dust and drove on home. No one followed me there."

Alys shook her head at this unpleasant description. She'd have to make it up to her people, somehow...

"You still got the note, yeah?" Briggs said.

"Sure thing, I do. Slid it inside the plastic pocket that has the Rover registration card in it. To preserve any fingerprints if there are any."

"Good job, Erik."

"Alright." He sounded proud. "See you when I do."

Alys was not surprised when he did not ask where she was, or if she was okay. It did not take very much to distract or over-whelm her excitable cousin. That business with the stalker's note and being given a mission by Briggs, who was the sort of person that he would want to impress, would be enough. She remained quiet, staring unseeingly at the road ahead.

"Are you okay, Ms. Huxley?" Briggs inquired.

"Yes, I am." Alys shrugged. "Always moody after a live gig. It's such a high, you know? Massive adrenaline rush. Just ignore me."

CHAPTER 12

Huxley obviously had no idea of what she was asking here... Tristan could no more ignore her than she could stop breathing. She also understood the sort of high that the singer described, way better than Huxley might have thought. Once upon a time, Detective Briggs survived on a steady regime of adrenaline and fear. She'd learned to deal with it. To control the crazy highs that might lead her to take too many risks, and the crushing lows that left her feeling exhausted for days on end, and often sick. Tristan was no stranger to living on the edge, and the sort of loneliness that this could create as well.

"I felt the energy tonight when you were on stage," she told her client. "It was powerful."

"Yeah, and that was only a small crowd. Wait until you're behind the scenes at a massive stadium!" Huxley chuckled, her excitement palpable. "I can still feel the rush right now. I am so totally *On*! Coming down after a show is a bitch, you know?"

"I can imagine." Tristan remembered having to go on long runs to recover from a rush. Ten, fifteen, even up to twenty miles one night. "How do you deal with this kind of pressure?"

"Oh..." Huxley shrugged unhappily. "When I don't have a stalker getting in the way of things, and I am with the rest of the band, I normally stay up all night, talking and partying with my crew."

"Getting rid of excess energy on the dance floor?"

"Sometimes. There are other ways to do it, too. Quicker and more relaxing ways to, uh..."

Tristan glanced at her when she did not finish and noticed a hint of challenge in her blue eyes. Huxley was clearly baiting her for a reaction.

"Like smoking dope and taking downers?" she prompted.

"Well." Huxley regarded her with an amused smile. "I will neither confirm nor deny that, Officer Briggs."

Tristan suppressed a smile at the blatant tease. Huxley sure did enjoy flirting with danger.

"Retired," she reminded her. "And anyway, smoking dope isn't illegal in this state. Whatever else you choose to do is up to you... I just hope you're careful."

As an Exit sign for the scenic coast road came up on the side of the freeway, Tristan automatically glanced in her rearview mirror.

"There's no one back there, Briggs," Huxley grumbled. "We got away clean."

"Just making sure, Ms. Huxley."

"Yeah, well. Like you said, it's the middle of the night now. And you know as well as I do that no stalker will be waiting for me at the beach."

Tristan kept up her speed, all the while wondering how she would feel in Huxley's shoes. *Probably frustrated enough to want to jump out the window by now.* The night was clear. Still in the mid-eighties, with only a gentle breeze blowing in from the ocean.

This was the sort of night when Tristan might take her bike out for a spin on that coast road, actually. She understood Huxley's desire to stay out, and she was correct as well; it would be safe, and there really was no reason not to facilitate the request. *I am her bodyguard, not her babysitter.* Huxley would be well within her right at this point to tell her to just shut up, and to take her to the beach, or anywhere of her choosing. Yet, she had not. Just asked, as if Tristan were a friend instead of someone paid to keep her safe.

"Hold on," she said, and veered off onto the exit lane with only a few yards of road left to spare.

"Alright!" Huxley yelled, beaming.

"Yeah, okay." Tristan laughed. "Where to, Ms. Huxley?"

"You pick, Briggs. Somewhere nice and sandy!"

• •

Tristan decided to head to Keller Point, a remote surfing spot on the outskirts of Lewiston which was bound to be nice and quiet at this time of night. A delighted if perhaps slightly over-excited Huxley insisted on picking up supplies along the way.

"A: I'm starving. And B: this is cause for celebration!"

"What is?"

"A rare night of freedom!" Huxley chuckled. "What's your poison of choice?"

"I don't drink, Ms. Huxley."

"When you're working or generally?"

"Generally."

"Oh?" When Tristan did not automatically fill in the blanks for her, Huxley just went on smoothly. "Well, that's okay. What can I get you instead?"

"Tell me what you want and I'll go into the store," Tristan replied. "Lock the doors and keep the engine running while I'm gone. Any problem, lay on the horn."

"Aye-aye, Captain," Huxley quipped. "But you know it's all fine, right? Please, relax!"

Twenty minutes later, Tristan followed her down a narrow sandy path to the beach below. Huxley was still in high spirits, eager to walk all the way to the water's edge and dip her toes in. Tristan remained close behind her, all senses on alert and keenly aware of their surroundings. The light of a splendid full moon illuminated several vehicles parked at the other end of the mile-long beach; the usual assortment of campervans and trucks with surfboards on the roof. She caught the smells of a bonfire and something nice cooking on someone's barbecue. Laughter on the breeze, the sound of a guitar. *Okay, then.* Tristan did relax a little more. This was fine, indeed. A typical summer's night out here, and a safe choice of location.

"It's really nice," Huxley announced, testing the water. "We should go skinny-dipping."

She walked in up to her mid-shins, holding up her dress in one hand and raking her fingers through her hair with the other. *She shines brighter than moonlight...* Tristan ignored the thought but she struggled to come up with an appropriate answer. 'Go ahead, I'll keep an eye on you', sounded weird given the topic.

"Huh-uh," she just mumbled, at a loss.

Huxley shot her a mischievous look in response.

"Are you up for it?"

"I'm on duty, Ms. Huxley."

"That's the worst excuse I ever heard!" Stepping back onto dry sand, Huxley started walking backwards, facing her with a teasing smile. "I didn't take you for the timid type, Briggs."

"Well… There you go."

"No, no… Don't give me that evasive line, it's not fair!" The singer chuckled, even as she fixed her intently. "Do you want to know what I think?"

Tristan shrugged at the rhetorical question, aware that she was about to be told, no matter what she answered. It occurred to her as well that she wanted to know, yes… And that it would not do. As if she could guess it all, Huxley pointed a knowing finger in her direction, her smile turning coy.

"I think that you must be the opposite of shy in private. Am I right?"

Not seeking an escape from her daring line of questioning, but genuinely alert to the sounds of people approaching, Tristan glanced over her head. *Dammit...* Did no one go to bed at night anymore? She spotted three men, not walking a too straight line. Rough laughter echoed after them, and two of them exchanged shoving gestures as they zig-zagged their way across the beach. They were clearly drunk. Definitely all over the place. Possibly friendly… And possibly not. Either way, Tristan did not want to risk her client being hassled.

"Ms. Huxley…" She instinctively held out her hand, and the singer just as naturally took it again, moving close. "I hate to tell you this, but I think we should go."

"No, it's fine," Huxley huffed in defeat. "I do know the line between exciting and stupid. Better not tempt fate. Let's go back to the car."

They sat on the tailgate, sharing nacho chips and sipping iced tea. Huxley had insisted on it after finding out that Tristan did not drink.

"I'm sorry we couldn't stay longer," she reflected.

"No, you're not," the singer snorted in reply. "Be honest."

"Well..." Tristan flashed a quick smile, amused at this way she had to call her out on the slightest inaccuracy. It was kinda nice, and she did not dwell on the reason why. "Let me rephrase that: I wish you could have had longer out there, but I'm happy to be back with the car. And for you to be safe."

"But you could have handled these guys, right?"

"In theory, yes." Tristan shrugged.

"Why in theory?"

"Because you never know who you might be facing. Their state of mind, if they have a weapon... Whenever you can, it's always best to walk away from this kind of potentially tricky situation. Then everybody's a winner."

"Very wise," Huxley approved.

"I'm glad you think so."

"Mmm, yes. And anyway, don't worry about it." Huxley made a sweeping gesture with her left arm. "Look! Here we are, with amazing views of the ocean out in front and a sea of stars over our heads. I don't need much more to be happy. And to feel free."

"Then I'm happy too."

"Hey, Briggs?"

As Huxley lowered her voice and pressed her naked thigh gently along the side of hers, Tristan unconsciously inclined her head toward her, and fought the urge to close her eyes.

"Yes, Ms. Huxley?" she murmured.

"Thanks for doing this."

"This? What do you mean?"

Huxley shrugged, looking uncharacteristically reluctant.

"This: sitting with me and sharing food. Just being here and being nice. In my world, people often treat you like an object. Do this, do that, stand here, smile at the camera... You know?"

"Yes, I have some idea." Tristan nodded, noting the slight dissociation in her sentence. *'In my world, people treat you like an object.* Huxley obviously sought to detach herself from the lack of human recognition involved. "I know you said people often see you as a brand, nothing else. And treat you accordingly."

"Yes..." Huxley looked up at the stars, biting on her lip.

Sensing a surge of subtle distress, Tristan gave her a gentle nudge, mimicking her previous gesture. Whether or not this was appropriate coming from her, in her official capacity as Huxley's bodyguard, only crossed her mind after the fact, when the singer squeezed her leg in recognition. Tristan was well aware that it was not her job to act as her friend, to *'Sit with me and share food'*, as Huxley thanked her for. And although it would be tempting to convince herself that she was only doing it out of professional concern and courtesy, Tristan knew that it would be lying. She wanted to be here now. And to be nice. For sure.

"Are you okay?" she asked, suppressing a sigh at her own self.

"Yes." Huxley glanced at her with glistening eyes. "I sound like I'm complaining a lot, don't I?"

"Not really. And I don't mind, anyway."

"Thanks... But I do. I understand how lucky I am to have been born in this life. From the age of twelve, when I first started performing, I never wanted for a single thing. I could pay off my parents' mortgage within a year, and move us to a better place the next. I've been able to support other members of my family. I sent two of my younger cousins to medical school, and gave Erik a job. I have been blessed in so many ways."

"Handling this level of fame and constant attention must be hard, though," Tristan prompted, sensing a *'But'* coming up and her hesitation.

"No, not even that." Huxley chuckled. "Apart from the odd freak from time to time, as we're having now, I handle this side of things just fine. Can't recall a time when I wasn't famous. And you won't like me saying this, Briggs, but I have my ways to go about incognito."

"You're right. I wish you didn't." *This won't be happening on my watch.*

"I just need regular clothes, a baseball cap, and sunglasses to fly under the radar, you know?"

Tristan shook her head at her naivete. She'd heard this sort of claim from other clients, and knew that they had no idea of the risks they were taking.

"You think I wouldn't recognize you in a crowd even if you wore a baseball cap? Simply from your build or the way that you walk?"

"Yeah, maybe you would," Huxley shrugged. "But it's your job."

"Not to mention the sound of your voice; it's better than a fingerprint to identify you."

"I usually stay quiet when I'm out."

"Oh. Can you do that?" Once again, despite the seriousness of the topic, Tristan could not help a gentle jibe.

"Hey!" Huxley laughed. "Don't forget your place!"

Tristan was joking, obviously, but it was sensible advice all the same. Huxley's flamboyant character was beyond attractive, and her more vulnerable side also triggered Tristan's protective instincts. She was aware of this, of course, and the danger of it. She had not felt the pull of attraction in quite this way in a long, long while. Even before the death of her partner, the job had taken its toll.

CHAPTER 13

It was probably normal to feel that one could trust their body-guard... Although with the last one, Alys discovered that it may not always be safe, nor wise, to do so. Tristan Briggs was clearly different, and one of a kind. Alys would not have suggested this outing at the beach otherwise. With anybody else, she probably would have just snuck out after arriving back home, and gone to visit Rose on her own, the way she often did. This was unusual, for sure, inviting a stranger along for the ride. She also did not usually feel the urge to confide in another human being the way that she did with Briggs. Alys was not entirely sure how to feel about that. Cautious, definitely. But the feeling was nice. And in the end, the urge proved irresistible.

"Can I tell you something really personal and a bit weird?" she asked.

Briggs met her gaze, green eyes sparkling beautifully in the moonlight and a faint smile dancing on her lips.

"It's kinda hard to say no when you put it like that."

"I'm going to risk it, then," Alys declared. "Remember that movie in which Mel Gibson can hear women's thoughts?"

"Ah… No, I'm not a big movie person."

"That's fine. Just to say that sometimes, when I'm talking to people, I can tell exactly what's on their mind. And half the time, it's absolutely not what they are telling me."

"Really?"

"Yes! Like, someone will be speaking emphatically, telling me how much they love and care for me, right?"

"Right."

"But at the same time, I'm totally aware that they think the complete opposite. A lot of people who claim to be my friends could not care less. Even family members, sometimes! They all think I don't know it, but I can see right through them. May as well be written above their heads: *Selfish sucker*. It's so—" Alys stopped abruptly when she noticed that Briggs was laughing. So, there she was, risking opening up to the woman for reasons that she did not even fully understand… And Briggs was *laughing?* Alys stared, wanting to be angry but feeling deflated instead. "What's so funny?"

"Nothing."

"Then why are you laughing at me?"

"I am not laughing at you, Ms. Huxley."

On that, Briggs pulled her close for a reassuring squeeze. Alys forgot the topic, and her indignation. Briggs' arm around her shoulders was something else… The woman was warm and strong, hard muscles in all the right places. Alys held her breath when she felt a softer and very female part of her bodyguard press against her side. She nearly gasped at the contact, but it was over in the blink of an eye when Briggs released her. Alys blinked hard a couple times. *Jesus, Al… Get a hold of yourself!*

"So, then what?" she demanded, hiding her fluster behind a harder tone.

"Just the way you describe it is funny," Briggs stated with a smile.

"The way I describe what, exactly?"

"Your ability to sense people's hidden motivation for being around you. Thank you for sharing something so personal with me, but there's nothing weird about it. In fact, it's often viewed as a higher form of intelligence."

Alys relaxed, realizing that Briggs sounded approving.

"You think so?" she prompted.

"It's a fact," the bodyguard grinned. "Want to know what cops call it in simple terms?"

"Sure, tell me."

"A good bullshit detector."

"Oh yeah," Alys chuckled. "I've heard of that before."

"It's a useful skill, worth cultivating. Communication on a higher level of mind and consciousness. Apparently, one of these days when we are all evolved enough, we won't even need to speak to communicate with each other."

Alys stared into her eyes, allowing her deepest thoughts to bubble to the surface. *Please, touch me again. Put your arm around me… Hold me…*

"What am I thinking now?" she challenged in a softer tone.

Briggs broke eye contact rather quickly, but not before Alys spotted a faint flush of color spreading across her cheeks. *Wow, did she get that?*

"Trying to trick me, I feel," Briggs said.

Those enigmatic green eyes locked back onto hers, and Alys felt heat rising in her own face.

"Absolutely not," she answered. *I was pleading, actually.* Her next question flew out of her mouth before she even knew what it would be. "Hey, why don't you drink?"

Far from looking away this time, Briggs narrowed her eyes slightly. She was very hard to read. Alys could not decide if the reaction was in warning, or assessment, or what... She raised a quick hand in apology.

"I'm sorry. Forget I asked that. I'm just—"

"It's okay," Briggs replied, glancing at the can of iced tea in her hand. Alys spotted a tiny muscle in her jaw twitch as she obviously considered her response carefully. It took several long seconds, during which she seemed stuck on a loop in her own head, unable to settle on a single answer. Until she looked over and actually smiled. "To put it simply, Ms. Huxley, I don't know how to stop with alcohol."

"I see... It's a common problem."

"Apparently so, yes."

"So, you just don't start, uh?"

"I don't start. It's too dangerous otherwise."

Briggs stared so hard, despite her easy expression, that Alys suddenly wondered if they were still on the same subject. But of course, they must be... Because, surely, her bodyguard was not sending her telepathic messages about not starting things which could only lead to trouble down the line. Alys glanced at her mouth and struggled to look away. She could not help a shiver. Briggs was dangerously attractive, indeed. It would be hard to stop with her, no doubt, if Alys were to start anything.

"Do you find it hard?" she murmured, pushing the thought aside.

It was strange, although not totally unpleasant, to discover that everything about Briggs aroused her curiosity. *And not just that...* Alys was far from shy, and her career afforded her plenty of opportunities to play. She did it openly and unapologetically. But this was different, she could feel. More than just lust.

"It gets easier," Briggs said.

That sixth sense of hers hinted at something more, deeper, and perhaps devastating, being left unsaid. Although this time, Alys realized that she was within sight of an important line. And that she should not cross it.

"I'm glad it does," she murmured. "Thank you for sharing."

"Sure." Briggs nodded sharply. "Let's go back to what you were saying to me before."

"Alright. What about it?"

"Being as rich and famous as you are is bound to attract all kinds of misguided people into your circle."

"Sharks and vampires," Alys snorted ironically. "Yeah, you got that right."

"Enemies?" Briggs insisted. "Jealous fake friends who may turn into stalkers one day?"

"Oh..." Alys had not been hinting at this, although with Briggs being a former cop, it made sense for her to zero in on the possibility. It was a good question, albeit a little disturbing for Alys to consider. She shook her head. "No, no... I can't think of anyone I know doing this. Some acquaintances may be jealous and try to profit from me from time to time... But never to the point of threats. Certainly, no one close to me would turn into a stalker!"

"Okay, that's fine." Briggs held her gaze, sympathy flashing across her handsome features. "You know it's part of my job to inquire about this sort of thing, right? I'm not accusing anyone in your team."

"Yes, I totally get it."

"Good. This aside, I also understand what you were trying to explain. I hope you have people you can trust and who love you in your life as well, not just stalkers and vampires."

"Yes." Alys laughed easily at the way she used her own words. "Erik does drive me nuts sometimes, but he does cares about me for real. Rose has been my best friend since I was nineteen. And Brad has stuck with me through thick and thin for years as well, even if he does not always agree with my creative choices. They love me no matter what, whether I'm a rock goddess or just a regular girl in love with her puppy."

"That's great," Briggs approved. "I'm glad to hear that. And Sex Pistol is a lucky pup."

The comment wasn't loaded, Alys knew that, and yet it hit her deep on the inside. She was dying to ask about Briggs... *Who do you love and trust? Who loves you back? What happened to put that wary look in your eyes?* Again, though, it felt as if the window had closed on confessions. So, she just opted for a safer question.

"Mind if we stay out here a bit longer and soak it in?"

"No problem, Ms. Huxley."

••

The last thing Alys remembered was Briggs retrieving a blanket from the truck's locker to wrap around her shoulders, and keep her warm. The sound of surf crashing on the beach brought her back some time later. Alys cracked an eye open. *Dawn.* Sunrise not far off on the horizon. She closed her eyes again, snug and sleepy, only for her heart to do a nice double-flip as she realized her position. She was resting with her cheek on something soft. Not a pillow. *Oh, my God...* Briggs. Alys remained very still, allowing her heartrate to settle. Soaking it in at the same time, despite a pulse of initial panic. Briggs had one arm around her shoulders again in a protective hold. Alys had laced both of hers around her waist, holding on tightly, as if she might lose her.

Her cheek was pressed gently between her breasts. In her sleep, she had apparently turned fully into Briggs and thrown one leg over hers. *Naked* leg. The slit in her concert dress did little to keep her covered, or stop her feeling the heat of that hard blue-jeaned thigh. *Fuck!* Briggs would have to be dead asleep not to feel her clitoris contract in reaction, and Alys had a feeling that this never happened. All of a sudden, she found herself hot and so, so incredibly tight! No wonder, really, since it looked as if she'd been crawling all over her bodyguard as she snoozed. Her hips rose of their own accord, her body responding to triggers beyond her control, and Alys froze in consternation. As casually as possible, she started to pull away.

"Alys."

The arm around her shoulders tightened gently, stopping her retreat, and Alys looked up into two pools of emerald green. Briggs was awake, you bet, and staring into her eyes.

"Oh. I'm sor—" Alys started to say.

"No," Briggs murmured. "It's okay."

It is? Alys stared wildly in return, feeling both hopeful and confused at the same time. Briggs traced a soothing finger over the line of her jaw. She placed a folded knuckle under her chin and softly tilted her head up a bit. Alys held her breath when she noticed her swallow and her lips part expectantly.

"Alys," Briggs whispered again, and damn if her name on these hot lips did not make Alys clench in reaction!

She sighed, her entire body relaxing into Briggs' embrace. The dynamic in this moment excited her more than she would have thought possible. Alys was the one in charge in all aspects of her life. Brad may play an important role behind the scenes, but she had the final say in every decision made. She was also never afraid to exercise it, and to be controversial in her choices.

When it came to relationships, and sexual encounters especially, Alys always liked to lead as well. Part of it, she knew, was massive trust issues. The stuff she'd mentioned. It was always hard for her to let go and surrender control. She rarely did. Right now, though, lying in Briggs' arms, all she wanted was to be held, protected, kissed... And really, whatever else Briggs may have in mind. This was so far off her usual M.O., and so startling to her, that Alys had no idea how to react. Granted, it was probably fine. Briggs had that sexy look in her eyes, fiercely focused and also a bit detached at the same time. Desire was written all over her face, and it was going to happen. She was going to kiss her, and everything would change. Alys would be lost. Somehow, she knew this with the utmost clarity. Far from frightening, the idea was a relief. She realized that she wanted it more in that instant than she had ever craved anything in her whole life.

CHAPTER
14

Alys rested one hand on the side of her neck, causing Briggs to shiver and her vibrant eyes to turn even more attractively hazy. Her skin was smooth and hot, like a fever. Damn, she looked so hungry... This was at once the most romantic and hottest prelude to a kiss which Alys had ever experienced. And Briggs was done waiting now. As Alys pressed into her a little more, in silent invitation, she closed the distance between them and took her mouth with staggering skill and authority. *Oh. My. God.* Not that Alys was in any mood to resist her at this point; but even if she had been, Briggs' commanding manner would have annihilated any last shred of reluctance. And the woman could kiss! Alys melted into her, opening up like a flower greeting sunshine after the rain. Briggs felt very much like it too: warm and gentle yet no less demanding, with the sort of energy coursing through her which hinted at scorching delights to be unleashed. Alys heard a languorous whimper and realized somewhere at the back of her mind that it came from her own mouth. She was stunned. Briggs had barely even touched her but she already had her moaning against her questing tongue. This was so incredibly different...

And so unbelievably good. Eager to test her in return, Alys slid her bare leg in between hers and pushed, nice and heavy. Briggs' reaction, a full-body shudder and instinctual rocking of the hips, was equally thrilling.

"Ms. Huxley…"

A hundred paparazzi showing up around the truck to snap them in action would not have stopped Alys in her tracks at this point. Briggs was hot and hard against her side and she wanted to touch her everywhere. She needed to run her fingers over her bare stomach, to cup her breasts into the palm of her hands and feel their weight. She wanted to flick her thumbs over nipples she already knew would be hard, and take them in her mouth. She ached to rip the buttons on her jeans and to find her, finally; hot, wet, and ready for her.

"Ms. Huxley."

Alys throbbed at the idea of making her aloof and focused bodyguard moan inside her mouth. She wanted to take her and be consumed by her in pretty equal measures, and was looking forward to a tussle to decide who got to do what first, if Briggs were that way inclined. Unfortunately, none of that was going to happen.

"Ms. Huxley?"

In the blink of an eye, it was all over, and Alys awoke with a startled jolt. *What the…* She blinked, disoriented. Briggs was no longer kissing her, let alone within touching distance. It was still dark. She was cold.

"Oh, gosh," she murmured.

Her right hip was sore from lying on the bare metal floor of the truck, and Briggs was just as immaculately in control of herself as before. Alys groaned inwardly. *Was this all a dream?* Even worse… *Did I moan out loud?*

"Sorry to wake you up," Briggs apologized. "But I think it's going to rain."

Alys glanced at the sky. Indeed, the stars had disappeared behind a layer of clouds. They were about to get wet, and not in the way that she preferred.

"Sorry for dozing off on you," she muttered.

"That's okay," Briggs smiled, totally nonplussed.

Same words as in the dream, but definitely no longer the same vibe. At least, she didn't look as if Alys had done anything to embarrass herself.

"How long was I snoring?" she asked.

"Forty minutes or so. No snoring that I noticed."

Alys knew from her studies that the mind did not register a difference between something real or imagined. She used that to her advantage often when visualizing a successful performance ahead of a big show. As she watched Briggs jump off the tailgate and extend a hand to help her, it occurred to her that she looked just as good as in the dream... Alys felt just as keen, her body reacting to the dream kiss as if it were real. Jumping off without taking Briggs' hand, she tightened the blanket around herself to hide obvious signs of major arousal going on.

"Let's go home," she declared.

●●

Tristan delivered a series of loaded punches to the training bag hanging in front of her. One good thing about living on Huxley's property was having access to her state-of-the-art private gym. Anyone training for the CrossFit Games would love the set-up. Tristan was not so much focused on this or her practice though, than on the way that the previous night with her client ended.

Huxley was very quiet on the way home, her impromptu snooze apparently having taken the wind out of her. Tristan remained equally silent as she drove the truck, paying attention to the road but also absorbed in thoughts. Even now, her mind kept looping back to that surprising evening. Huxley revealed herself to be extremely open in conversation, and not afraid to ask questions either. The fact that Tristan was okay with that left her feeling puzzled. She rarely talked about herself, and usually shut down conversations about alcohol before they could even start. But she'd been fine telling Huxley. Tristan also struggled to wrap her mind around what happened next, and her own reaction to it. One minute, they were talking and looking at the stars. Then, Huxley dozed off with her head on her shoulder. Before long, she snuggled close with her arms locked tightly around Tristan's waist. *Didn't put up much of a defense, did you?* Tristan stepped away from the punching bag before raising her knee, pivoting swiftly, and snapping her leg outward to deliver her strike. *And when was the last time you held a woman like that?* Frankly, she could not remember. Tristan did vividly recall the way she felt while holding Huxley. Sitting in the dark with one arm around her shoulders, listening to her slow breathing, she'd felt calmer and more settled than she had in a long time. And then, Huxley shifted position... Tristan slammed her fist into the bag again. *Dammit.* The embrace quickly became challenging for her after that, as she stared at her client's bare leg thrown over hers. Tristan became hyper-aware of the heat of Huxley's body. She imagined caressing the inside of her slender thigh, and going all the way... Like a treasure map tracing an inviting path to a forbidden destination, the party dress revealed way too much. When Huxley moaned softly in her sleep and tightened against her breasts, Tristan almost hissed and she bit hard on her lip.

Good thing it was about to rain, giving her an excuse to wake the woman up. But temptation did not end there. Huxley seemed a little lost and confused when she opened her eyes and looked at her... *Sexy as hell.* Tristan came very close to fisting her fingers in her hair, pulling her back into her arms, and kissing her as if it were their last minute of life on the planet. *But you didn't. You're fine. Stop thinking about this stuff!* Refocusing, she crushed the bag with two front kicks and some heavy cross punches. *There you go! Much better.* Right on cue, a familiar voice sounded behind her.

"Hey, Briggs. Nice moves you got there!"

Erik appeared, wearing a pair of shorts, training shoes, and an appreciative smile on his face.

"Hey, thanks," she nodded. Were she wired any differently, Tristan might also feel appreciative of him. Huxley's sometime goofy cousin looked like he'd stepped off the cover of a fitness magazine. As it was, Tristan was immune to his naked chest and the rippling muscles in his stomach. She just wondered if he could move as well as he looked, and grabbed a fresh towel to wipe the sweat off her face. "Are you into martial arts?"

"Yep. Taekwondo, mainly. A little kick-boxing. What about you?"

Tristan held a black belt in Taekwondo as well as Brazilian Jiu Jitsu. She was also qualified to instructor-level in Krav Maga, a lethal combat mix of many different disciplines favored by the Israeli army.

"Me too," she replied evasively. "Fancy a dance, Erik?"

"Oh, man!" He cracked his knuckles in anticipation. "Yeah, you bet!"

She threw her towel aside and moved to the center of the room, essentially designed as an open ring.

"Alright. Put me down if you can."

"Uh… You might regret saying that, Briggs."

He came at her smiling, fists up to his chest and rolling his shoulders. For sure, he had the stance and all the moves down right. And he was light on his feet for such a big guy.

"Very nice, now quit showing off," she teased him.

"Gotta be careful, eh…" He threw a couple of lazy warm-up punches that she easily deflected. "Alys won't be happy if I hurt her bodyguard."

"I don't think that's going to happen somehow."

"Okay." He breathed in and exhaled sharply, coming into focus. "Let's do this dance."

It was a nice surprise. Erik turned out to be very good, and enthusiastic as well, once he realized that Tristan could take care of herself and that he would not hurt her. A couple of times, he even came close to landing a damaging punch, and he laughed when she vanished from in front of him like a mirage.

"Fuck, Briggs, you're so damn quick!"

"And you…" Tristan pulled back from a disabling kick just enough not to hurt as she made contact with the side of his jaw. "You talk too much. Focus if you want to get me!"

"Alright, alright!" He shot her a sweaty grin, clearly having fun. "Bring it!"

Soon, he was all in and really trying to put her down. Good training, for sure. Tristan deflected a nasty kick and she blocked his follow-up punch, forcing him back a safe distance with two jabs delivered in quick succession. Erik would be a nice guy to have on her side in a punch-up. She recalled him saying that they would be partners, and instantly thought of Jake. But it was only brief, and she did not allow the subsequent stab of sadness from throwing her off-guard. What happened next did, though…

"Hey, whose bike is that sexy Kawasaki out there?"

The deep and rich timbre of Huxley's voice penetrated her consciousness like a hot knife slicing through butter. Tristan kept her guard up but she also instinctively took her eyes off Erik for a second, to glance aside and see her walk in. The singer must have just been for a swim in the pool. Her hair was wet. Tristan had never seen her in a bikini top before, with a purple and pink sarong tied around her waist, and flip flops. But she did not get a chance to smile or even reply. The next thing she was aware of was a stiff blow to the side of her head, a brief loss of vision, and she hit the deck. *Oh, shit!*

"Woops!" Erik knelt beside her, his face looming large and blurry until she blinked and regained clarity. "I'm sorry, Briggs! Hey, you okay?"

"Yeah," she grunted, fighting a wave of dizziness. "Fine."

"You sure?" He looked genuinely upset but also puzzled at the same time. "Sorry I didn't hold back on the kick… I was sure you'd block that one easily."

"Well…" Tristan tested her jaw. Still attached and working fine. Dizziness receding. She flashed him a rueful grin. "I said to take me down, didn't I?"

Reassured to see her smile, he patted her on the back with a chuckle.

"Told you that you might regret it."

"Yep. I know."

"And what was that you said about staying focused?"

She took the friendly ribbing, knowing that she deserved it, and the kick in the face as well. *So, all it takes now to shatter your concentration is a woman in a bikini?* Tristan promised herself that it would not happen again, only for her resolve to crumble when Huxley laid a cooling hand over her flaming cheek.

"Are you okay, really?"

Erik could ask her all night long and not generate a tenth of the relief that Tristan felt when Huxley inquired. She fought the impulse to close her eyes and lean into her touch. Tried to move away but Huxley followed. Even worse, she rested her free hand over the back of her head.

"I'm alright," Tristan murmured, feeling sluggish all of a sudden in spite of herself.

"You need some ice."

"No, no, it's—"

"Erik," Huxley interrupted. "Get us an ice pack from the studio, please."

"Sure thing," he approved, and flew out the door.

CHAPTER 15

A few minutes later, Tristan sat with a Koolpak over her eye and a concerned Huxley by her side.

"How come you keep ice packs in your studio?" she asked.

"Dancers often need a little TLC after a video shoot. I like to be prepared for them."

"You do take good care of your people."

"Definitely. I do care. How are you feeling?"

"I'm okay." Tristan shrugged, uncomfortable about getting so much attention. "It's not the first time I get kicked in the head, eh…"

"Well, I'm sorry to hear that. Let me see."

Truth be told, Tristan's issue at this point was not receiving attention, her throbbing cheek, or the headache brewing behind her eyes, but how much she enjoyed having Huxley fussing over her. She should be fighting it, she knew; not encouraging her. Well… Allowing wasn't encouraging as such, was it? *Semantics, Tris. AKA bullshit, as you well know.*

"… your clients, in the line of duty?"

Tristan looked up, realizing that Huxley was speaking.

"I'm sorry, what did you say?"

The question earned her a pointed, almost suspicious look in return.

"Are you sure that we shouldn't take a quick trip to the ER? You took a nasty hit and now you keep fading on me. You may have a concussion."

Not fading. Just distracted because you're half-naked and almost sitting on top of me. Again.

"It's not a concussion. I'm fine." Hoping to shift the topic of conversation away from herself, Tristan added; "Erik's a skilled fighter. Very good indeed."

"He almost knocked you out." Huxley snorted in obvious disapproval, as predicted. "Is this supposed to happen during a round of friendly practice?"

"I lost concentration. It's my fault he got me down."

"Mm." Huxley touched light fingers to her cheekbone and winced in dismay. "You're very hot in that spot. And bruising all around your eye already."

"It's nothing to worry about," Tristan assured her.

"Right. So, I was asking about the other times you got hit in the head. Did that happen when protecting clients?"

"No. In training, mostly. And only a couple of times, to be honest."

"You never took a hit for a client?"

"Once or twice, I was caught in the way of a good punch meant for one of them, yes." Tristan held her deep blue gaze as Huxley went totally still to simply stare at her. She tended to do that a lot. "Why do you ask?"

The singer shrugged, maintaining eye contact.

"Just in case you haven't realized it yet, I am quite insanely curious about you, Briggs."

Tristan was grateful for the pouch of ice that hid half her face and, hopefully, her blushing as well. She was sure that the sudden heat she was experiencing was not related to her injury. *Get a grip, for God's sake!*

"Don't let what just happened lead you into thinking that I can't protect you, Ms. Huxley," she stated. "It takes a lot more to put me down in real life."

"Can I ask you a delicate question?"

"You can ask…" Tristan nodded, suddenly wary.

Huxley leaned forward, her expression intent.

"Is it true what they say about bodyguards?"

"Who's '*They*'?"

"People… You know."

"What do people say about bodyguards?"

"Would you take a bullet for me?" Tristan looked away on a light shake of the head, and Huxley immediately reached for her hand, holding her back. "I'm sorry. Is this a rude question to ask you?"

"No, you're fine." Tristan smiled, prompting the singer to do the same. "It's not rude, just way off the mark."

"Explain it to me."

"Well. Elon Musk gave a good analogy for it, actually."

"Oh, really?"

"Yes." The Koolpak was warm against her face now, and Tristan removed it. "How expensive would air travel be if you had to replace the aircraft after each trip, uh?"

Huxley shrugged, apparently none the wiser.

"My goal isn't to wait until someone tries to shoot you, Ms. Huxley, and then jump in front and hope for the best. That may look good in the movies, but the cost would be too high."

"Absolutely," Huxley nodded tensely.

"The cyber sleuths at Lewiston P.D. are working to identify your stalker. Granted, we had no luck finding fingerprints on the piece of paper he left on the Rover, but we'll get him some other way. I'm sure of it."

"Yes..."

"In the meantime, there are plenty of measures we can take to keep you safe."

"Like good preparation and getaway cars?" Huxley smiled wanly.

"Yes. And a switched-on bodyguard. Ms. Huxley, I think we can—"

Tristan went quiet, and she totally lost her train of thought, when the singer unexpectedly reached up to cradle her cheek in the palm of her hand once more. This was no check for swelling or temperature, she realized; the gesture was too tender and her eyes too grave for it to be that simple. Tristan laced her fingers around her wrist, gently pulling her hand off in order to be able to think.

"What's wrong?" she asked.

"I don't like the thought of you getting hurt."

"I told you: I don't jump in the way of bullets. Prevention is my game."

"But you got in the way of a punch before," Huxley pointed out.

Tristan really wished that she'd not told her this now. And it suddenly dawned on her as well that this was no random line of questioning.

"Ms. Huxley..." She watched her client gnaw on her bottom lip, her eyes brighter than usual. She looked ready to burst into tears, something Tristan suspected must not happen often. "Talk to me, please," she prompted. "What's going on?"

"I received another letter from the stalker," Huxley finally confessed.

Tristan blew air out sharply. *Goddammit.*

"When?"

"Just now, as I was checking my emails. That's why I came to find you."

"Show me. Is he threatening to hurt you again?"

"No." Huxley shook her head, grabbing on to Tristan again as if she might be about to be snatched out of her universe. "This time he's threatening you!"

••

Tristan stood with her arms crossed in front of her chest behind a row of screens at Lewiston P.D., watching a computer analyst attempt to trace the stalker's IP address. The officer in charge of the case, a rangy blonde with intelligent blue eyes going by the name of Cody Miller, was new to the department but no less experienced as an investigator.

"Is it the first time he emailed you directly instead of going via your website, Ms. Huxley?" she asked.

"Yep. First time he's ever tried that."

Tristan hid a smile at her tone of voice. Huxley had been genuinely upset earlier when she told her about the email. But now she sounded defiant once again, and the attitude suited her. Tristan caught a glint in Miller's eye in reaction which had very little to do with professional approval. No surprise. Huxley was sexy as sin in her jeans and fitted leather jacket, the biker look definitely a winner on her. She'd insisted on riding the Kawasaki to the station and quickly disabled any reservations Tristan may have about it.

'It'll be much quicker and we won't be stationary in traffic. It's unexpected. And no one will recognize me with a helmet on. Let's go, Briggs!'

All good arguments, and Tristan let herself be convinced. It was not lost on her that the line between the mission and real life was very blurred when it came to Huxley... Then again, Tristan was never much of a rule follower to begin with. She did not get hung up on details and procedure. She liked to keep track of the big picture and act accordingly. As long as she could get the job done, and keep her client safe, she was happy to improvise.

"It's no good," the analyst sighed. "No matter what I try, I keep getting pinged back to a location in Japan. He's using VPN, for sure. And a solid one at that."

"Can you tell which one?" Miller asked.

"Not at the moment, but I'm not done yet."

"Alright, keep at it. Ms. Huxley, I'm going to require a list of all the people who have your private email address, and your relationship status with them."

The rock star instantly bristled at the request.

"This email is only for family and close friends."

"I understand," Miller said gently. "But I still need a list."

Huxley glanced at her, a question in her eyes, and Tristan nodded in confirmation.

"Yes, it'll be helpful."

"Alright," Huxley conceded.

As she grabbed a pen and paper and started to write, Miller turned to her.

"So, Briggs. What's on your mind?"

Tristan re-read the single line of the email on display on the center screen: *YOUR NEW BODYGUARD MAKES A TASTY TARGET.*

"He wants to let us know he's paying attention."

"For sure. Has he threatened anyone close to her before?"

"I'm still here, Detective," Huxley snapped without looking up from her list. "And the answer is no. It's only ever been just me."

Miller grimaced in reaction and mouthed a silent '*Oops!*' to Tristan, prompting her to grin in sympathy. The detective would likely not forget who was in the room again any time soon.

"No matter what his email says, I don't think I'm this guy's new target," she concluded.

"No, I agree with you. Thank you, Ms. Huxley." Miller took the list from the singer and quickly scanned through it. "This is perfect."

"Look, I don't want you to get in touch with anyone on this list," Huxley warned. "Apart from my best friend, Rose Carling, no one else knows what's been going on. My family aren't local. I don't want them to worry unnecessarily."

A note of anxiety was well-hidden under her authoritative tone, but Tristan was paying attention and she picked up on it. Huxley stood very close to her, their shoulders almost touching. She held back from putting an arm around her.

"We shouldn't need to contact your folks," Miller assured her. "But in case we have to, I promise to come to you first, Ms. Huxley."

"That's fine, Detective."

"Okay." Tristan ended on a friendly smile, grateful to Miller for not mentioning the worst-case scenario; that family members and close friends may need to be informed at some point, simply for their own safety. "Thanks for your help, Miller. You've got my number."

"And you too, Briggs. You both take care now."

••

Alys noticed the ease with which her bodyguard interacted with everyone at the police station, as if they all had some secret code to recognize each other by. It was pretty obvious that regardless of her current job title and occupation, Briggs was still a cop through and through.

"Were you based here?" she inquired, intrigued.

"Sometimes, yes."

Briggs seemed too intimately familiar with the layout of the place, as she led her down a flight of stairs and through an area that was off-limits to the public, for this answer to be totally true. But Alys, despite being insanely curious for real, did not insist. Finding out that the stalker had got a hold of her private email address did not upset her quite as much as the fact that he had threatened Briggs. It might be funny to say, but Alys had not considered the matter to be personal until then. Before, it really was just one more weirdo fan. *Been there, done that.* But now, one of her team had been dragged into it. *Tristan.* Alys was not sure exactly when she'd started to think of her as more than just Briggs, the security woman. For sure, her dark handsome looks made her stand out... But it was more than just that. And if she were truly honest with herself, Alys had to admit that Briggs had got under her skin a little bit from the first moment she laid her eyes on her.

"After you, Ms. Huxley."

Her ever polite and attentive escort held open an unmarked door which turned out to lead back into the parking lot. For sure, she knew this building like the back of her hand.

"Thanks," Alys nodded, feeling subdued.

Briggs met her gaze as they reached the Kawasaki parked next to a Lewiston P.D. unit.

"How are you feeling?"

"Better than your eye looks," Alys smirked.

Briggs laughed, genuinely entertained. *Gosh,* Alys reflected, charmed and perplexed at the same time. *The woman even laughs at my jokes...*

CHAPTER 16

"But I mean seriously, though," Briggs went on, clearly unaware of her appeal or the thrilling effect of a warming note of concern in her cool green eyes. "Are you okay?"

"Yes." Alys shrugged, glancing away. "Fine."

Briggs folded her arms over her chest, right hip tilted to the side, and watched her with a faint yet patient smile on her lips. This was all it took for Alys to blurt out the rest.

"I didn't like the way the detective implied that some of my family and close friends may be involved."

"Ah, that's not it, Ms. Huxley."

"Why else would she ask me for a list?"

"Because the fact that the stalker was able to acquire your private and confidential email address goes in our favor."

"Explain that to me, Briggs."

"It narrows down the field of investigation. It was massive before, but not so vague now. Our analyst will have a good go at tracing the guy through email networks."

"Miller is going to want to talk to my people face to face, isn't she?" Alys prompted.

"You know, it's the best way," Briggs nodded.

"I understand, but..." Alys exhaled sharply. "I hate having people I love involved in sordid business. If it were only me, that would be one thing. But this... It makes my skin crawl."

"And I do understand that," Briggs assured. "Miller does as well. One of your friends may have given out your email to this guy in good faith. Or their account was hacked..."

"Or they made a genuine mistake."

"Yes, that could be."

Alys was grateful for the few different options offered here. The thought of betrayal from a loved one would hurt a lot more, and she pushed it to the back of her mind.

"So," Briggs concluded, "the quicker we find out the truth of the matter, the faster we will get our hands on that guy. And then everyone can be safe."

Alys knew what she was not saying, and she tensed at this too.

"I don't want you or anyone else to be hurt."

"No one will be hurt, Ms. Huxley," Briggs promised.

Alys took a deep breath in and let it out slowly. They'd had this talk already, and Briggs' conviction was reassuring.

"Okay." She held her gaze. "Do you miss being a cop?"

"What makes you ask?"

"Because," Alys replied, noting a layer of caution dropping over those vivid green eyes. "You say 'We' all the time when you talk about the police."

"Well. We're all one team on this case, aren't we?"

More evasiveness and, this time, Alys wanted to ask. Before she could do so, a happy yell sounding from across the parking lot interrupted their conversation.

"Hey, Tris!"

Alys turned to see a dark-blonde woman in tight jeans and running shoes, a white t-shirt, and chest body armor, striding up toward them. Tall, fit, and grinning wide, the newcomer pulled Briggs into her arms for a tight hug.

"Tristan. Damn, it's good to see you!"

"Hey, Quinn..." Briggs smiled, obviously pleased to see the woman too.

But as the embrace went on, Alys was surprised to catch a swift rush of emotion in her face. Briggs closed her eyes, caught her bottom lip in between her teeth, and tightened her grip on her friend. The cop who obviously knew her well enough to call her *'Tris'* responded the same. It did not take a genius to realize the strong bond between the two. *Ex-lovers?* No, Alys did not get that vibe. More like sisters in arms. Partners. The officer was the first to let go, and apparently decided to get over her emotion by hitting Briggs on the shoulder. Playfully, though it still looked rough to Alys. Briggs did not seem to mind.

"What happened to your face, Tristan?"

"Took one during a sparring session this morning."

"Ah... Getting soft in your retirement, uh?"

"Nope, just training hard." Tristan grinned and she patted her smugly on the cheek. "You wouldn't understand."

Quinn chuckled at the good-natured joke before turning to her.

"Hi."

"Hello," Alys nodded.

She was used to people examining her with that, *'Hey, don't I know you from somewhere?'* searching expression on their face; but this one clearly was wondering something else as she looked approvingly back at her friend. Briggs dispelled any wrong ideas about the nature of their relationship.

"Quinn, this is my client, Alys Huxley."

"Nice to meet you." Alys offered her hand.

"You too, Ms. Huxley." The police officer obviously knew who she was, but her demeanor did not change. She just looked relaxed. Powerful and in control. Very much like Briggs, and it occurred to Alys that she liked that sort of thing very much. "I heard about your stalker... I'm sorry about that."

"Thank you."

"And don't worry," Quinn was quick to add with a lively grin. "With Miller and Briggs on the case, you really have two of the best in your corner."

Alys looked aside, catching thoughtful green eyes watching her.

"Yes," she mused. "I think so too."

"Anyway, gotta go," Quinn announced. "You let me know if you need any extra help on this stalker thing, Tristan."

"Roger that. Thanks."

"And don't be such a stranger, okay? Come over for dinner one night. Lia would love to see you. Since we got married, I've been—"

"Whoa, hang on," Briggs cut in, clearly flabbergasted at the news. "You two got married?"

Quinn chuckled, her face radiating happiness.

"Don't look so shocked. I swear I was a willing participant."

Alys laughed at that but she noticed that Briggs still looked perplexed. *Interesting...*

"How the hell did I miss that?" she muttered. "I'm sorry, Quinn. I was—"

"Relax, Tris. No one knew about it. We eloped."

"Good for you!" Alys exclaimed, earning herself a lingering glance from her bodyguard.

••

Tristan stood listening as Quinn chatted easily about her recent wedding, a trip to Mexico, and private vows exchanged on the beach during a fiery sunset. It all sounded amazing... And she hadn't known. True, Quinn and Lia decided to elope, but all the same... She felt uncomfortable. This was definitely a case of, *'Long time, no see'*, between her and Wesley. And nothing to do with Quinn, for sure. Tristan had just deliberately avoided her after the murder of her partner. Too many memories, none of them good. Even now, it still felt like yesterday... Quinn was in charge of the scene that night, inside the warehouse where Jake was discovered to have been tortured and killed. Tristan was not supposed to be there. For sure, no one called her in. She still showed up, unannounced and loaded full of lethal fury. Quinn spotted her instantly as she arrived and she did her best to keep her away. It was for her own good, of course. *He's gone, Tris. There's nothing you can do. I'll fill you in later, okay?* But Tristan refused to walk away. She had to know it all. She needed to see for herself. She would have punched her way past Quinn if she had to, although thankfully, it did not come to that... But it was close. Now, she pulled her back into her arms for a warm hug.

"Congratulations. That's great for you and Lia."

"Thank you, my friend."

"I'll come to see you both soon, I promise."

"Make sure you do." A laughing Quinn pointed to her face, leaving her on a tease. "Keep your guard up and your eye on the ball, woman. Bye, Ms. Huxley."

"Bye!" Her client nodded to her after Quinn went into the building. "Hey, she's nice."

"Yep." Tristan left it at that and she reached for her helmet, eager to avoid a bunch of personal questions on the back of the encounter. "Shall we, Ms. Huxley?"

"I'm ready to get out of here." With a hot daring grin, the singer added: "Take the coast road and open up that throttle, will you? You were so careful on the way in that it felt like I was riding with my grandma."

"It's my job to be careful," Tristan stated.

"Indulge me, beautiful," Huxley countered with a wink and a throaty laugh.

The coast road wasn't the most direct way home but Tristan took it anyway because she could not think of a reason not to. Nothing to do with the fact that Huxley called her *'Beautiful'*, of course, although this was kind of nice. The day was sunny and warm, the road nice and grippy under the bike's new tires. Not much traffic either, and overall perfect conditions for a fast ride. Tristan allowed the Kawasaki to come to life on the return trip, not taking unnecessary risks but riding with purpose all the same. Huxley was having fun. She could tell from the way that she anticipated every bend and subtle change in speed. She was an alert pillion rider, at one with the experience. Tristan enjoyed her solo rides. She loved the sense of freedom that riding gave her when she was on her own. Now, she was very much aware of Huxley, pressed tightly into her body. The back seat on the powerful sports bike was tiny and set a bit higher. Probably designed with speed and performance in mind, it still very much encouraged intimacy. Huxley was not the kind to shy away from that. Tristan was exceedingly conscious of her cradling embrace, strong thighs pressed against the outside of her own. Huxley kept both arms around her for safety, but her hands wandered to different places. Unusual spots, definitely *not* for added security.

The palm of her right hand rested over Tristan's lower abdomen, a gesture as thrilling as it was possessive. She kept the other one pressed against her chest, very close to cupping her breast. Did she even realize what she was doing? Tristan chuckled inside of her helmet. *Of course she does.* The fiery Alys Huxley liked to tease and play, and live life on the edge. Tristan both knew and appreciated that about her. Living life to the full... *When was the last time you allowed yourself to do that?* Steamy encounters with strangers at The Club probably did not count. Shifting down a few gears as they caught up with a slower truck, Tristan sat up to check on her passenger, prompting Huxley to shift position as well.

"You okay?"

"Hell, yes!" the singer shouted over the noise of the engine.

Tristan could hear it in her voice, how much Huxley really was enjoying the ride, and this pleased her more than she knew it should.

"Almost home, Briggs," her passenger added, and pointed at the truck in front. "Go on, smoke this guy!"

Tristan did not even think about arguing this one.

"Close your helmet and hold on to me properly."

Huxley squeezed her with her legs, possibly acknowledging with that response that she knew what Tristan referred to with that word, *'Properly'*. She slapped her visor shut and clasped her tightly around the waist. Another more gentle squeeze followed, her signal to say she was ready. Tristan briefly laid her gloved hand over her thigh, feeling the immediate tightening of muscles under her touch. Riding on her own after this would never be as good, she was sure of it. Spotting an opening in incoming traffic, she pulled her visor down. Huxley leaned forward again, ready for the burst of acceleration. Tristan did not hold back this time.

She twisted the throttle, quickly hitting sixth gear and shooting up to 100mph in the outside lane. In less than two seconds, the truck was reduced to a small dot in the distance. Feeling Huxley tethered safely to her, Tristan slid back into the right lane, now free of traffic, but she kept up her speed, wanting to give her a better taste of what Huxley had asked for. When they got home, Tristan did not need to ask if she had enjoyed the ride.

"That's it! I'm getting one!" Huxley whipped off her helmet, face beautifully flushed and her eyes sparkling in excitement.

"You're buying a Ninja?" Tristan chuckled.

"Is that what she's called? Nice!" Huxley trailed her fingers over the top of the Kawasaki's tank before meeting her eyes and smiling softly. "Thank you for an exhilarating ride, Briggs. And for making me feel like a regular girl."

Tristan understood what she meant by that but an added response still shot out of her mouth before she had a chance to re-evaluate it.

"I think you are an extraordinary woman, Ms. Huxley."

CHAPTER 17

Tristan decided to go for a run around the outside perimeter of the property that evening, the need to check on security also a good excuse to clear her mind. *You are an extraordinary woman...* Good thing Huxley took the comment lightly, just with an ironic chuckle. But then, she also rested her fingers over the bruise on Tristan's cheek and looked deeply into her eyes.

'I'll be in the studio for the rest of the day. Get some rest.'

Well. Fair to say that Tristan had never felt more splendidly restless because of a woman than she did now. The run helped her to settle, as exercise always did. But not for long. She arrived back at the annex to find a tube of Aloe Vera cream on her bed, and a pink Post-It note. *'For your eye'*, the note said. It was simply signed, *'A.'* Tristan kicked off her running shoes, sat on the bed, and stared at the note. *Alys.* Huxley had not invited her to call her by her first name yet, and Tristan hoped that she would not. It was a fine line between caring professionally for a client and getting in over her head. As it was, Tristan knew that she surfed a razor-sharp edge with Alys Huxley. There was a lot about the woman which made her want to care for real. *A lot...*

••

After a few weeks, Alys was no longer too sure if she wanted to caress her bodyguard's face or give her another black eye. Briggs was only doing her job, she knew, and exceedingly well too. But with an increase in traveling, concerts, and exposure to her fans at Live gigs, perhaps a clash between the two was inevitable at some point. It happened at the end of a ten-day stretch during which Alys flew around the US to perform at sold-out events in New York, Miami, Denver, San Francisco, and Las Vegas. Her new album, GUTS-Y, was out and topping music charts, both at home and abroad. In another month or so, she would head to the southern hemisphere for a tour of Australia and New Zealand. Brad had also scheduled dates, and booked stadiums, in Europe: Berlin, Paris, Rome, and London, were all on the list. This would be the biggest trip of her career to date, and Alys was excited. Life was good, you betcha! Even better still, her stalker had gone quiet.

"He's given up on me," she declared triumphantly. "I knew he would!"

Briggs was cautiously optimistic, probably just to be polite. She was keen to emphasize that Detective Miller and her team remained on the case. When questioned, she admitted that she believed the threat was still real, and that the stalker's silence may actually be a worrying sign of worse things to come. Alys just wanted to forget about it all and focus on her music. On the plane back to Lewiston, she dropped into the seat next to Briggs and eyed her coolly.

"Everything alright, Ms. Huxley?" her bodyguard enquired in return.

"Apart from the fact that you injured one of my followers in Vegas, everything's fine," Alys snapped, and proceeded to drop a newspaper onto her lap.

Briggs arched an eyebrow at the title. *Trigger-Happy Security At Huxley Concert Results In A Broken Nose.*

"You were mobbed in Vegas, Ms. Huxley."

She was right, of course. Before the concert, Alys had been signing autographs in front of the venue when two enterprising fans leaped over the security barriers and ran to her to take an impromptu selfie. They were both young and totally harmless, and Alys did not allow Briggs to scare them off. Of course, this was encouraging mayhem. Soon, not just two, but a handful of people, surrounded her. And it wasn't long before the rest of the crowd also pushed forward. Among the jostling and heaving, Alys was grateful for her bodyguard's strong arm around her shoulders, and for the two additional security guys leading the way to the entrance door. She understood the need to be firm in these situations... But when a burly fan with long hair and a bushy beard stood in her way, and did not respond to one of the guards' curt, *'Step aside, please'*, Briggs did her own thing. She did not slow down or repeat the request. Just used her elbow to create some space, and walked right through.

"I don't like this kind of publicity," Alys stated.

"Sorry, Ms. Huxley, I didn't mean to break his nose. Just to get you quickly out of a potentially dangerous situation."

It was hard to stay mad at a woman who was so quick to apologize, and so disarmingly genuine with it too. Alys was not going to reveal that a huge part of her actually enjoyed having Briggs by her side more or less 24/7. It was a case of resenting the need for a bodyguard, but secretly relishing the presence of this particular woman in her life.

"Anyway, just to make you aware of a slight change to our schedule." Alys spoke briskly, eager not to acknowledge feelings and emotions that would only make everything more awkward if she allowed herself to dwell. "The Actors Guild's Awards are taking place in town tonight, and Carin Davies just won for Best Actress. She's a close acquaintance of mine, so we're going to the after-party. It's held at *Spirit Incognita*. You know the place?"

Briggs looked like she'd just been told that the jet was going to crash.

"I know the place. It's an exclusive club in the harbor area," she said.

"Correct." Alys moved to stand up because staring into her eyes was a risky option, especially when they were so close. She wondered how Briggs knew of the club and was curious to find out. How did she relax, other than riding her bike and going on solo runs? Did she have someone? Enjoy sex? Alys wondered about all this stuff, for sure. "I told Erik. He'll pick us up and drive us straight there when we land."

"Ms. Huxley. I don't think this is a good idea."

Alys turned back, perplexed and irritated.

"Why not?" Briggs constantly had issues with her schedule or the places that she wanted to go, but she did not expect *Spirit* to be one.

"I haven't had a chance to recce the premises." The body-guard shrugged as if it were all very obvious. "I don't have a list of attendees. Not sure of the level of security in place at the club, and —"

"Oh, come on!" Alys exclaimed. "We're not going to some dive in Old-Lewiston! This is an official after-party for the AGA. The event is on par with the Golden Globes. There's bound to be more security roaming around than actual guests!"

"Yes, but I really don't think you should—"

"No, Briggs," Alys snapped. "I'm going."

The party was not much fun, in the end... And she would not have lingered long under different circumstances. But Briggs had come dangerously close to saying *'No'*. And even though it was childish, Alys was pushed to make a point. As she mingled with A-Listers who still tripped all over themselves for a photo opportunity with the Rock Goddess, she was doing everything that she should: smiling, flirting irreverently, coming back with the perfect one-liner at the perfect moment... But part of her was also detached, observing. Fake looks and smiles, scared people clinging to their celebrity like a shield or a life jacket. Alys was aware of her own act here too. Singing was everything to her, as well as connecting with the people who *'got'* her and her music. The rest, she could really do without. *I'd rather be at home with Sex Pistol...* The thought of him warmed her up from the inside out. And someone else, too. It was impossible to forget about Briggs watching her, even though the security guard was indeed skilled at blending into the background. Alys was always aware of her, as if they were linked by some intangible thread. It felt good. Reassuring, as it should. *Exciting.* Every once in a while, Alys would look to find a pair of blazing green eyes fixed on her. Briggs' intensity was palpable, even from across a room full of sparkly people. Alys was amused and a little annoyed to find that she attracted many admiring glances. A couple of beautiful women even went up to her and exchanged a few words. Briggs was obviously polite with them in return, but her attention never wavered. She only had eyes for one woman in the room. *Don't I know the feeling...*

"Having fun?" Martini in hand, Rose leaned an arm around her shoulders.

"Highly debatable," Alys replied, and her friend chuckled.

"Well, at least you haven't burst into flames yet."

"What do you mean?"

"From the way your hired muscle keeps looking at you." Rose nodded toward Briggs, who was leaning against the side of a marble column, looking like a more attractive version of James Bond. "Mm, those sizzling eyes and brooding expression... She's smoking hot, definitely."

"Just doing her job," Alys muttered.

Rose kissed her on the cheek and went on, her words just a little bit slurred.

"You don't really believe that, do you, Al?"

"How many of these have you had, babe?" Alys inquired, glancing at the drink in her hand.

"Just enough to survive this boring party," Rose laughed. "I think you should start singing."

"I'm off-duty tonight."

"Haha! Yeah, fair enough. Anyway, don't try to weasel out of this topic. I've got eyes, you know? Your protector in shining armor is doing way more than just her job. Look at her, watching you... She's feeding!"

"You're weird, Rosie," Alys declared, although she had to smile.

Briggs did look hungry out there, and she would not mind being the one to satisfy her.

"Don't tell me you haven't thought about it." Rose swayed lightly against her side, speaking as if she could read her mind. "Because I know I have, more than once. But she's so remote... Aloof. What's the deal with her?"

Briggs kept a lot under wraps, it was true. Rose was correct about her being hard to reach. *But not all the time... Not with me.*

Alys could recall many times when Tristan's sense of humor had come to the surface, and the shining light in her eyes when she smiled. Nothing at all distant or unapproachable about her then. *And here I am, thinking of her as 'Tristan' once again…*

"So, you thought about it, uh?" she prompted.

"More than just thinking. Sadly, she turned me down."

"What did you do, exactly?"

"Grabbed her and tried to kiss her." Rose chuckled, clearly amused.

"You're kidding?" Alys exclaimed with a quick rush of displeasure.

"Nope!"

"When?"

"In Miami. I invited her back to my room after the show. Bit tipsy that night, to be fair…"

"What a surprise, hey?"

"Maybe not, but anyway, she was incorruptible. The perfect gentlewoman. Just walked me back to my room, made sure that I was safe, and said goodnight. That alone was incredibly sexy, by the way. I had to… You know. Take care of things myself in the shower."

"Oh, thanks for keeping me informed," Alys smirked.

"Yeah, well… I'm telling you, darling: I think she's got the hots for you big time."

Alys watched Briggs smile and nod patiently as yet another starlet accosted her.

"Let's go home," she decided.

"You go on without me, darling. The winner for Best Writer invited a bunch of us back to his place for a bit more interesting stuff."

"Interesting stuff?"

"You know…" Rose raised her glass. "Better than this."

Alys pulled her into her arms for a heartfelt hug. Rose was an amazing woman, and an incredible dancer. But she had her demons. And she liked to party hard. Sometimes, the two did not mix all that well.

"Be careful, okay? Call me in the morning."

"Always am," Rose winked. "And I will, I promise."

Alys walked up to Briggs, enjoying the look of surprise and quick irritation on the other woman's face when her bodyguard stopped paying attention to whatever she was saying and turned to look at her instead.

"Ms. Huxley?"

It might be wishful thinking, but it seemed to Alys that the warmth in her voice was only reserved for her. Keen to hide the effect that this idea had on her, she raised a confronting eyebrow at her security officer.

"Seems like I survived the party despite your being unable to *'Recce'* the place."

"Are you ready to go home?" Briggs answered politely.

"You sound hopeful," Alys remarked. She could not resist another tease. "What's the matter, Briggs? Too many gorgeous women hitting on you making you uncomfortable?"

The corner of Briggs' mouth twitched before she could hide her smile. This happened more often than she probably wanted it to, and Alys loved to be the cause of it.

"It's okay," Briggs shrugged. "I'm used to it."

Alys caught the subtle glint in her eyes, only there for her to see. Briggs was joking, quite obviously. The moment was warm and intimate in a way that made Alys think of doing what Rose had attempted. She held back, but it cost her.

CHAPTER 18

"How's it going, Tris?" Angie inquired a week later when she called for an update.

"Uh. It's going."

"Wow… As good as that, uh?"

"No, it's okay." Tristan shrugged. "I just wish I didn't feel so much in the dark, that's all."

"Still no new letter from the stalker?"

"Not since his last message, sent to Huxley's private email three weeks ago and threatening me."

"Maybe he got wind of the investigation. Perhaps the cops got a little too close and scared some sense into him."

"Yeah, maybe. I hope so."

"Doesn't sound like you believe it though."

"You know me, Angie. If it feels too good to be true, I won't relax. People like that generally don't tend to stop. They only get worse and become more obsessed as time goes on."

"True… And yes, I do know you, Tris," Angie replied with a smile in her voice. "Which is why I assigned you to Huxley in the first place. If anyone can keep her safe, it's you."

"Is there a reason you're buttering me up like that?" Tristan groaned.

"I'm just paying you a compliment, Briggs. Damn!"

"Huh-uh. Sure. Thank you very much. And?"

"I need a favor," Angie laughed.

"No kidding. Shoot."

"Would you consider staying on a bit longer with Huxley and going with her on her Australian tour?"

Tristan wished her heartrate didn't start racing so much at the question. *Of course, I would...*

"Did she ask?" she prompted.

"Her manager called me to do it. He seems pleased with the work that you've been doing."

Ah. Wright. Yeah, it made sense for him to want to extend her contract beyond the initial period.

"Glad to hear it. I'm also not as displeased with this guy as I thought I would be," Tristan admitted. "He's on the ball despite his arrogant attitude. So, yes."

"Yes? You'll go?" Angie sounded stunned and suspicious at the same time, as if she'd expected a hard battle and was not too sure that it might not still be coming.

"Sure, I'll go. Like I said, I don't think we've heard the last from this stalker. I'm not going to jump ship before the situation is resolved." *She probably didn't ask for me, but I don't want to leave her. I'm not going to mess up this time, and let her get hurt.*

Just as the thought occurred to her, and her heart tightened in reaction, Angie hit her with the usual question.

"How are you feeling?"

"You've got to stop asking me that, Ange."

"Sorry. But you know I'm only doing it because I care about you, right?"

"Yes, I know." Tristan swallowed her impatience. "But once and for all, I'm fine. And for the record, I haven't been attending AA meetings. I don't need this stuff. What happened before, how messed-up I got, it was a one-off. It won't happen again. I'm stronger than that. You understand?"

Angie answered without missing a beat.

"Yes, I sure do. Do you understand that you're in breach of contract?"

Are you fucking kidding me? With a flush of irritation, Tristan drew in a breath to ask exactly that; but then she heard Angie's telling chuckle, and she relaxed.

"Haha. You're hilarious."

"Yep. But seriously, Tris, you sound solid."

"I keep telling you!"

"Any particular reason at this time?"

"Not really," Tristan lied, thinking about Huxley.

"Even better." Angie sounded fully reassured. "And thank you for representing Dagger so well. Just please, try not to break too many noses, okay?"

"I'll take that under consideration."

Tristan hung up with a smile, feeling very good indeed. On impulse, she texted Quinn. *'Come on over. Lia's cooking'*, came the answer. Tristan got on her bike and went before she could come up with a twisted reason not to. It was great to catch up with her friends after so many months apart, and the reunion went well. Dropping in on Katie afterwards, she also got a chance to meet her new partner, Mark Lee, for the first time. And if ever a man were in love, completely head over heels over his new girlfriend, it was him... Not only that, but Lee was just as caring and affectionate toward Jake Jr. And Jake himself seemed at ease in his new role as big brother to Mark's daughter.

"He's definitely a keeper, Kate," Tristan told her friend on the way out.

What she truly meant was that Jake would approve of the relationship. He only ever wanted the best for his wife and child.

"Thank you for saying that," Katie replied with glistening eyes. She understood what Tristan left unsaid. "It means a lot to us. Are you okay too, Tris? You seem relaxed."

"You know what?" Tristan smiled. "Yes, I am."

She was not naïve enough to believe what she'd told Angie; that there was no particular reason for it. For sure, there was. But it would not turn into a problem. Tristan was convinced of this, simply because she would not allow it. The job came first, now and always. It had to.

••

Huxley celebrated her twenty-ninth birthday in style with a Live performance sponsored by iTunes, streamed conveniently from her own backyard to the likes of Apple TV and YouTube. In the evening, she held a private pool party for some friends and band members. Tristan made herself scarce during that time, keeping an eye on things from a reasonable distance. She had not been officially invited, after all. Rose came to find her after a while, as Tristan leaned against a tree in the shadows of the pool house. In killer heels and a gold satin dress that highlighted her smooth chocolate skin, with dark curly hair flowing over her shoulders and a killer smile on her red lips, she looked magnificent.

"Hey, stranger!" she greeted her.

"Hi Rose," Tristan nodded.

"What are you doing out here on your own?" the woman asked. "You okay?"

She seemed genuinely concerned, and Tristan smiled. Rose had come on to her hard in Miami. But to her credit, she'd been nothing but warm and friendly since Tristan made it clear that she was not interested. She really was a beautiful soul.

"I'm fine, yes. Just making sure that no one gets out of line, you know?"

"Are you ever not working?" Rose sounded puzzled.

"Not really, no," Tristan chuckled.

By the side of the pool, Erik was showing off to a group of attractive women, the personal trainer who was sharing his bed not that long ago now nowhere to be seen. Erik liked girls; no surprise there. Tristan's attention drifted to Huxley. The singer was also clad in a stunning party dress, but she had kicked off her heels. Sex Pistol was in her arms, happily, and drawing quite a crowd. Even the women who were talking to Erik eventually moved to Huxley and her puppy. Tristan grinned. *Yep, this makes sense as well.*

"Hey, Tristan?"

"Mm?"

As Tristan turned to her, Rose clasped her fingers, emotion suddenly rising into her face.

"Alys showed me the sick and nasty stuff that this stalker sent her. You won't let him get to her. Right?"

Tristan held her hand, squeezing gently.

"I won't let him touch her, Rose. I promise."

Rose flashed a shaky smile, eyes sparkling with reluctant tears.

"You sound like you mean it."

"I certainly do. We're going to nail this guy."

"Good. Soon, I hope… She's amazing, you know."

"I know," Tristan said gently. "You're very special too."

"Ah!" Rose shrugged, looking away quickly in reluctance and embarrassment. "Yeah, yeah... Gosh, I need a drink!"

Her pupils were wide enough for Tristan to realize that she must be on something else. It was not her place to comment or give advice, but Rose sounded sad, and she knew only too well what that was like.

"Once upon a time, staying drunk around the clock felt like the only way to cope for me," she offered.

"What... You?"

Rose was obviously startled at the admission.

"Yeah." Tristan nodded. "It almost killed me."

"Wow. That's huge, I had no idea. What happened to make you sober up?"

"I had a good friend who cared very much. Eventually, she forced me to talk to her. It helped."

"Lucky you," Rose murmured.

"Yes, I was. Rose, I know you've got Alys. But if you ever need to talk to someone else, I'm here for you. Any time."

A single tear escaped, rolling down the side of the dancer's face, but she wiped it away quickly. She was tough; Tristan did not doubt it. Rose looked her in the eye, long and deep, before leaning over and kissing her softly on the cheek.

"Thank you, Tristan. You are very special too. I'll see you later."

Tristan smiled faintly, knowing that she would go for that drink. Nothing she could do about it right now, but maybe she had planted a seed. She kept a discreet eye on Rose as the party went on, making sure she was okay, and on everybody else as well. The birthday bash ended reasonably, some time around one-thirty a.m. In the still and fragrant night, Tristan sat alone on one of the loungers, enjoying the peace and quiet which ensued.

Sex Pistol soon trotted into view.

"Hey, puppy." Eager to prevent an accidental fall into the pool, Tristan clicked her fingers to get his attention. She picked him up, earning herself a lick on the nose, and settled him over her lap. "What are you doing out here on your own so late, little guy?"

"He's not on his own." Huxley adopted the smooth tones of a late-night talk show host as she came into view. "But thanks for looking out for him."

"No problem." The puppy curled up against her chest, and Tristan smiled. "He's cute."

"So are you, Briggs."

"I'm sorry?" Tristan looked up, alert.

"What?" Huxley shrugged, looking both amused and ironic at the same time. "It's true. All tough on the outside, but melting like ice cream as soon as a puppy licks your face. You're cute. Deal with it."

Tristan relaxed, since she was obviously teasing.

"Yeah, I'll deal." Huxley was still in her glitzy black dress, with one of the spaghetti straps probably intentionally fallen off of one shoulder. Still shoeless in an attractively careless fashion. And carrying a plate. "Enjoying a late-night snack, Ms. Huxley?"

"This is for you."

"Oh?"

The singer smiled almost shyly as she offered her the plate.

"I know you were working tonight. Didn't even make time for a slice of birthday cake. So, I saved you one."

Tristan did her level best to keep a straight face and not let Huxley see that she was touched by the gesture. But she really was. *Hard as nails, uh? Yeah, right!* On impulse, she stood up and handed her the puppy. Huxley raised an eyebrow in wonder.

151

"Just give me a second please?" Tristan asked. "I'll be right back with you."

"Okay... Sure."

Tristan raced back to her studio to pick up the present that she had bought but then decided not to give to Huxley. Birthday or not, never before had she felt inclined to buy anything for a client. Let alone wrap the gift in glittery pink paper! It did not seem wise or appropriate to start. Yet, in the blink of an eye, Huxley's kind gesture destroyed any hesitation she previously had. *Nothing wrong with being nice, is there?* Of course, there was more to it. Tristan resolutely pushed the thought out of her mind as she rejoined her.

"Happy birthday."

Huxley looked at her with eyes wide before breaking into the sweetest smile.

"Oh... Thanks!"

Seeing this look on her face; a mix of surprised, curious, and genuinely moved, made Tristan glad that she had gone to get the gift. And worried as well. She sat back down.

"Don't get too excited. It's not diamond earrings."

"Don't get the wrong idea," Huxley chuckled. "The earrings aren't really a gift. Brad just buys me things to wear on stage and passes them off as a special thing. It's just business."

"Really? I thought you two were closer than that."

"We're close business associates," Huxley confirmed. "But my friends know I don't care much for flashy expensive gifts. You know what Rose got me? Compression socks for the flight to Australia!"

Huxley sounded so genuinely pleased and excited about it that Tristan laughed. Hard not to appreciate a woman who was so complex and also down to earth at the same time.

"Socks over diamonds?" she grinned. "Nice."

"Oh yeah! I'm a practical kind of girl. Here, I brought you a fork. Dig in."

Tristan wolfed down the birthday cake, especially delicious since she had missed dinner, and she enjoyed watching Huxley unwrap her present. She worked with meticulous care.

"Are you trying to keep the paper intact?"

"Yep. Quirky, I know."

"You'd be a good asset to the bomb squad."

This triggered a laugh from the woman.

"You say the weirdest things, Briggs."

"Thanks, I think," Tristan nodded.

Huxley flashed her a sparkling glance.

"Weird is good," she said. "I like people who are different."

CHAPTER 19

The last thing Alys expected when she went to find Briggs, after helping a terminally drunk Rose to bed in her guest room, was a present from her. At the back of her mind, she kept wondering if her security officer even liked her. Sure, she was friendly... And even warm at times. Alys figured her own insecurities must be to blame for making her fear that Briggs might only regard her as a spoiled and uninteresting character. Sharing this moment together now, she was keen to make it last. In an ideal world, maybe she'd also kiss the tiny spot of chocolate cream left on the side of Briggs' attractive mouth. Too late; Briggs licked it off herself. Alys returned her attention to unwrapping her present, and she laughed in delight when she finally discovered what it was.

"Oh, this is so cool!" Briggs had got her a plush toy. A little stuffed koala with a cheeky grin, dressed in an Australian flag t-shirt. Sex Pistol clearly thought that the gift was for him. "Sorry babe," Alys chuckled. "This one's off limits."

"Come here, boy." Briggs tempted the inquisitive pup back to her with a chocolate-smeared finger.

As Alys considered her new birthday gift, she was aware of a light prickling sensation at the back of her eyes. Certainly, this was not due to a lifelong passion for either plush toys or koalas. Without stopping to consider, she threw her arm around Briggs' shoulders.

"I've never toured Australia or Europe before. Not only is this one big for my career, but personally, as well. I've dreamt of taking my music around the world since I was a little kid. Now I get to do it for real, in person. This is huge."

"I know." Briggs nodded softly. "That's why I got you this. A little mascot. And a souvenir to mark the year of an incredible achievement."

Alys kept her eyes riveted onto her face.

"Such a thoughtful present. Thank you."

"I'm glad you like it, Ms. Huxley."

For a split second, Alys glimpsed naked emotion behind her steady green eyes. It also occurred to her how ridiculous and unfounded her own fears were. Could it be that Rose was correct in her observation? And that Briggs was attracted to her? In that instant, everything changed. Alys became acutely aware of how close they were. She had her arm around Briggs. The bodyguard felt warm and relaxed against her side. As Alys went quiet and met her eyes for a full-on stare, Briggs did not make a single move. She just swallowed and her lips parted ever so slightly, as if searching for more oxygen. Alys waited a fraction of a second more, heart pounding in her own chest. But when the woman still did not move, she gently curled her arm a bit tighter around her neck. Briggs looked like her eyelids were suddenly heavy. She finally twitched, and blinked a couple times.

"Ms. Huxley—"

"Sshhh…"

••

If Tristan had been able to think, she might have wondered how they'd gone from sitting together, talking about Australia and eating birthday cake, to sharing the same breath. *'Extremely well'*, could have been the answer. On a lovely slide. Huxley only kissed her once but it had to be the best, richest, softest, most focused kiss that Tristan ever received. The singer was gentle, yet decisive. The instant she tightened her arm around her, and looked so deep into her eyes, Tristan slipped into a light trance. It felt great to be held, and especially by this particular woman. It was getting late, and she was tired. It took her a bit longer than normal to realize where this was all headed. When she did, and tried to pull out of her daze, it was too late. Huxley touched her lips to hers. Incredibly lightly at first, and then pressing more firmly. Tristan closed her eyes and she fell again. Soundly into the kiss this time, every cell and instinctual particle of her being attuned to Huxley. She raised her hand to touch her face. She caressed the elegant line of her jaw, and found her cheek aflame. Soft skin burning the palm of her hand. Desire awakened, and Tristan trembled. Just like so many times before with Huxley, she was aroused against her will.

"Tristan..." Huxley pulled back with a murmur.

First time using her name, and Tristan knew that she would never forget the tone of her voice as she said it. Huxley sounded turned on, sexy, sultry, and also strangely relieved. Never before had Tristan wanted to kiss a woman back so much as she did now. She stared at her lips, swollen full of blood and moist with the memory of their first kiss. Huxley looked back at her with hooded eyes and a longing smile.

'Dammit, Tristan. She's your client!'

Jake's voice sounded in her head like a gunshot. A series of brutal images flashed in front of her eyes. The man who was like a brother, dead. The terror in Katie's eyes when Tristan knocked on her door. Jake's wife knew before his devastated partner even said a word. Tristan fixed on a memory of Jake Jr at the funeral. The kid was too young to understand, but he could feel. He cried as he watched his father be buried. *All because I dropped the ball. If only I'd listened to Jake, he would still be here.*

"Hey, hey..." Huxley called to her in concern. "Briggs? Are you okay?"

Tristan was appalled to find her eyes filling with tears. She swallowed them back.

"I'm fine. Look, I just—" She turned to face Huxley, intent on apologizing for what had just happened and taking full responsibility. But the expression in her eyes stopped her short. *Alys.* So open and unguarded in this moment. So pure. Tristan saw her truly then. Not as a client, a rock goddess, or whatever else. She was just Alys, a beautiful woman with a kind heart and an infectious zest for life. Tristan exhaled. "I'm sorry."

"Why?" Huxley sounded fierce, although her smile belied a hint of genuine sadness. "I wanted to kiss you, Briggs. I'm glad I did."

"So am I," Tristan murmured. She could no more deny this than she could move out of Huxley's embrace at the moment. But she knew that she had to, and soon. "I'm sorry that it can't happen ever again."

Huxley moved away first, dropping her arm from around her shoulders and standing up. Tristan felt cold. She forced herself to remain seated where she was, instead of rising and going to her.

"Tell me why not," Huxley prompted.

"Because I'm in charge of keeping you safe. I can't afford to make a mistake."

"What are you talking about? Why would you?"

"Mistakes happen when feelings are involved."

"You have feelings for me?"

It was a heartfelt question, delivered wrapped up in a good slice of attitude, for protection. Tristan wanted to show her with a kiss of her own how much she wanted her... But instead, she forced herself to lie.

"I don't have feelings for you, Ms. Huxley."

"Don't worry then, Briggs," Huxley chuckled, although her eyes had gone flat. "We're fine on that count. Come on, puppy. Let's go!"

She walked off on that, leaving Tristan to stare after her in regret.

••

The next few days were tense and difficult, definitely on the cool side. Huxley turned argumentative, quibbling over small details for no good reason. She seemed intent on making last minute changes to her schedule. Nothing to the degree that it would compromise her overall safety, but enough to give Tristan more work and, on at least a couple of occasions, a headache. One of these annoying tweaks included deciding to spend half the night partying at a new club downtown, and making out with one of the dancers there. Tristan hated every second of having to watch the performance. *You know that's your own damn fault.* She had crossed a line and this was payback. The following evening, she considered riding to The Club and getting rid of some tension.

Pretty sure it would be more effective than roaming the outside walls of the property like a lion in a cage, checking on the CCTV system. This was Erik's job now and he clearly took it seriously. Tristan found no fault with the cameras. Everything was clean and working well. At almost midnight, she made up her mind to at least take the Kawasaki out for a ride, if nothing else. The idea of anonymous sex at The Club left her feeling cold tonight, but she was too edgy to try to sleep. On her way to grab her helmet, she just happened to glance toward the house. Lucky move, too. She spotted Huxley, in jeans and a t-shirt, flying out the front door. Tristan went still, on alert. *What now?* Her client rarely if ever went out again after calling it a night. Contrary to her rebel rocker image, she liked to spend quiet evenings in front of the TV with Sex Pistol. Also, she was not stupid enough to take this kind of risk. *She would tell me if she had to go out. Surely, she would.* Or maybe not... Tristan swore under her breath when Huxley jumped behind the wheel of the Range Rover and gunned the engine. *What in hell does she think she's doing?* There was no time to ponder and figure it out, and Tristan was too far from the house to just shout and ask her politely to wait. Given her recent moods, Huxley was likely to ignore her, anyway. The next best option would be to sprint across the bottom lawn and intercept the Rover before it went out the gates.

"STOP!"

Huxley hit the brakes, causing the heavy vehicle to slide a bit further on the gravel path before stopping, only inches from Tristan's raised hand. Holding onto the steering wheel with a white-knuckle grip, the singer glared at her through the windshield.

"Ms Hux—"

"Move, Briggs! Get out of the way!"

Tristan did, although probably not in the way that Huxley meant. Not wasting her breath to ask questions at this point, she leaped to the side, grabbed hold of the door handle, and hoisted herself onto the passenger seat, just as her client stuck her foot to the floor again. They were rolling before she was fully in... And fast, too. Tristan yanked her door shut, barely in time to save it smashing into the side post. *Glad it's not my leg.* She took a deep breath and turned to stare at her client. Something must be very wrong to cause this sort of a reaction. Huxley may be keen to remind her of who was boss from time to time, but there was a difference between choosing to go to a different restaurant at the last minute, to assert her authority and control, and doing this. In jeans, a wrinkled t-shirt, and battered running shoes, Huxley was not dressed for an event or to party. She wore no makeup, and she was actually quite pale. Tristan counted her lucky stars that she had spotted her leaving when she did, and was able to jump onboard. She decided to remain silent, aware that Huxley seemed upset. The last thing she would need right now was for her bodyguard to demand to know what she was doing, as if Tristan had any right to know. Or to be reminded that she was not supposed to go out without an escort. Tristan knew what her own answer would be if the roles were reversed. Maybe because she chose to be patient and not treat her like an object, as many others did, Huxley soon opened up.

"It's Rose," she related in an anxious voice. "She left me a load of messages earlier this evening, but I was very focused on writing a new song and I didn't find them until now."

"Okay." Tristan's stomach tightened. "Is she alright?"

"No. Not at all."

CHAPTER 20

Huxley replayed the messages on her phone for her benefit. Four of them in a row. Starting with Rose asking her friend to call her back, and getting progressively more desperate until the last one she left.

'Please, Al, I really need you. I'm so messed up tonight, I don't know what's going on. I'm sorry... Please, pick up the phone. Darling, I feel so alone...'

Rose was crying and she also sounded drunk. Rambling on about crazy stuff. If Huxley had not already been tearing down the freeway like a Formula One race driver, Tristan might have told her to step on it.

"Has this happened before?" she asked.

"Yes, a couple times. Rose suffers from chronic depression. The last time she got really down was two years ago, when she came off a month-long tour with another singer. The change in pace got to her."

As Huxley took the exit road toward downtown Lewiston, Tristan checked her mirror, noting with a measure of relief that they were the only car on the road here.

"Does she call you when she's bad?"

"Yes, she does. I wouldn't usually miss a call from her but I was so immersed in my work tonight..." Huxley bit on her lip with a shake of the head, concern for her friend obvious in the tense line of her shoulders. "I'm sorry I forgot to let you know, Briggs. But I was only thinking of Rose and wanting to get to her ASAP."

"That's okay, I understand." *I know what that's like...* Tristan reached across the space to lay a comforting hand on the back of her shoulder. She was reluctant to ask the next question, aware of what a negative answer might mean, but she forced herself to do it. "Did you call her back and manage to speak to her?"

"Yes," Huxley confirmed.

"Oh, great! How was she?"

"Drunk out of her mind but I told her that I was on the way. She got that, I know. She sounded relieved."

"Excellent."

"Just you wait until the woman sobers up," Huxley added with a mix of an affectionate and irritated chuckle. "I almost got a heart attack listening to her messages! I know it's totally out of her control, but... Damn, she scares me sometimes!"

Tristan knew for sure that they were on the same page with that.

"Is she on medication?" she pressed.

"No." Huxley shrugged. "Not the kind you're asking about, anyway."

Such a shame. Rose had so much going for her, yet she still struggled with a lot, and used alcohol and legal pills in order to alleviate her pain. It certainly did not have to be like this, and Tristan decided that she would talk to her. She could share some of her story, take her to an AA meeting if Rose was open to it...

Granted, this might blur the lines between the professional and personal even more. But Rose was not her client. Also, it might save her life in the long run.

"Slow down here," Tristan instructed as her driver went on as if the speed limit were just a starting point.

"What?" Huxley snapped, instantly pissed off at being told what to do.

"Just around this corner, Ms. Huxley. Unless you want a cop on your tail."

Huxley muttered under her breath but she did reduce her speed. Sure enough, right where she thought it might be, Tristan spotted a police cruiser parked in the shadows on the side of a convenience store.

"Wow." Huxley smacked her on the thigh, her usual spirit making a comeback. "Saved us a ticket and a waste of time here, Briggs. Do you know all the spots where cops lie in ambush?"

"Not all, but some. And this was no ambush, by the way. Only a criminal would think it."

"Obviously not!" Huxley laughed. "But thanks for warning me. I'm glad to have you onboard."

"I do have my uses," Tristan remarked, her eyes on the cop car receding slowly in her side mirror.

"That's not what I meant."

"No?"

"No." Huxley flashed her another look, this one penetrating and warm. "I am glad to have you with me, Briggs. Period."

She still had her right hand over her leg, nice and relaxed, and the simple touch felt amazing. Tristan just nodded though, unwilling to acknowledge the comment for what it could be; the start of something else that would lead to distractions she could not afford.

"Me too," she said. "No one followed us down the freeway, but you never know."

At this subtle reminder that she was working here, not as a friend or anything else, Huxley moved her fingers calmly back to the steering wheel.

"Yeah, you never know," she smirked.

Tristan noticed her lips tighten in displeasure. She fought the urge to touch her again, and apologize... But for what? The paradox was not lost on her that she had to be a little bit unkind in order to keep her client safe. She would never have imagined that she would face this sort of problem on a job. Just like the idea of *'Taking a bullet'* for one's client was far from the norm, developing feelings for them also was not as common as they liked to portray in the movies. Tristan knew the price of not keeping a cool head in the field. No matter what, she would not pay it twice.

••

Alys had caught a glimpse of a different side of Briggs when she kissed her that night. Not so sure, tough, or distant. Instead, she was warm, welcoming, and deliciously receptive. Alys could still taste her; heated lips and a hint of chocolate. Briggs did not say no that first time. She did not remind her of the rules, duty, or obligation. She just fell hard and deep into the kiss. Beautifully. There had to be something else to explain her reluctance besides her dedication to the job. *To me...* For sure, Briggs had made it clear that her ability to keep her safe could not be compromised. This was sexy too, and perhaps Alys should not look further. Glancing at her again, meeting those calm green eyes as Briggs looked back, she almost said it again; *I'm really glad you're here.*

Having to rush over to Rose in the middle of the night to deal with one of her episodes would be daunting, even at the best of times. But even more so now. As Alys climbed out of the Rover in front of her apartment complex, she could not help a shiver of apprehension. They were alone here. The street seemed empty. But who knew what danger might be lurking in the shadows?

"Are you alright, Ms. Huxley?"

Briggs stood by her side, very much like a shield. Attentive and alert, as always. Alys resisted the urge to clasp her hand and move even closer.

"Yes," she said. "Just that when I least expect it sometimes, one of the threats that this idiot wrote to me will jump into my head. It's unsettling."

"Mmm." Briggs stared down the street, eyes intent and her expression fierce. "He won't get anywhere near you, I promise you that."

She spoke with such strength and confidence... Encouraged, Alys took a deep breath and she squared her shoulders.

"Alright, let's go quickly."

Aware that Rose may be passed out by the time she got to her place, she had brought her own key. She knocked first, and announced their presence, but then unlocked the door without waiting for a reply. Briggs followed closely on her heels.

"Rose?" Alys called. "It's me, darling. Rosie?"

Rose was indeed fast asleep on the couch, an empty bottle of vodka and a knocked down vial of pills on the coffee table in front of her. Alys sighed in resignation.

"Oh, babe. Rosie, do you—"

"Ms. Huxley." Briggs cut in sharply and stepped in front of her. "Call 911 and ask for an ambulance."

"What?"

It took a second for Alys to understand what she was doing, as Briggs pushed her fingers against the side of her friend's neck and visibly waited to feel something. It was the first time Alys had seen this done in real life. And it was surreal. *No.* Her blood went cold at the realization of what it meant. *No, there's no need for this! She's just asleep!*

"She barely has a pulse," Briggs announced, turning to flash her an urgent look. "Make that call, Ms. Huxley, please."

Alys reached for her phone and dialed 911 with trembling fingers. Meanwhile, Briggs went on to whip the soft blanket that covered Rose off of her, revealing a plastic tie around her bicep and a needle still dangling from her right arm. *Jesus, Rosie... What did you do?*

"Yes! Ambulance please!" Alys requested frantically when an operator picked up. "My friend is unconscious! We just found her in her apartment."

"Tell them it's an opioid overdose," Briggs said as if she'd diagnosed this sort of thing hundreds of times before. "Irregular breathing, weak pulse, constricted pupils. Totally unresponsive to stimuli. She's icy cold. Rose? Rose!"

Alys relayed the information to the 911 operator as Briggs continued to try to rouse her friend.

"Alcohol was also involved. We're at 9103 Bex Hill Drive. Apartment 7A." Alys nodded to her bodyguard. "They'll be here in five minutes."

"Okay." Briggs continued her efforts, slapping Rose's face and the top of her hands and arms harder now. "Wake up. Come on, Rose, come back to me!"

Alys moved next to her, clasping her friend's hand tightly in hers. Rose was freezing cold, definitely, her lips and fingertips already blue.

"Rose, it's me. Open your eyes!" She shook her head when no response came. "Dammit, I just spoke to her! Why did she do this?"

Briggs did not offer any reassurances this time, and actually just swore under her breath.

"Fuck!"

"What?" Alys yelled in panic.

"She stopped breathing. No pulse."

She pulled Rose off the couch in one swift motion, laid her flat on the floor, and started to do chest compressions. Alys kept holding her hand. She felt helpless. Terrified. Meanwhile, Briggs went on doing CPR like her own life depended on it.

"Come on. Come on, Rose!"

But Rose remained just as still. This was a total nightmare, all of Alys's worst fears realized. Until…

"Yes, got her!" Briggs finally uttered in triumph. "I have a pulse."

Alys automatically drifted to her after she quickly briefed the two paramedics who took over. She leaned against her side while Briggs passed a protective arm around her shoulders.

"They're going to stabilize her, okay?"

"Okay," Alys murmured, biting on her lip.

"We'll follow in the Rover to the hospital."

"Yes."

"Ms. Huxley?"

Alys tore her gaze away from Rose, now with an oxygen mask over her pale face and an IV line in her forearm instead of a needle full of drugs, as she was secured onto a stretcher. Briggs regarded her with such warmth and compassion in her eyes that it almost made her break, finally, and burst into tears. She just managed not to, but she was close.

"You just saved her life. If I'd been on my own here..."

A shadow passed over Briggs' brilliant eyes, so fleeting that Alys was not even sure she'd not dreamed it.

"Do you want me to drive?"

She was offering, not instructing, as others might be keen to do; and so gentle with it. *I'm really glad you're here, Tristan.* Alys nodded in reply, tears burning harder at the back of her eyes.

"Yes, please."

"Okay." Briggs gave her a brief but heartfelt squeeze. "Let's go then."

Alys would barely remember the drive to the hospital. They followed behind the ambulance. Briggs drove sure and safe, the same way she rode her bike. Alys noticed that. She also found a measure of comfort in the memory of that day on the Kawasaki. Then they were there, parking illegally in front of the entrance and jumping out of the Rover. Rose was rushed to a treatment room. A nurse stopped her from following in when Alys tried.

"Sorry, you can't go in there."

"But I—"

"Someone will be out to talk to you as soon as possible."

The nurse disappeared behind a set of revolving doors that clicked shut behind her. In the sudden silence and stillness that ensued, Alys could only stare. *Oh, Rose...*

CHAPTER 21

They sat to wait on a couple of chairs in the hallway, at an angle from the nurses' station and, hopefully, out of the way of prying eyes. It was not enough. Tristan soon spotted movement around the corner. Two guys were taking turns popping their heads out from behind the wall. Staring and giggling excitedly. *I'm telling you, it's her!* They certainly weren't subtle about it, and Huxley groaned in reaction.

"I can't. Briggs... Not now."

"Leave it with me, Ms. Huxley."

With two quick strides, Tristan crossed over to ask them to respect her client's privacy. She was polite, understanding. But when one tried to snap a shot of Huxley, she grabbed his wrist, ignored the sound of the expensive phone clattering to the floor, and twisted his fingers back into a painful lock.

"Ow!" the guy hissed. "Ow, ow, stop! OW!"

"Hey, what are you doing?" his buddy protested.

Tristan forced them both to take some steps back.

"Ms. Huxley isn't here to entertain you tonight, guys. This is private business. Understood?"

"Let go, dammit!"

Tristan released the guy and she repeated her question.

"Do you understand me? Are we clear?"

The two were young and probably harmless. Just a little too keen and thoughtless in their enthusiasm.

"Yeah, fine," the first misguided admirer huffed.

"Don't break our noses, eh!" the other one chuckled.

Obviously, they read the trash mags. Tristan kept her eyes on them as they retreated down the hallway and went to hook up with another dude, coming out of an exam room on crutches. The one who'd tried to snap a pic and got his fingers squeezed glanced back, flashed an irreverent salute, and galloped after his friends on their way out. *Okay, fine.* These two had been waiting on an injured friend and happened to recognize Huxley. Clearly only a coincidence, nothing sinister about it. Reassured, Tristan walked back in time to see a woman in maroon scrubs walk out of the ER, glance around, and head straight toward Huxley.

"Are you with the young woman who was recently brought in?" she inquired. "A Ms. Rose Carling?"

Huxley shot to her feet in response.

"Yes, we are. How is she? Can I see her?"

Tristan recognized the expression on the doctor's face with a sinking feeling. Her stomach tightened and she instinctively moved closer to her client. Quinn's voice sounded in her head, as loud and clear as if she had been standing in front of her. *'He's gone, Tris... There's nothing you can do.'*

"Your friend arrested a second time in the ambulance, and once more on arrival," the doctor explained in a soft, practiced voice. "We did everything we could to bring her back, but the third time, we were unable to." She clasped Huxley's shoulder in sympathy. "I am very sorry for your loss."

Tristan nodded once in acknowledgment when she glanced at her, but she kept her main attention focused on Huxley. She heard her shocked exhale at the news and watched the rest of the color drain out of her face. The singer's shoulders dropped. Her head followed her eyes as she looked down. For a moment, she looked as if her knees would buckle and she might just crumble to the floor. Tristan was ready in case this happened, though she also knew that she was made of more resilient stuff. She was not surprised when, past the first piercing hit of the arrow, Huxley straightened up.

"I want to see her."

"Of course, you can do that. Follow me, please," the doctor invited.

Huxley took two steps forward before turning abruptly to look at her. Her usually clear blue eyes were stormy and hot, full of pain, glistening with a film of tears that she was obviously working hard to keep inside. Tristan felt her own emotion rise in response.

"I need a few moments alone with Rosie. Okay?"

The fact that she even bothered to check at this point was pretty unbelievable... And Tristan did not think it had anything to do with protocol. Probably not due to safety concerns either. She held Huxley's gaze intently, hoping to convey to her at least a tiny part of what she would not allow herself to say out loud. Not here, anyway. Not right now. *You are so beautiful. So strong. I'm so proud of you!*

"I'll be right here, Ms. Huxley," she replied instead. "Take as long as you need."

Huxley fixed her sharply for a couple more seconds before letting out a big sigh. But her gaze softened and she murmured a grateful, *'Thank you'*.

••

The show must go on.

This included organizing a quiet funeral for Rose, who had no family of her own. Huxley hosted an intimate gathering at the house afterwards, with all her friend's favorite people assembled together to honor and remember her. Over the next week, she performed Live at two different events: one in Texas, the other in Georgia. Both dates had sold out months in advance and could not easily be canceled. Doing so would only create more hassle anyway, and so, Huxley just got on with the job. She did what she did best, delivered brilliant performances. It was not lost on Tristan that she kept pushing herself hard with interviews and TV appearances, going on full-steam ahead. Outwardly, no one could have guessed that she had just lost someone extremely close to her to tragic circumstances. She was slightly more quiet than usual in private, but not overly so. Bradley Wright carried on as if nothing of any consequence had taken place. Even Erik, who cried openly at Rose's funeral, did not seem too concerned about his cousin.

'Yeah, that's Alys for you,' he stated when Tristan remarked on it. 'She's a tough girl. She'll digest this one in her own way and be just fine, you'll see.'

Tristan was not totally convinced, but she certainly hoped so. A week later, she'd just finished a call with Detective Miller when a knock came on the door of her annex. It turned out to be Huxley. For once, without Sex Pistol in tow. She was dressed in jeans, boots, and a leather jacket. Carrying the bike helmet that Tristan had lent to her, and looking more gorgeous than even the word could describe.

"Hello, Ms. Huxley."

"Hi." The singer stepped almost aggressively past her and into the lounge, then she threw the helmet onto the couch. "Can I come in?"

"You are in," Tristan nodded.

"Yeah, well." Huxley stared at bits of disassembled weapon on the table, her expression turning even darker. "What are you doing with that?"

"Cleaning my back-up weapon."

"Huh."

Huxley took off her jacket and flung that over the couch as well. She appeared wired as hell, and Tristan risked an obvious question.

"Were you thinking of going for a bike ride?"

"Well, I, uh…" Huxley turned her back on her and began to pace across the lounge. She sank her fingers into her hair, shook the wavy strands loose, and smoothed them out of her face as she turned around. "I was going to ask you… Um…"

"Ms. Huxley." Tristan stepped forward when she struggled to catch her breath. "Would you like to sit down?"

"No."

"Okay."

"I was going to ask you to take me out on your bike, yes." Huxley completed her sentence. "To ride hard and fast down the freeway and… And… Forget about all this!"

She made a vague gesture across the room. Tristan did not ask what she meant by it, and *'All this'*. She knew that Huxley probably referred to the pressure and demands of her career. Or of life in general. The two were intimately linked in her case, and the pace, of late, had been pretty relentless.

"If you want to, we can—"

"No, I don't want to anymore," Huxley interrupted.

"That's fine." Tristan nodded soothingly. "I'll take you out whenever you feel like it."

Huxley did sit on the couch, finally, and regarded her with a blank expression. Something was going on with her for sure, and Tristan had to ask her at least one question.

"Did you receive another email, Ms. Huxley?"

"No idea." The singer shrugged. "I didn't check. But since your cop friends are monitoring my inbox now, you'll probably be the first to know if I do."

Tristan quickly and silently put her weapon back together and locked it into the safe. Meanwhile, Huxley stood up again to pace in front of the window. She remained quiet, absorbed in her own thoughts, and Tristan did not ask. Whatever had her client feeling so agitated was bound to come out if she did not push her. After awhile, Huxley grew still.

"Briggs," she murmured.

"Yes, Ms. Huxley," Tristan answered calmly.

After another heavy silence, the singer turned around to face her again.

"I just had a massive fight with Brad," she announced.

Tristan narrowed her eyes, wondering what kind.

"Do you mean a work-related argument?" she asked.

"Yes. I shared with him that I was thinking about canceling the upcoming world tour." Huxley took a hard breath and blew it out. "Maybe even quit everything for good."

"Everything?"

"My career."

"Right." Tristan stayed calm. "And what would you do?"

"I don't know." Huxley shrugged. "Just disappear, I guess. You ever felt that way, Briggs?"

Back to this yearning she had of not being famous anymore, or so special. Huxley sounded like she might welcome a nice and deep black hole to leap into. And it was not hard to imagine how Wright would react to this kind of talk. Although not concerned about him, Tristan could sympathize. Wright was also totally invested in the Huxley enterprise. In a way, it was his life too. Tristan held the singer's gaze, whose face had morphed into a solid mask of misery and bitter regret. Now they might get to the bottom of things. She gave her a gentle smile and avoided the question. This was not about her.

"We can talk if you'd like to," she prompted.

Huxley's mouth quivered and she gasped for air.

"I failed her, Briggs," she blurted out. "Rosie... It's all my fault!"

Tristan pursed her lips at the astonishing level of pain that she perceived laced in that one statement. Huxley was skilled at modulating a full range of emotions when she sang. It was not just her incredible voice that made her stand out from so many other talented performers in the field, but her ability to sing from the heart, as it were. Now, every bit of anguish and remorse that she felt could be heard in her tone. She sounded exhausted and raw. Broken, really. Tristan let out a soft breath in reaction but otherwise remained silent. Her client may well have hoped that throwing herself into her work like she did the past few weeks, and burning the candle at both ends, would help her to get over this painful event in her life. *If only it were that easy...* It sounded as if it was all going to come out now, and Tristan needed to allow it.

"It took me two-and-a-half hours," Huxley recalled, a river of tears flowing down her face. "I took a fucking eternity before I looked up from my work and picked up her messages!"

Tristan did not move from her position on the couch, even though she ached to close the distance between them, and pull the woman into her arms.

"I always told Rose that if she needed me in an emergency, I'd be there for her," Huxley went on. "You know? She knew it. All she had to do was call."

"I know," Tristan whispered.

"But when she did call... The one time it was deadly serious and she really needed me..." Huxley bit hard enough on her bottom lip to make herself flinch. "I was not there for her. Too busy writing that stupid song! When I imagine how lonely and desperate she must have felt... Bad enough to stick that needle in her arm! It's my fault. I kill—"

"Ms. Huxley. Please, stop."

Now, Tristan went to her. Huxley did not resist when she embraced her. Just laced her arms around her waist, as painful sobs racked through her body, and cried as if she might break into pieces. When Tristan moved them back to sit down on the sofa, Huxley pulled her legs up across her lap and she wrapped herself around her body, holding on as if she were drowning.

"I can't do it anymore," she moaned. "It's too much, I just can't!"

CHAPTER 22

Of course, she was in no way responsible for her friend's death. She did not get her drunk on vodka, wrap a tie around her arm, and push a lethal dose of heroin into her system. She did answer her calls for help, even if there was a slight delay. And she also went over to take care of Rose, as she always did. Huxley should not be blaming herself for the way that it ended. It just seemed as if all the pain of loss, grief, and the added stress of her very unusual life, finally accumulated in a single charge and got her to breaking point. So, Tristan kept it simple.

"You don't have to do anything," she assured. "Right now, it's okay. You can rest."

Huxley went through a few cycles of this. She would cry for a while, calm down, then start sobbing again. Tristan held her, allowing emotions to come out without saying much in between breaks. Every time Huxley apologized for her tears, she just told her that it was fine.

"Shh. Let it all go."

Huxley fell asleep in what seemed to be a favorite position; snuggled against Tristan's side with one leg thrown over hers.

Her face was still wet with tears and fever hot. She lay with her cheek pressed into the side of her neck, soft lips just brushing Tristan's skin. It was the second time that Alys Huxley ended up falling asleep in her arms, and just as challenging. Tristan closed her eyes, focused on breathing slow, and tried to relax. *Don't think about how it feels.* But holding Alys felt amazingly good, for sure. It was hard not to remember the kiss they had shared... *Don't think about it, dammit!*

••

It was dark in the room when Alys opened her eyes. She knew immediately where she was, and remained unmoving as she also recalled who was present there. *Gosh... I can't believe I fell asleep with her again!* And actually: *On* her. Alys lay still, listening to the steady rhythm of Briggs' breathing. She sounded fast asleep too. Slowly, she lifted her head to check. Yes, her security chief was asleep, face turned toward her and her lips softly parted. Alys stared in wonder as she remembered their first kiss. *First* kiss... *As if there's bound to be another one.* She wanted it to happen now. How about if she gently brushed her lips over hers? Woke her up in this way, and watched a smile blossom in her green eyes? Alys rubbed her face, tight from previous tears, and she allowed her gaze to travel down the length of Briggs' body. Her t-shirt had ridden up a bit on one side to reveal smooth skin and hard muscles. The waistband of her jeans followed the smooth curve of her hip. It would be tempting to trace the small hollow there, and not just with her eyes... Alys shivered a little, causing Briggs to turn sideways into her. She held her breath in reaction. *Okay...* Now their roles had changed. Her tough bodyguard was the one who nestled against her side, unconsciously seeking to be held.

Alys closed her arm around her, surprised at the sudden wave of protectiveness that this triggered. Briggs was the one supposed to keep her safe, after all... But of course, she was only human. Alys suspected that there was a lot she probably didn't know about her past, and that some of it might be painful. Anyway. *Since when do I cuddle with my staff?* It occurred to her that she had stopped thinking of Briggs as just another employee a good while ago. Even before the kiss, which wouldn't have happened otherwise. Having her around for travel, events, and at home as well, felt as right and natural to Alys now as drinking water. She closed her eyes, focusing on the reassuring feel of the woman in her arms. *Keeping each other safe.* She drifted off on that thought, and one of the most vivid dreams she ever had ensued. It was Rose. She was standing on her favorite beach, dressed in a short white dress. Coming to take her hands with a gorgeous smile on her face. Alys held on to her in almost desperation.

'I am so sorry, Rosie! I let you down! I miss you so much!'

'It's okay, Al.' Her best friend smiled sweetly. *'It wasn't your fault. Please, don't worry about me. I'm fine now. I miss you too. I will see you again.'*

'Promise?'

'Yes, I do. I love you.'

"I love you too," Alys murmured.

In her sleep, Briggs squeezed her tightly.

●●

When Alys woke up again, what felt like only minutes later, the room was full of bright sunshine. Briggs was gone off the couch. Given the smell of fresh coffee in the air though, she could not be too far. Alys got up, stretched, and quickly went in search of her.

Briggs stood in another pool of sunshine outside the little studio, with her hands in her pockets and her face tilted toward the sky. Alys smiled, instantly distracted at the sight of her. It felt like the morning after. For sure, the night had been intimate. She walked up to her, laced both arms around her waist from behind, and rested her face against her shoulder.

"Hey... Good morning, Briggs."

The greeting was unplanned. Bold and personal. She was not entirely sure of how Briggs might react. Not unexpectedly perhaps, the bodyguard tensed a little at first. But not for long. Alys soon felt her relax, and Briggs did even better. She pressed one hand over hers in what felt like a silent acknowledgment of a new level of connection between the two of them, and turned her head to the side.

"Good morning, Ms. Huxley."

For a moment, they were both silent. Alys was only aware of Briggs' solid strength as she leaned against her, of the heat of her fingers, and the sense of utter completeness and well-being that she felt in return. She forced herself to speak when the urge to kiss the back of her neck and nibble behind her ear became too strong and dangerous.

"Thank you for last night. I wasn't quite myself."

"You're welcome. Don't worry, I know what it feels like."

She rarely shared anything personal, and Alys was so taken aback at the comment that she missed the opportunity to ask for clarification. What did Briggs mean exactly? That she knew what it was like to not feel like herself? To lose a close friend? Or to feel guilty? Before Alys could ask, she went on.

"I was going to wake you up with a cup of coffee, but then I had another idea."

"Oh, yeah?"

"Yeah." Briggs turned around, staying close but no longer touching her. She did smile invitingly. "The coast road will be nice and clear at this time of the morning. I know a little coffee shop in Myers Creek that makes the best muffins. We could take the bike, if you like, and—"

"Yes," Alys interrupted as excitement flooded through her. Relief, too... She had not wanted to leave and get back to normal just yet. Didn't want to leave *her*. "Yes, yes, yes!"

••

Tristan was well aware that she was pushing it. Taking her client for a ride before 7 a.m., the way she might do with a new girl-friend, was absolutely not what the rulebook prescribed! But it was the human thing to do. She had felt her pain acutely the previous night. She knew how intense and destructive feelings of guilt could be. Watching Huxley light up like a Christmas tree when she suggested the quick road trip was worth bending the rules. No question about it. Tristan treated her to a relaxed ride up to Myers Creek, some thirty-five miles north of Lewiston, and the little café that she knew. The owner was a Harley enthusiast who never wasted a chance to tease her about her preferences. Today was no exception.

"Still on your Japanese toy, I see," she remarked after taking their order. "When are you going to get yourself a proper bike, girl?"

"When I do, it won't be a tractor on two wheels," Tristan replied easily, glancing at her gleaming cruiser parked in front.

Maddy, as her name was, snorted ironically, and she looked to Huxley for support. Incredibly, she seemed to have no idea of who the singer was.

"Would be a comfier ride for you, honey. That hot seat can't be very good for your back, uh?"

"That's okay," Huxley grinned. "Comfy's good but I prefer fast and wild."

Tristan chuckled when Maddy flashed her a glance as if to say, *'What have you got yourself here?'*. She paid for the coffees and blueberry muffins, and followed Huxley to a table on the terrace, facing the ocean. From there, she had a good view of the road in the back, and also of the beach in front. It was a safe spot.

"She was fun," Huxley remarked as they sat down.

"Yep, Maddy's alright."

"And you know the best thing? She didn't recognize me!"

Tristan smiled again at the innocent joy in her voice. Huxley was in her jeans and leather jacket with a red bandana around her neck, no makeup, and her hair flowing loose. Gorgeous, but as her own self, not her stage persona. Maddy also probably did not expect Tristan to bring round a world-famous rock singer on the back of her crappy Japanese toy.

"Good," Huxley nodded when she shared that with her. "I like being a regular biker chick. I also much prefer the look of your bike to hers, by the way. And the way she goes."

"Fast and wild, uh?" Tristan laughed.

"Yeah. She has a nice roar too."

"Takes one to know one."

"Are you comparing me to your bike?" Huxley chuckled.

Were she to be doing that, it might turn inappropriate and downright dirty in just a few words. Tristan shook her head no, slowly. Huxley lingered with her eyes on her and a thoughtful expression.

"Sometimes, I like soft and cuddly too."

"Yes, you do. It's okay."

"I know that." Huxley jerked her chin at her in a friendly challenge. "What about you? What do you like?"

Tristan had woken up all wrapped up in her arms. In her sleep, she'd turned into Huxley and slid down her side, so that she lay with her cheek softly pressed against her breasts.

"Sometimes," she admitted. "It's nice to cuddle."

"Good on you, Briggs." Huxley grinned again in approval and took a bite of muffin. "I might have to buy a bike just so that I can come back to this place. This is delicious!"

Tristan reached for her coffee, realizing that she was feeling a bit hot. The ride with Huxley had been comfortable and easy, but yeah, still hot. It was a thing with her, definitely.

"You could come back in the Rover," she remarked.

"Nah, wouldn't taste the same! You know what I mean?"

"I think I do. You mean the taste of freedom?"

"You got it," Huxley talked with her mouth full. Again, it was weirdly enticing. "So, how old were you when you got your first bike?"

"Twenty."

"Uh-uh?"

"I bought a second-hand 600cc Yamaha at ten a.m., and it was in bits by two p.m."

"What?" Huxley frowned. "Why? Did you get conned?"

"No." Tristan laughed. "I crashed the thing. To be honest, it was too much for me without any experience. Didn't realize how fast I was going around a bend until it became a choice between dropping the bike and sliding into bushes, or slamming into a semi-truck coming the other way."

"Ouch." Huxley winced and she touched her arm.

"Yes. Needless to say, I wasn't wearing protective kit. I lost quite a bit of skin, as well as all my money, on that day."

"You still don't wear protective gear."

"No, but I've learned to ride."

Huxley seemed entertained. She was definitely curious.

"Now I see that the advice you gave me the other day about starting on a less powerful bike was from your own hard-earned experience."

"Totally. Are you really going to learn how to ride?"

"When I find the time... Yes, I would like to." Huxley gazed out over the beach and the ocean before returning her eyes to her with a wondering smile. "Hey, have you ever been on a longer road trip?"

"I took my second bike up to Vancouver one summer."

"Wow... Did you stay at motels along the way?"

"I had a tent, so I wild-camped on the side of the road. Only used a motel from time to time when I started to feel feral and needed a proper wash. Otherwise, I bathed in lakes or streams. I saw a bear one morning upon waking up. He took a good look at me and went on his way."

"That's amazing!" Huxley stared in fascination and delight. "I'd love to go on a road trip with you someday!"

CHAPTER 23

Huxley said, *'With you'*, and sounded like she meant it. For the first time, Tristan allowed herself to consider what it might be like to be with her for real. Not just in the roles of bodyguard and client. Dangerous thoughts. But it was incredibly easy to picture herself on a trip with Alys. Riding back roads, sharing a tent and cuddles under the stars on the side of a lake... Tristan drew the line at imagining anything else.

"Can I get you a refill?" the singer asked.

"I'm good for coffee but I wouldn't mind another muffin."

"Me too! You stay here and relax. I'll go.

Aware that it mattered to Huxley to do the little things that everybody else took for granted, Tristan let her go back inside on her own. It was safe here, and she knew for sure that they had not been followed. They took their second round of muffins onto the beach. Sitting in a sheltered spot, watching surfers gliding on the waves, Huxley told her about the dream she'd had.

"It seemed as real as the beach in front of us now. And the relief I felt when Rose told me that she was fine, and that she still loved me, was out of this world."

"That's wonderful. I'm glad it happened."

"Yes..." Huxley's smile faded. "But it was only a dream."

Tristan shook her head as she observed ripples of sunshine over the water.

"Who's to say that this isn't a dream too? It all disappears at night when we go to sleep, doesn't it?"

"Yes, but it's always there in the morning. We simply pick up where we left off."

"True. I guess as long as it felt real to you in here..." Tristan pressed her hand over her own heart, "I think you should trust it. Maybe it was different from this reality. But also, more than a regular dream."

"It felt very special. Like a gift. Even now, talking about it, I can feel Rose in me."

"There you go." Tristan smiled. "Beautiful. I wish I had the same experience with—" *Ah, damn.*

She stopped abruptly, shocked at her own words. She never brought up her own stuff in conversation. Never talked about Jake to anyone. It was too sad. Too raw and painful. She tried to shrug it off, but Huxley rested a hand over the back of her neck.

"You know, Tristan, sometimes you look really sad."

"I'm okay." *Tristan...*

"I know. But something happened to you, didn't it? Was it something similar to me and Rose? You can tell me, you know? If you want to."

Tristan's walls would have gone up at the speed of light if she'd started making demands. But Huxley was not. She offered. She dropped the official *'Briggs'*. Not telling her anything would surely ruin the morning and perhaps drive a permanent wedge between them. Tristan also wanted to tell her. On a deeper level, she trusted Huxley more than she had anyone in a long time.

"I was working undercover at the time," she recalled. "My team and I were investigating an international drugs cartel with links to the local mafia. I was in deep…"

"I heard undercover work is the most dangerous for a cop," Huxley stated.

"Where did you hear that?"

The singer flashed a sheepish smile.

"True crime online podcasts. Sorry for interrupting you."

"That's okay. What do you like about these podcasts?"

"Oh, well… If I had to start over, I think I would study to become a forensic psychologist. I am fascinated by the mind, and the full spectrum of human behavior, as it plays out in real life." When Tristan did not reply straight away, Huxley paled. "Please don't take this the wrong way. I'm not saying that I find tragedy entertaining."

"Of course not. That never crossed my mind." Tristan was also never going to admit that her hesitation was only due to the fact that for a moment there, all she wanted to do was lean over and kiss her. What came out of her mouth next was kind of even worse. "I like the way you think. I like you. Alys." *Oh, for God's sake!* "Anyway…"

••

Alys let her carry on despite spotting a flicker of something that looked very much like arousal in her eyes. But it was there and gone in a flash. She was aware that her interruption had come at a crucial point and did not want the conversation to turn back to herself again. Now she only wanted to know about Tristan. The only reason she'd remarked on the undercover part was because she hated the thought of her taking risks.

"Jake… My partner. He thought I was in too deep and that I should pull out. He was right. Only the day before, the leader of the drugs gang executed one of his own men, thinking he may be a spy. But I wouldn't quit. Still thought I had a bit more time to gather the evidence we needed. We argued about it." Briggs stared out at the ocean with a glazed, far-away look in her eyes. "The next time I saw Jake, he was dead."

Alys clasped her hand for support but otherwise remained silent. The story was not over, she suspected.

"I'll say this quick," Briggs went on, squeezing her fingers briefly in acknowledgment. "The gang took him."

"Took him?"

"He was kidnapped."

"Oh, no…"

"They tortured him to make him reveal the identity of the undercover cop. Jake never said a word. He protected me until the end and he died a horrible death."

Briggs held her gaze before looking away. She wouldn't cry, obviously, but it was easy to see how cruelly and deeply the memories of that time still affected her.

"Is that why you left the police?" Alys inquired.

"Huh-uh. I was drinking heavily. One night, Angie found me staring into the barrel of my own gun. For some reason, she decided to give me a job." Briggs sighed. "I stopped drinking. I got better."

Alys stared, astonished. The admission left her speechless. Without thinking, as seemed to happen a lot around the woman, she pulled her into a rough embrace.

"I'm sorry about your partner." *You need to get your hands off of her. Stop it with the hugs and the hand holding!* Alys pulled back, eyes still hot and fierce. "Thank you for telling me your story."

Briggs watched her with a colorless smile.

"That's okay. I wanted to tell you."

"Great. Now tell me why."

The smile grew a bit easier.

"Because no matter how bad things are, they do get better. And it felt like the right time to share. I hope it's okay."

"Yes. It means a lot. Thank you for talking to me, for the ride, for last night... And all the rest."

"You're welcome, Ms. Huxley."

There it was, another subtle reminder of their status with each other. Alys stared some more, unwilling to take the hint.

"Hey, you know something?"

"Mm?" Briggs prompted.

"I like you too, Tristan. A hell of a lot."

Forget about status, rules, and job titles between them; Alys was going to kiss her again. She knew it with absolute certainty. And from the sudden tight expression in Briggs' bright eyes, she realized it too. Alys leaned slowly toward her, giving her time. It was reassuring when Briggs only broke eye contact to glance at her mouth. She exhaled. Every muscle in her body relaxed. Alys touched her cheek and found her hot. They were so close now. *So close...* Then, Briggs' phone started to ring, startling them both and breaking the spell.

"It's Erik," she announced, and took the call.

Alys considered grabbing the phone and throwing it aside. This was their morning, their time, their moment. *Dammit!* She had visions of straddling Briggs' lap, wrapping both arms tightly around her neck, and kissing her to her heart's content. She was certain by now that she would kiss her back. Alys might have given in to the impulse, and to hell with any consequences, if her bodyguard had not suddenly spoken ominous words.

"It's okay Erik, don't panic. Call Detective Miller and wait for us. Yes, Alys is with me. We'll be back at the house in thirty minutes or so."

Briggs was grim as she hung up and met her eyes.

"What's going on now?" Alys exclaimed. "Tell me!"

"Somebody sent you a dead rat in the mail. And a message. We need to get back to the house."

"Fuck!" Alys jumped to her feet. "Is Erik safe?"

"Yeah. He's fine. Just a little spooked."

"It's him again! That goddamn stalker! What does the note say?"

Briggs turned to her as they reached the bike, and this time she looked both angry and reluctant. To her credit though, she came right out with the truth.

"It says: *'Your puppy will be next to join your friend in hell.'*"

Alys gasped in shock and an involuntary rise of tears, but she quickly swallowed them back. *I am done with crying and being weak!*

"That's not going to happen," she snapped.

"Correct." Briggs flashed her an unexpectedly bright smile as she passed her helmet to her. "I'll let you have a cheeky go on the bike another time. Okay, Alys?"

Alys flushed in pleasure. Not because she offered to teach her, but because she kept the connection going.

"Okay, Tristan." *And I will kiss you another time.*

Briggs straddled the bike, started the engine and kicked off the stand, then nodded to her to get on. Alys was used to these steps by now. Everything looked the same, as well. But it still felt entirely different, like a brand-new energy between them. Briggs stopped on the edge of the parking lot as they were about to re-join the main road, and twisted back for a quick check.

"Open throttle all the way, okay?"

No deferential *'Ms. Huxley'* this time, which was a relief. No question either. Briggs simply told her, talking as she would to a friend. Alys allowed herself to think and hope that it may even be deeper than that.

"Go for it," she replied intently.

"Hold on tight then."

The ride back made Alys question getting her own bike. She liked having Briggs as her pilot, as well as an excuse to hold her like this. For sure, a tight grip was necessary when weaving in and out of traffic at 70mph, or faster on the straight bits. But the embrace also satisfied Alys's growing urge to take care of Tristan and keep her safe. Sure, she was strong. Tough. *Fully weaponized as well.* If Alys dropped her arms a little, she would feel the gun in its holster attached to Briggs' belt. No doubt she was a perfect shot too. Everything about the woman tasted of excellence, and she certainly did not act as if she needed a protector. But now that Alys knew about her story, if only probably just the tip of the iceberg, it made her eager to shelter her. A little bit, at least. She could well imagine the extent of the trauma and guilt that Briggs must have suffered with the tragic death of her partner. *His murder... God!* She shivered at the thought. Instantly, Briggs slowed the bike down and pressed her left hand over her thigh. *Talking about protective...*

"What?" she yelled over the wind. "You okay?"

Alys patted her on the shoulder in reassurance. She was sure that if anybody else tried to act this way with her, like Erik or Brad sometimes did, she would growl in irritation and remind them that she could take care of herself, thank you very much. Coming from Briggs, such attentiveness and care did not feel restrictive. Just good. Attractive. And Alys wanted it.

"I'm fine," she shouted. "Keep going!"

Weirdly perhaps, although thankfully, she felt no shame or guilt in enjoying the moment. In a few more minutes, they'd be back at the house and forced to deal with difficulties. Alys knew that Rose would approve of her making the most of this respite. For sure, the stalker's latest threat had the power to shake her to the core if she let it. She would not. With Tristan by her side, Alys felt safer. Stronger. She would focus on that. *Everything's going to be okay.*

CHAPTER 24

Erik was waiting for them on the drive when they arrived back at the house. Hands on hips, frowning. Looking pissed-off.

"Thanks for letting me know that you were sneaking out for a ride, uh!" he snapped at his cousin.

"Oh, should I?" Huxley growled in return, immediately uncooperative.

"Come on Al, I couldn't find you! When I opened that box and saw what was inside, I thought you might have been—"

"I'm fine, as you can see. So chill, okay?"

"You chill! Man! Don't talk to me like that. Anything could have happened to you!"

He sounded outraged. Huxley's face grew darker. Sensing a spectacular fight about to erupt, Tristan stepped forward to ease the tension.

"This one's on me, Erik. I should have told you. Sorry."

His anger dissipated, replaced by sheer relief.

"Okay, Briggs. Yeah, no worries. At least you picked up the phone, uh! I was kinda freaked out after opening that package, I can tell you."

"Obviously." For some reason, probably heightened levels of stress now that they were back, Huxley would not relent. "So, you opened my mail because…" she prompted.

"Because it fucking stank of rotting flesh, Your Highness," he yelled. "And you were AWOL!"

"Okay, guys. Please," Tristan intervened. "That's enough."

"I'm going upstairs to get Sex Pistol," the singer announced with a dismissive snort aimed at her cousin.

"Damn," Erik muttered under his breath as he watched her storm into the house. "I love her to bits but she can be a piece of work sometimes! You know?"

Tristan murmured in sympathy, unwilling to take sides and reflecting that Huxley's temper was very attractive, actually. She wasn't sure about her being a piece of work… But gutsy? Yeah, for sure. And she liked it.

"Everybody's a little tense right now," she nodded.

"Sure." He blew air out and gave her a look. "So, you went for coffee?"

"Yes."

"Hey, that's nice…"

Whether or not he suspected that there was more to it, he did not say and Tristan did not volunteer. She was unclear of where she stood with Huxley. They were a lot closer, for sure. As for anything else, she would try to figure it out later, maybe on a solo run. In the meantime, Miller pulled up in an unmarked cruiser with a CSI tech to handle the package. Tristan had a brief look at it. Non-descript cardboard box, brown tape, the house address typed on a regular label. Inside the box was an extra-large rodent, decomposing fast. No obvious cause of death. The threatening note, also typed and all in caps, was on the table next to the open package.

"Take care of it please, Jace," Miller requested of her tech guy. "The rest of us, let's go outside to talk, shall we?"

Wright joined them in the backyard, his face pinched as if he'd been forced to lick a particularly sour lemon. Huxley came back from her apartment, holding her puppy tightly in her arms. As she took a seat next to her, Tristan noticed that she looked a little pale.

"Are you alright?" she murmured.

"Yes." Alys flashed a forced grin. "I'm just relieved that my little one is, too."

Tristan returned her smile, as Sex Pistol snoozed against her chest.

"No one will get to either of you," she reminded her gently. "Not as long as I'm in charge."

"Thanks, Tristan," Alys murmured.

"Alright, then." Miller took the lead for the meeting. "Run me through it in detail. Erik, is it?"

"Yeah. So, look: I don't normally open her private mail," he announced, frowning at his cousin. "But the stench coming from that box was something else, man!"

Wright coughed as if it were stuck in his throat, although he had been nowhere near the package. Huxley had insisted to have a look, as Tristan knew she would; *'Just to see what we are facing.'* She was brave, definitely.

"I understand," Miller said. "Carry on."

Erik did not have too much more to add. He got the mail, opened the package, *'freaked out a bit',* in his own words, and made an emergency call to Tristan. Fingerprints were discovered all over the box, as expected. Probably his and a bunch of mail employees'. More interestingly, the CSI tech was able to recover a partial one from the note.

"This one won't be mine!" Erik declared in triumph. "Once I realized what the package was, I used gloves to pull the note out of the box!"

"Good job," Tristan approved when he glanced at her.

"Sounds promising," Miller nodded as well. "We'll check it out and let you know what we come up with. In the meantime, we may have a lead on the stalker. Do you know a guy named Ethan Kisin, Ms. Huxley?"

"No," Huxley answered categorically.

"That's okay. Does his face ring a bell?"

The singer shook her head after Miller showed her a picture of a tall blond guy with longish hair and pale blue eyes.

"No, I've never met him."

"Dude looks weird if you ask me," Erik commented. "Don't know him either."

"Mr. Wright?" Miller inquired of the manager too.

"No," Wright assured, his mouth curled in distaste. "And I would know. I never forget a face."

Tristan stared at the photo, noting the tiny mole on the left side of the guy's mouth. Nice identifying mark. She, too, would not forget this face in a hurry.

"What's the deal with him?" she asked.

"His name and credit card were used to buy tickets to every performance you gave in the last six months, Ms. Huxley," Miller answered. "Even better, he worked as a computer repair guy on the street opposite Holson Medical Center in Dallas…"

"Where my cousin Joan worked part of her medical internship," Huxley nodded tightly.

"Yes, indeed. We would like your permission to contact her and find out if she ever used his services. This may be how he was able to get hold of your email address."

"Wow, that's twisted," Erik groaned.

Next to her, Tristan felt Huxley shiver.

"My cousin recently transferred to the University Medical Center in Tucson, Arizona," she advised. "Go ahead and contact her if you want, but please, make sure that nothing you do puts her a risk over there!"

"Absolutely," Miller assured. "You have my word on that. Perhaps you wouldn't mind giving her a quick heads-up before I call?"

"I'll do it right after we're done here. If you're right about your theory, this is even more screwed-up than we previously thought," Huxley murmured, echoing Erik's sentiment.

Tristan knew that it had taken her awhile to take the threat seriously. For sure, it had to be sinking in fast now.

"Have you got eyes on the suspect?" she asked Miller.

"Unfortunately, no." Miller sighed. "He sold his business three weeks ago and also terminated the lease at his apartment. His card was used to book a flight to LA. Nothing since."

"Gone dark, uh?" Tristan almost let out an aggressive growl of her own. *You son of a bitch.*

"We'll soon get a fix on his location. In the meantime," Miller turned back to Huxley. "Is there any chance you could go away for a while? Take a little vacation? I know this is probably asking a lot with your schedule, but..."

"You people have no idea," Wright muttered. He turned to Huxley, impatience and frustration written all over his face. "But then again, I don't know. Are you calling it quits, Alys?"

"What?" Erik roared. "What the hell, Al?"

Clearly, no one had bothered to enlighten him. After a few seconds, when all eyes were turned to her, Huxley sighed.

"Just give us a few minutes, please."

••

"I'll make sure a cruiser stays in the vicinity tonight, just to be on the safe side," Miller offered as they walked away. "Until further notice as decided by you, Tristan."

"Okay, thanks. Anything else I should know that you didn't want to share in front of everyone?"

The detective gave a light shrug.

"Not really, other than it's never good when a stalker goes off the grid like this. I don't need to tell you."

"No, you don't."

"Fair to say he didn't book himself on a meditation retreat, eh?"

"That's fair," Tristan agreed and her stomach tightened. "If he follows the usual trend, he may try to make contact soon. Call her on the phone or attempt to meet her in some way."

"Yes, that's what I was thinking too. It really would be ideal if you could convince her to disappear for a bit, you know?"

"I'll do my best."

"I heard she can be difficult. Not keen on people trying to tell her what to do."

"Why? Do you enjoy it?" Tristan smirked.

"Of course not. But the situation warrants it here. And you are her bodyguard too."

"True..."

"Anyway, I'm sure you'll do fine," Miller grinned.

Tristan stared at her with a cool eyebrow raised.

"What's that supposed to mean?"

"Sorry, Briggs; not a criticism. Just that she seems to really respect and trust you. That's good as far as I'm concerned."

Yeah, right! Good recovery, Miller.

"Thanks," Tristan simply nodded.

"One more question that I forgot to ask her."

"Go ahead."

"I assume it's common knowledge that she owns a puppy; but can you confirm?"

"Good question. And yeah, Huxley talks about him a lot. I think he's even been on the cover of a magazine with her once or twice before."

"Okay." Miller approved. "See you later then, I'm off."

"See you. Thanks for your help, Cody."

The detective flashed her a thumbs-up and left. Going back into the house, Tristan bumped into Erik coming out. He did not look happy.

"Hey, everything alright with you?" she asked.

"Yeah." He shrugged almost aggressively. "Why wouldn't it be?"

"Just asking, buddy. You did really good today."

He paused at the door, turned back with a suspicious look.

"You think so?"

"I wouldn't say it otherwise."

"Thanks, Briggs." His shoulders relaxed and he blew out a loud exhale. "Thanks for noticing."

"Of course. I'm not the only one who did."

His usual smile made a slow comeback.

"It's all happening today, isn't it?"

"Sure is, my friend."

"Alys is still in the office with Brad. I think they might be in there for a while, looking at the schedule. Don't worry too much if they start shouting at each other, okay?"

Tristan threw a thoughtful glance at the door.

"I probably will. It's kinda my job to worry."

"Yeah." He chuckled. "But that's their love language!"

Wright came out of the office twenty minutes later, shot her a dark look, and walked off without a word. Sex Pistol was next, looking a lot more agreeable, followed by his owner. Huxley seemed a bit tense as she glanced around the room, although her expression cleared as soon as she saw her.

"Hey, Tristan."

"Hey," Tristan nodded softly. "How are you doing?"

"Better." The singer smiled. "Much better."

"Excellent. Everything go okay with Bradley?"

"Yes." Huxley took two quick steps forward, as if she were going to embrace her, before stopping abruptly in the middle of the room. Still smiling, but a reasonable distance away. "Mainly, I'm still a bit high from the bike ride."

"Good. I'm glad you enjoyed it."

"Made me feel like we were on a real trip. All of a sudden, all the stress that I was feeling sort of receded to the background. I felt relaxed and care-free... I guess it helped me to realize that even without this looming threat, I could do with a bit of time off, probably."

She sounded a mix of puzzled and uncertain, as if this were a great discovery to her, and Tristan smiled.

"You know, before having you as a client, I might have said that rock stars had it pretty easy in life. Minimum work required for maximum reward."

"Huh!" Huxley snorted. "Now you know better, right?"

"For sure." Tristan grinned. "I've seen how hard you work and I don't think you should feel an ounce of guilt about taking a break. Not in this situation. And it'll benefit your creativity as well, won't it?"

"Yes." Huxley clearly appreciated this. "You're right about that too. I admit it's been a while since I had any time off."

"How long?"

"Oh..." Her eyes glazed over as she tried to remember and could not even. "A few years, I think."

"Right. So, it's not so bad then."

"I guess not... I just hate being forced to do it now because some asshole is acting out. And please, don't lecture me about the benefits of keeping a positive mental attitude. I'm not in the mood for that right now."

"Fair enough. I'm not the lecturing kind anyway."

"Don't want to go for a run either, or hit the gym."

"That's okay. Sometimes you just gotta feel the suck."

"Exactly." Huxley laughed. "I'm glad you understand."

"So how 'bout pizza and TV?" Tristan suggested, knowing where this might lead and yet unable to stop herself.

She should leave her client to it, really... Huxley was safe in her own home and did not need an escort in the same room as her. Tristan knew that; she just didn't want to leave. Huxley was on the same page. She stepped forward with a hopeful grin.

"Great idea! Shall we get half-and-half?"

CHAPTER 25

Tristan did not want to book a regular vacation rental house for this getaway, or an Airbnb, as Erik suggested. At the same time, Huxley flat-out refused to use the safe house owned by Dagger Inc., claiming that she did not want to, quote, *'Stay at a fricking jail!'*. Until, that is, Tristan showed her pictures of the luxurious waterfront residence in Jacques Harbor, Maine.

"Of course," Angie declared proudly. "I will not house our clients in jail, a motel room, or anything of the sort. Only the best for us. Here are the keys to the house, Tris."

"Thanks."

"I've sent the security codes to your phone and connected it as the main controller. The house is fully automated, as you well know."

"Yep."

"A vetted driver will pick you up at the airport. His name's Rob, a retired cop. Ask him what the weather is like downtown. He'll answer pink."

"Wow. Very 007, Angie."

"I know but it works, eh. How many in your party?"

"Just Alys and her dog. And me."

"Ah." Angie lingered with her eyes on her. "Cozy."

Oh, you have no idea... Huxley actually suggested that they take the bike and cut loose. Just go on that road trip, ride into the sunset, so to speak. Tristan would have struggled to find reasons not to do exactly that if she had insisted, but the singer did not. *'Better to wait until this asshole is caught'*, she decided. Tristan kept her face nicely neutral as she went on speaking to Angie.

"It's the best-case scenario as far as I'm concerned. This way I won't have to worry about anyone else. The house has its own swimming pool and private beach, which should limit the need for excursions as well..."

"Yeah, that's the whole point of a safe house," Angie cut in, satisfied. "It's perfectly self-contained. And totally safe, indeed. Looks just like a regular house from the outside but in fact, it's more like a bunker. State-of-the-art security system, bullet-proof glass all through the house, re-enforced walls... And all mod-cons on the inside. Very nice indeed."

"Yeah. So, my plan is to hole up for a while. There might be family visiting at some point, but not sure yet. With a bit of luck, Miller will get her hands on the stalker while we're there and life can resume its normal flow. Alys has made up her mind. We're all set to fly first thing tomorrow morning."

"And she'll post a few decoy pictures on her social media, as discussed?"

"Yeah, she's cool with that. She'll make it appear as if she's in LA creating new music. She was doing that just before I got hired and she's not posted anything about it yet. So, it works."

"Excellent." Angie sat on the couch in Tristan's apartment, on Huxley's property, and leaned her elbows over her thighs. "So..."

"So?" Tristan prompted.

"Alys, uh?"

Angie did not miss much and she must be paying particular attention on this one. Tristan cursed herself for letting the name slip. Twice. She shrugged as if it were nothing.

"Yeah. Alys, Huxley, whatever."

"You seem to be getting on well with her."

"I'm doing alright. And she's not stupid either. She resents the need for protection, but she's smart enough to recognize that she needs it. It's been okay."

"So this assignment isn't as bad as you first thought, is it?" Angie laughed. "Remember when you yelled at me and said that you didn't want to babysit a bubble-gum pop star? Or chaperone her lunches with equally unworthy girlfriends?"

Tristan relaxed a fraction at the reminder. *Entitled, annoying, insipid…* All words she'd used before she even met the singer in real life. *That'll teach me.* She could imagine how Huxley would laugh if she told her of her previous misconceptions.

"I don't remember yelling at you, but yeah, she's nothing like I thought." *Alys… Fast asleep in her arms. Laughing on the bike, urging her to go faster. Giving her shivers just by saying her name…* Tristan suppressed a sigh of longing and she made sure to keep her tone in check. "I'll admit: the job is keeping me interested, which I didn't think it would."

"Interested." Angie flashed her another piercing look. "You are, uh?"

"Yeah." Tristan shrugged. "Of course."

Angie had a hunch and was fishing for info, obviously, and she hesitated to tell her more. She'd allowed Huxley to kiss her. They'd slept together. Fully clothed, yes… But all the same; *we slept together.* Even less likely, Tristan had fully opened up to her.

Not only did she tell Huxley about Jake, but also how low she'd dropped in the aftermath. To say that she was *'interested'* was an understatement. She bit on her lip. *I shouldn't be doing this.*

"Hey." No doubt noticing her unease, Angie stood up and came to her. "Don't go so pale on me all of a sudden."

"I'm fine."

"I hope so. Just know as well that whatever's going on, I trust you to handle it, Tristan. I'm saying this to you as a friend, okay?"

Tristan could have told her that nothing was going on, but it would be lying. That, she didn't do.

"Maybe you shouldn't," she murmured with a sudden flash of clarity.

"What?" Angie frowned. "What do you mean?"

"When it comes to a client's safety, there's no room for this kind of allowance. You're right, Ange, I…" Tristan swallowed. "I feel close to Huxley. A lot closer than I should."

"Oh, Tris," Angie said, her gaze softening. "It's alright."

"It's against the rules. Dagger's policy." Tristan shook her head as a wall of solid resolve settled across her mind. *I dropped the ball once and Jake died. Never again.* "I won't let her get hurt."

"I know."

"I won't take that risk."

"I do know that," Angie said firmly. "And I will uphold the rules that I set myself for Dagger personnel. But Huxley won't always be at risk, and you won't be her bodyguard forever."

"What are you saying?"

"That I trust you to keep her safe. But also, that you should keep sight of the big picture and not shut any doors. It's been a while since you felt close to anyone, hasn't it?"

"Yeah." Tristan shivered. "It has."

"Then keep this advice in mind." Angie winced a little. "I mean, if you feel like it. I'm aware that you didn't ask me for it. And I was like a bull in a china shop, prodding you for details. Sorry about that."

"That's okay. I invited it."

"Alright, then." A relieved Angie smiled and gave a quick hug. "Keep me posted. And if you need anything when you get to Maine, just yell."

"Okay. Will do."

"What time do you think—"

A sharp knock on the door preceded Huxley's unplanned and unexpected arrival.

"Hey, Tristan. Do you know if..." She stopped dead in her tracks when she spotted Angie, and their close proximity to each other. "Oh."

Huxley looked fierce as she came to stand close. Almost in between the two women, and closer to her. The positioning, Tristan realized, was not random. In actual fact, it felt extremely proprietary. Even with her resolve to keep her personal feelings in check and focus solely on the job, Tristan could not help but react to this. Huxley's move made her feel hot from head to toe; she just hoped it didn't show. The singer's blue eyes flashed as she took in Angie. Fixing her as if she were assessing a threat. A rival. Certainly, competition. No one, female or male, for that matter, would fail to get this message. Even though silent, it still came through loud and clear. *'I don't know who the hell you are, but BACK OFF'.*

"Ms. Huxley." Angie broke into a practiced smile. "Hello. I am Angie Cristoforetti, the CEO of Dagger Inc. I spoke at length to your manager, but it's a pleasure to finally meet you. How are you?"

••

The only inconvenient thing about the safe house was that there was no recording studio there. *'You mean the* best *thing... Right, darling? Aren't you here for a vacation?'* Rose's voice echoed across her mind, as well as a ripple of laughter.

"Technically, I am here to hide," Alys murmured under her breath.

For sure, a little humility was in order. It was not lost on her how lucky she was. *A:* Simply to be alive. And *B:* Not many people who encountered problems in their personal life were privileged enough to just hop onto their own plane and fly to a luxury house on the other side of the country until things calmed down. This place, too... A prized vacation spot on the rugged coast of Maine, was absolutely gorgeous. The house included four bedrooms, six bathrooms, an indoor swimming pool. Stone or hardwood floors throughout. A modern gym. There was also a well-equipped professional kitchen. Super-nice, indeed. There was a small wood at the back of the property, and the entire front of the house afforded amazing views of the ocean. Alys was pleased about that, yet quite surprised to discover so many panoramic windows.

"The first time you came up to my place, didn't you tell me that it was dangerous?" she reflected. "And now, we've got this at a safe house?"

"Yes, but this glass is bulletproof. And reflective, as well," Briggs said. "We can see out, but from the other side, it'll be like looking at a mirror. Totally private and safe."

"I might invest in this for home then."

"I think it would be a good idea, yes."

"Have you been here before with a client?"

"No, this is the first time, Ms. Huxley."

Briggs was back to her regular routine. She'd barely cracked a smile, and also been cool and distant, since her boss's visit. The change left Alys feeling both perplexed and frustrated. She did try to put her moody bodyguard, and everything else, out of her mind for the first few days of their stay in Maine. And to relax, indeed. She was more tired than she thought, and catching up on sleep was actually quite good. She swam in the pool. Meditated. Read a Sci-Fi novel. The sort of things that people supposedly did on vacation to chill out. But by the morning of Day 4, she was bored out of her mind and ready to climb the walls. Erik had declined to come on this trip, saying he'd take time off too, and go to Mexico with a bunch of friends. *As if being with me were such hard work...* Alys understood his need to see his buddies, of course. She'd considered inviting a couple of women she knew to keep her company, but they were acquaintances rather than intimate friends. The only person she wanted to be with right now was Rose, as always... And Tristan Briggs, definitely. Alys found her in the front yard that morning, busy doing a round of circuit training on the lawn. Dressed in shorts and a Nike sports bra, with sweat glistening attractively over her hard muscles, she looked amazing. Alys might have lingered a while watching her, but Sex Pistol gave her away by trotting over to drop his tennis ball at her feet.

"Hey, pup," Briggs said in welcome.

Doggy mouth open in a grin, tongue out, his tail wagging harder than his little body could handle: the invitation was clear. *Play with me!*

"Hey, Tristan," Alys nodded.

"Good morning, Ms. Huxley."

Tristan picked up the ball and she faked a couple of throws, causing Sex Pistol to whine excitedly. Then she lobbed an easy one for him. Alys chuckled when he tripped in his haste to get it, went rolling, and struggled comically for a moment to get back on his feet.

"He's still such a puppy. And so eager!"

Tristan nodded approvingly as Sex Pistol brought the ball back to her and sat waiting expectantly.

"Good boy! He's very well trained. You did a good job with him."

"Wish I could take credit but I didn't do anything. He's just smart and he loves to play. Hey. Let's go out today, okay?"

Briggs eyed her as if she'd just suggested a weekend trip to Mars.

"Out?" she repeated.

"Yes! This place is nice but I need some air. Let's go for a beach walk and ice cream. I'll wear sunglasses and a floppy hat. With the puppy with us, we'll look like any other couple out for a stroll."

Briggs dropped the ball when she said that. It rolled into the pool, sending Sex Pistol into a small puppy panic. Alys fished it out for him. By the time she turned back around to look at her, Briggs seemed recovered, albeit less than enthusiastic.

"I guess we could go for a walk," she mumbled.

"Great! Let's do it."

CHAPTER 26

Just like any other couple... Huxley's words rumbled in Tristan's mind as they followed the rocky shoreline. She knew for sure that Alys had not deliberately engineered this time alone with her. In fact, the look on the singer's face when she admitted that the only friend she really wanted to accompany her was Rose, was heartbreaking. She'd been subdued the first few days, and Tristan assumed that she must be working on stuff. Feelings and emotions. Good for Huxley. It also gave her a chance to settle. But now... *Just like a couple.* Tristan had never entertained this kind of thought before. In the past, her career always came first. After Jake, she simply stopped wanting to be close to people. Anonymous encounters at The Club were good enough for her, and a lot less emotionally risky. Alys Huxley was a massive risk on at least two major levels. Still, Tristan could not help it. She was attracted to her, more and more each day. Just looking at Huxley now, in her incognito attire and with her puppy in a chest sling, because it was too hot for Sex Pistol to walk along on a day like this, made her smile. As she did, Huxley pointed at the sky.

"Look!" she exclaimed.

"What?" Tristan inquired, instantly on guard.

"Blue moon rising." Huxley grinned.

"What?"

"You smiled, Briggs."

"Haha… Yeah, very funny."

Huxley jumped over a rock pool and landed much closer to her. Tristan had been keeping a reasonable distance in between them. Not anymore.

"Why are you so tense? And don't tell me that it's your job, okay? You already served me that one a hundred times. I don't need it again with a different sauce."

Tristan smiled. Again. Impossible not to.

"I'm just focused," she said.

"On the job?"

"Yes."

"There you go," Huxley groaned. "Different sauce. Let's get you an ice cream and see if that does anything to improve your mood. Want an ice cream too, Sex Pistol?"

The puppy gave an agreeable bark.

"Rum and raisin? No, you're too young. How 'bout vanilla instead? Oh, look at this: Tristan's smiling again! You think she's too serious, puppy? Yeah, me too."

Safe behind a pair of Oakleys, Tristan rolled her eyes at the monologue. But yes, she was smiling. She relaxed a little more as they bought ice cream and sat in the shade of a cluster of trees to enjoy it. Sex Pistol got his own and Huxley also poured water in a collapsible bowl she'd brought for him. The view over the harbor was magnificent. Brilliant sunshine, azure sky, and not a cloud in sight. Sailboats drifted over calm water. People swam. Kids ran about on the beach, throwing ball or playing Frisbee.

All of it pretty idyllic, and Huxley gave a languid sigh. It was the sort of hot day which incited torpor, for sure, although she must have no idea of how alluring and sexy it sounded when she did that.

"Doing okay?" Tristan prompted.

"Mmm... Yes. Vacation not so bad after all. Just had to get out of the house. Can you sail?"

"No. Why?"

"Just thought we could hire a boat and get out there on the water. Maybe we still can..."

"Can you sail?"

"No." Huxley grinned. "But how hard can it be, uh? Maybe I'll do that some day. Learn how to sail properly and then take a yacht around the world. Live a simple life. Maybe shave my hair off like you."

Adventure, travel, and a nomadic life... It was a theme with Huxley's dreams, and Tristan would lie if she said that she did not find it exciting. She chuckled at the mention of shaving one's head though.

"What's that got to do with sailing?"

"Low maintenance, you know. Liveaboard-style."

"Ah... I might get dreadlocks for this kind of an adventure, actually. That's low maintenance too, right?"

Huxley had taken off her sunglasses and she fixed her with sparkling eyes.

"You'd still look sexy." She moved on before Tristan could react. "I guess it'd be similar to being on the road on your bike, uh? What was that you said to me the other day? You got a hotel to shower when you started to feel feral?"

"Yep."

"Feral," Huxley repeated with relish. "I love that word!"

"I know you'd be happier on a different kind of vacation," Tristan remarked with a smile. "This is too tame and boring for you."

"And of course, it is not a vacation."

"No, I know."

"But life works better without labels to restrict it. No matter what this is, I can still make the best out of every moment. Rose would want me to."

"Yes..." Tristan could only agree with this statement.

Once again, the singer rested her intense blue eyes on her.

"I wouldn't be able to take Sex Pistol with me on a motorbike trip. That's the only downside I can see so far."

"You could always road trip in a campervan if you wanted to take him along. Maybe not as exciting as a motorbike all the time, but loads better in bad weather. Riding in the pouring rain for several days in a row is no fun, believe me."

"I can imagine," Huxley laughed. "But with a camper, yes; lots of options." Her smile turned dreamy. "We could definitely do it."

That 'We' hit deeper than Tristan would have liked again, since she was pretty certain that Huxley was not only referring to herself and her puppy. Tristan could picture it all way more vividly than it was safe for her to entertain. *On the road with Alys Huxley...* Driving easy, cooking dinner at the back of the van, watching the sun rise in a new place every morning. Sleeping together. If she was not careful, she would start wanting it. As a lone guy in a baseball cap lingered while looking toward them, Tristan stood up.

"Let's move on, shall we?"

They went all the way around the harbor and stopped at a market on the way back to allow Huxley to buy some stuff.

"I like cooking but I never do it much when I'm at home. I'll make chili tonight, what do you think?"

"Sounds good," Tristan replied evasively. "I'll leave you to it."

Huxley managed a hard stare even from behind her pair of dark glasses. Clearly, this was not the answer she'd wanted. *I'm sorry...* Regardless of what had already happened between them, Angie's opinion, and even her own feelings, Tristan needed to be clear. She would not let this turn into something other than what it was: a security job. No less – no more.

●●

Safe... And free. Not for the first time, Alys reflected on the way that Briggs made her feel. Her escort was uncomfortable around her now, she could feel it. And she knew why. Something had changed that day on the beach, when they went for coffee. For a short while, it seemed as if Briggs might go with it, and it was thrilling. Then, she shut right down. This also was easy to figure out. Tristan Briggs: skilled, smart, and strong, was scared. Given her scarred history, it should come as no surprise. If she believed that she was to blame for the death of the most important person in her life, no doubt she'd be reluctant to take what she would view as a risk, and step out of line. Alys remembered that Briggs was friends with her boss too. She may have confided in her. Perhaps the woman gave her a reality check, and a reminder of the rules. *Knowing Tristan, she probably reminded her own self.* Alys sighed. For the first time in her life, she was a little scared as well. Relationships were nice and easy for her in the past. Short and sweet... Basically, they did not even deserve the name. She yearned for more with Briggs. Better. Long-term. *The real thing.*

The realization was stunning, and it brought her to tears. Staring at the supplies on the kitchen counter, feeling lonelier than ever before, Alys cried.

"Ms. Huxley?"

Goddammit!

"Yes!" Alys said roughly, keeping her back to her. "Didn't you tell me earlier that you had some work to do?"

"Yes. I've done it."

"Of course you did." She brushed her eyes as Briggs circled around the counter to face her. "Forgot you were the super-fast efficient type."

"Is everything okay?"

"Sure." Alys shrugged. "It's the onions."

"Ah." Briggs glanced at the bag of groceries, still unopened on the other side of the table. "Heard they can be quite ferocious. Especially in Maine at this time of year."

There she goes, being all charming again. The only thing with it this time was that Alys did not feel strong enough to handle it.

"Briggs," she exhaled. "What do you want?"

"To tell you that I spoke to Miller, and they have a lead on our suspect's location. She's confident it won't be long until they can bring him in for questioning."

"Thank God!" Alys exclaimed. "I mean, thank Miller and her team! I have to tell you... I was handling the situation pretty well until he threatened Sex Pistol. But after that, not so much."

"Yes." Briggs nodded softly. "Why are you crying?"

"Because I feel so—" Alys stopped herself short.

Briggs was a great listener. It would be easy to confide in her. She might stick around then... But Alys did not want that kind of comfort or pity. She wanted Briggs to stay because she wanted to. And admit to it. *Just ask her!* Alys did.

"Would you like to have dinner with me tonight?"

Briggs averted her gaze. Pursed her lips and even winced a little. *Right then.* Didn't take a genius to figure this one out either.

"Never mind. Forget I asked," Alys muttered.

"I wish I could," Briggs murmured. When she met her gaze again, Alys was taken aback by the depth of the sorrow that she saw in her eyes. Not just a flash of it this time. The emotion was there, lingering. "I'm sorry."

On that, she turned around and left the kitchen. Deflated, Alys stared after her. *Ah, Tristan...* She'd caught another glimpse of her true feelings. Briggs wanted to be with her. Damn, she'd just said it out loud! Although disappointed and frustrated at her continuing resistance, Alys could not help also be impressed by the strength of her resolve.

"This kind of self-control is annoying," she muttered under her breath. "But sexy, too."

No longer all that hungry, she still cooked the chili because it helped her to think. She cried with the onions, which did turn out to be ferocious. And poured her heart out to Sex Pistol, who made all the right puppy faces at her in return and really seemed to understand every word.

"I guess I shouldn't push," Alys reflected. "What happened to her partner was awful, and I don't even know all the details of it. I'm sure the last thing she needs is pressure, or to be reminded of that event."

She let Sex Pistol lick tomato sauce off of her fingers.

"Then again... I don't think punishing herself for the rest of her life is a solution. Might be different if she weren't in charge of keeping me alive. Take the pressure off. Maybe I should fire her." Alys chuckled without humor. "What say you, puppy?"

"Woof!" Sex Pistol wagged his tail.

Later on that night, she spoke to her manager. Brad shared some great news about the Australia tour.

"Sydney and Melbourne are already sold out. Brisbane will be soon. Couldn't hope for a better response to early ticket sales, kid!"

He always called her that when he was excited, and it made her smile.

"Did I tell you lately how much I appreciate everything that you do for me, Brad?"

"Nope," he snorted. "Do you ever?"

"Well, consider it done now," she laughed. "Goodnight. See you soon."

Alys lay in bed, eyes wide open. The house was quiet. Sex Pistol was asleep, twisted half in and half out of his basket, in his favorite position. Was Tristan fast asleep too? Alys knew that she liked to stay up late. Would it be wrong to go find out what she was doing? *Probably not...* But did she want to deal with another rejection? *Not really.* With a heavy sigh, Alys turned over onto her stomach, both arms wrapped around her pillow, wishing that she were hugging a live woman instead. *I wonder what she's thinking...* Would Briggs resist her so much if she understood that Alys was not simply after sex? Minutes and hours dragged by, and still, she could not fall asleep. Around one-thirty in the morning, Alys got up to go get herself a glass of water from the kitchen. Perhaps this would help...

CHAPTER 27

No such luck, as it turned out, although Alys was thrilled at the alternative. Having decided to respect Briggs's professionalism, and keep her distance, at least for the time being, bumping into her in the kitchen was a wonderful twist of fate. Even better: Briggs, who possessed an almost supernatural instinct for being able to sense people in her vicinity, did not notice her come in. Seizing the opportunity, Alys paused to watch. Her bodyguard was barefoot, clad only in boxer briefs just visible under a loose t-shirt with *LEWISTON P.D.* printed in block letters on the back. A blast from her own past, obviously. Alys took another second to admire well-muscled calves and tight buttocks flexing nicely, as Briggs investigated the contents of the fridge.

"Looking for something?" she finally asked.

The answer was brisk and not what she'd expected. In one fluid instinctive move, Briggs spun around and reached for the holstered weapon on the kitchen counter.

"Whoa!" Alys squeaked. "It's only me!"

Briggs settled down immediately. But even though she did not say it out loud, her expression was clear. *What the fuck?!*

"It's never a good idea to creep up on me in the middle of the night."

"I realize that now." Alys favored her with a little sheepish smile. "But I wasn't creeping. You usually hear a pin drop from a mile away, so…"

Briggs placed the gun back on the counter.

"I was lost in thoughts. That'll teach me, uh."

Alys did not miss the subtle flick of heated green eyes over her body. She, too, was dressed in briefs and an oversized t-shirt. Night attire. In the next instant, she could confirm from Briggs' reaction to the look that she had no bra on.

"Looking for the chili? If you are, it's in the freezer."

"No." Briggs pulled a Powerade out of the fridge. "Just this, thanks."

"Can't sleep?" Alys prodded.

"I haven't been to bed yet. You?"

"Can't sleep." *Thinking about you.* "What's keeping you up?"

Briggs gnawed on her bottom lip and eyed her silently for what seemed like an eternity before shrugging.

"Nothing much. I just finished a workout."

She stood by the side of the fridge, on the other side of the counter from her. Alys wondered how she might react, were she to step forward and put her arms around her.

"Can I tell you something?" she murmured.

Perhaps sensing what may be on the way, Briggs shook her head.

"I don't think it's—"

"I want to kiss you, Tristan," Alys interrupted. "To tell you the truth, I've thought of nothing else for the past three days. I want to kiss you, pull that t-shirt over your head, get you naked and make love to you all night." *There. THERE!*

"Ms. Huxley—"

"*Alys.* Will you at least call me Alys when we're discussing being naked together?"

"Alys," Briggs answered through gritted teeth. "I can't."

"But you want to." Alys stepped boldly toward her. "Right? You want to?"

"What I want has nothing to do with it."

"Yes, it does. Anyway, what do you think I'm after?"

"I think you just told me." Briggs stepped back as Alys took another step. "Alys. Please, don't."

Alys stopped, recognizing a genuine warning in her tone. She stared into Briggs' stormy eyes and noted regret, frustration, as well as raw, heated desire.

"It occurred to me earlier that I should fire you, Tristan."

"What?"

"If I released you from your service, would you be with me then?"

Briggs' expression darkened even more.

"Do you really think that I could walk away from the job now, knowing what this guy has threatened to do to you?" she snapped. "Just for a night of sex?"

"Don't insult me. You think that's all I want?"

"Frankly, I have no idea. And—"

"I'll make it clear to you then," Alys interrupted.

With one last step, she closed the distance between them. Then, eager to soothe the volatile atmosphere, she raised gentle fingers to touch her cheek. Tristan blinked. She swallowed hard, but stayed in place. Her skin radiated heat. Her body had gone rigid, nipples peeking hard under her t-shirt. She may be slightly pissed off, but she was aroused as well. Still, she did not move. That iron control only made Alys want her more.

"I won't lie to you," she murmured. "Everything about you, I find attractive. Yes, I want to kiss you. Touch you. Caress you. And I want you to do the same to me."

"Don't." Briggs warned again when she moved her fingers to her lips.

"I want to reveal the untamed part of you. I know it's there, just under the surface. And you're so beautiful." Alys carried on, ignoring her request to stop. She brushed her thumb over her mouth, leaned into her a little more, and made her sigh in spite of herself. Briggs was like marble, hard and unyielding... But some little things, she could not help. "Then, in the morning, I want to go for coffee again. Find a little place for that, just the two of us. I want to watch the sun rise over the ocean. Walk on the beach, holding hands. Later, I want to go home and cook you dinner. And—"

"Stop. Ms. Huxley."

Tristan wrapped her fingers around her wrist to pull her hand away. She was gentle but firm.

"You're trembling," Alys remarked. "Look, it's okay..."

"No, it's not," Briggs snapped, voice a bit rough now. "You have no idea."

"Wait." Alys tried to hold her back as she moved past her. Briggs shook her off; again, carefully but no less resolutely. She grabbed her weapon off the counter and headed for the door.

"Tristan. Hey."

"I'm sorry, I can't do this."

"But what's really the problem here?"

"No problem."

"What are you scared of?"

When Briggs halted at the door and glanced back, Alys held her breath in anticipation. Had she hit a raw nerve with this one?

224

"I'm not scared of anything," Tristan shot back.

She sounded proud. Fierce. Probably had no idea that a hint of uncertainty still pierced through her assurance. Granted, Alys was extremely attuned to her at this point. Anybody else may well have missed it. But she did not.

"I think you're shouldering blame that doesn't belong to you," she said to her gently. "From what you explained to me the other day, I really don't think that what happened with your partner was entirely your fault. Maybe not at all. Tristan, please, don't go..."

But she must have gone too far, crossed a line, and Briggs walked off without a word or another glance back at her. Left on her own once again, Alys leaned against the counter for balance, aware that she was trembling as well. *What the hell did I just do?* From deciding not to push Tristan, to pulling a stunt like this? She was amazed at her own self. And regretted her words, too! *What right did I have to say all this to her? And to make demands?* For sure, Briggs would want to stay away from her now! Quitting was not her style, but Alys feared that things may never be the same between them again. For a few moments there, she found it hard to breathe.

••

Goddammit! Who the hell does she think she is, talking to me like this?

Tristan stormed back to her bedroom and just paced around furiously for a while. Her usual ways to deal with stuff were not available to her here. She could not go for a run because she did not want to leave Huxley alone, no matter how secure the house might be. A bike ride or The Club weren't options either, though for sure, Tristan felt like the latter, with Huxley's tantalizing talk.

225

Unleashing my wild side... Man! The rest of Huxley's wants and desires, as she expressed so clearly, all contributed to making Tristan ache inside in a decidedly novel and unsettling manner. Holding hands on the beach, cooking together in the evening... *Just you and me.* Huxley was not only offering a one-off then, but something infinitely more intimate. Richer. And Tristan wanted it with startling intensity. All of it, including the naked part. Even better, she could have it now, no doubt about it. She sat on her bed, stared at the gun on the side table for a moment, a reminder of her duty. Then she closed her eyes and dropped her face into her hands.

'What are you scared of?'

The question had burned like a bullet when Huxley asked. Hopefully, Tristan managed to hide it from her... But the words, especially coming from a woman whose affection and respect she craved, were incredibly potent. She huffed in irritation as she recalled her own answer. What a load of bullshit. Yeah, she was scared. You bet. Since Jake's murder, she had done nothing but contract and hide. And Huxley was spot on with the other thing that she said as well, about her feeling guilty. Tristan must have asked herself the same question a million times. *Why did he go to that damn warehouse on his own?* The drugs gang had not simply abducted him in the middle of the street in broad daylight. They lured him in. For some reason, Jake had not told anyone where he was going that night, or why. Tristan always assumed that it must have had something to do with her... But she could never be certain. And Jake should have called. He had made a massive error of judgement. *Are you shouldering blame that doesn't belong to you?*

"Dammit..." After a few more seconds of reflection, Tristan got up and went to knock on Huxley's door.

••

"I'm sorry, Tristan. I was out of line."

Huxley had been crying, this was obvious to Tristan as soon as she opened the door. And looking very beautiful too, with her hair a bit messed up from the pillow and that loose Metallica t-shirt still on, which would be so much better off.

"No, I'm sorry," Tristan murmured. "You were right."

Huxley took her hand but the vibe was completely different this time. Not so demanding or overtly sexual. This was much softer and caring, as if she sensed that Tristan needed it. And dammit, she did. *I'm so tired of pretending…*

"Come on in," Huxley prompted softly.

One part of the room was bathed in clear moonlight and the other in soft shadows, inviting intimacy. Tristan stepped inside, barely glancing at the King-size bed at the far end, and the white curtains shifting in the breeze in front of the open French doors. She never broke eye contact. *Wasted enough time with stupid fears.* Letting go of Huxley's hand, she framed her face in both of hers. She noted the look of surprise, followed by tentative delight, which crossed the singer's face.

"Hello, Alys," she whispered, and kissed her.

Just a firm press of the lips, nothing too hot or challenging. Although she'd thought of taking Huxley's mouth in a very different manner before. Tristan had dreamt of kissing her rough and hard just as she came off stage, still high and supercharged from a performance. She knew how Huxley might respond to this sort of move: with relish. At the moment though, she longed for a slightly different sort of connection. Huxley had kissed her first, and opened up to her. She'd been honest about her feelings.

She spoke from the heart. And all Tristan had been able to give her in return was reluctance and push-back. For good reasons, of course, and some of them still stood... But now, before saying anything else, she just wanted to deliver the first kiss. And oh, gosh, was it worth it! Tristan kept it brief but it was still intense. Frankly, she didn't see how she could do it any other way with this woman. When she pulled back, Huxley kept her eyes closed for a second longer. She touched the tip of her tongue to her top lip, as if to savor the lingering taste of her. Then she opened her eyes, focused on her, and smiled.

"Hi, Tris..."

CHAPTER 28

Tristan stood in the middle of the bedroom, still cradling her face and feeling a bit breathless.

"You're right, I'm scared," she admitted.

"Oh, baby." Huxley immediately held her in the same way. "But I know you, Tristan. Allowing yourself to be close to me is never going to affect your performance on the job. I'm sure of it. You're way too switched-on for—"

"That's not it." Tristan closed her eyes, feeling her emotion rise. "That's not what I'm afraid of. Well, it's a concern, but I'll deal with it."

"Then what?" Alys inquired softly. "Don't worry, you can tell me."

"I'm afraid..." Tristan almost sobbed and her voice caught in her throat. She leaned her forehead against Huxley's and kept her eyes closed. "Sorry. Dammit, this is pathetic. I don't want to add to your—"

"It's okay. Hey, you're shaking again, you know that?"

"No..." Tristan had not noticed it but it was true.

"Just don't speak for a second," Huxley advised in a gentle voice. "Come."

She laced an arm around her waist and led her to the couch in a pool of darker shadows. Once there, she sat behind her and pulled her close, sheltering her in her embrace. Tristan allowed all this to happen even though it was bloody scary, alright. *Since when do I break down mid-sentence and require a cuddle?* Her brain may balk at the idea, but her body was doing its own thing. She was shaking, indeed. And when Huxley touched her fingers to her cheek, Tristan realized that she was crying too.

"Goddammit. I am so sor—"

"Don't say it," Huxley ordered. "What is it, Briggs? You got a problem with showing emotion? Are you the strong and silent bull-headed-type? Or is it accepting care from another woman that's the issue here?"

She tightened her hold, rested a protective hand on the back of her neck, and kissed her again gently on the lips. Tristan could feel a monster headache boiling behind her eyes. *Inflammation of the brain.* That's really what headaches were, she knew. *You're a fucking disaster, Briggs.*

"Are you yelling at me?" she mumbled.

"What would make you think that?"

"Called me Briggs again." Resting with her cheek pressed on Huxley's warm breast was beyond comforting, and yet she could not get the shaking under control.

"When I'm yelling at you for real, you won't need to ask for clarification," Alys replied with a soft chuckle. "Trust me, you'll know."

"Right."

"Anyway, consider it payback for all the times you insisted on calling me Ms. Huxley. Close your eyes if you want."

Tristan obeyed, sinking deeper into her arms.

"I have no problem with emotions," she murmured. "Or accepting care from another woman."

"Good." Huxley stroked her cheek, her voice both soothing and tender. "Do you want to talk about it, Tris?"

Tristan adjusted her position to look her in the eye. So close that she could feel her breath on her mouth, the lure of another kiss almost impossible to resist. But she needed to do the talking first.

"I lost one person I was close to and fell apart. And now I'm terrified of being with you because I fear the pain of another loss. It's weak. Stupid. Also, self-centered, and I hate feeling like that even more."

It was easier to put into words than expected. Huxley was calm, too, which helped.

"Self-centered?" she repeated. "How so?"

"Because you just lost Rose and I realize how much it hurts you. And yet, here I am, going on about my own stuff." Tristan blew air out sharply. "Damn pathetic."

Alys smiled and she caressed her lips.

"It's the second time you said this now. So, hear me: you are *NOT* pathetic."

"Huh," Tristan grunted.

"It's a fact, babe. Better believe it. And it's also not a case of either/or. We are allowed to each experience our own emotions without feeling guilty about the other. As for being scared of losing me..." Alys kissed her again, infinitely gently. "Don't go believing all the hype about Alys Huxley, the Rock Goddess. I don't go through life breaking strings of hearts. I don't even kiss girls as often as you might think. You should know by now that all I do is work."

Tristan traced the line of her jaw with a light finger.

"With the odd break on the back of a fast bike."

"Currently, yes."

"So, what are you saying?"

Huxley's liquid blue eyes remained warm and gentle but her expression grew slightly more serious.

"Two things."

"Okay..."

Tristan slid one arm around her shoulders and pulled her even closer. A very comfortable gesture and a strong anchor too, which made Huxley smile.

"I don't sleep around," she reflected. "I don't chase women. I've been more intimate and open with you, fully clothed, than with some of my lovers in the past."

"What does that mean?" Tristan murmured.

"I'm not sure." Alys flashed an almost shy grin. "Not sure where I was going with this. Just letting you know, I guess, that I take this very seriously with you."

"Thank you," Tristan murmured. "And me too. What's the second thing?"

••

"You won't lose me," Alys whispered.

Just when she was convinced that *she* may have lost Briggs as a consequence of her pushy behavior, Tristan had come to her with a beautiful admission. Laying herself wide open, which of course cannot have come easy for such an intensely private and controlled woman. But still, Tristan did it. *She did it for me.* Alys was touched beyond words and desperate to find the right ones in return.

"You won't lose me," she repeated. "First of all, nothing's going to happen to me. And then, there's this: I may not have many friends, but the ones that I do have, I tend to keep for the long term. Sure, the relationships shift and change over time. It's all pretty fluid. But I don't walk away from my friends and the people I love."

Alys added this last sentence because she wanted Tristan to realize that what she felt for her was real. No flash in the pan. She understood how seriously she took her job, and she would not push for her to break her own rules out of sheer selfishness. This was not to test her and see what would happen, or because she collected women as trophies. It was because she liked her. *A lot.* By the way that Tristan finally relaxed in her arms, and as the shaking stopped, Alys thought the message might be sinking in at last. Tristan even smiled.

"Thanks for telling me this."

"You're welcome. Does it help at all?"

"Yes."

"Great!"

"It's a lot of talking though."

"Oh, you tell me!" Alys rolled her eyes. "For all your tough attitude, you're kinda high maintenance, aren't you?"

"No way!" Tristan blushed crimson despite her protest.

"Yes, way." Alys chuckled. "Very cute, Briggs."

"So are you. Cute and sexy."

"You do like me then?"

"Already told you that."

"A while back, as I recall. Wouldn't hurt you to repeat it."

"I like you with a capital L, Alys. And I really think that we should stop talking now."

"Agreed! I thought you'd never—"

Tristan stole her words with a smiling kiss and now, at long last, Alys was treated to a taste of what she was really like when she allowed herself to be free. Briggs kissed hot and sensual. The single-mindedness that she put into her job translated into this as well. She took the lead and Alys happily let her, focusing on every sensation. Soft pressure made her part her lips. Briggs slid in smoothly to meet her tongue in a tender touch as thrilling as it was brief. Alys did not chase women, it was true; but she did chase that velvety tongue just now, causing Tristan to groan. As far as Alys was concerned, this sound was the best ever, not the least of all because it was so erotically charged. The kiss turned hungry then, until she was forced to wrench her mouth away to catch some air.

"So," she panted. "That's how you really kiss? Wow!"

"Did you like it?"

"You need to ask?"

"No."

"Hold on."

Alys stopped her as she leaned in to resume, by placing a firm hand in the middle of her chest. Tristan paused to raise a quizzical eyebrow.

"Now you want me to wait? I thought we—"

"Stop protesting and come with me," Alys laughed as she stood up. "Let's go to your room."

"What's wrong with this one?"

"We're not doing this in front of Sex Pistol."

"This?" Tristan chuckled. "You think he'll be traumatized if he sees us kissing?"

"Not kissing." Alys led her by the hand down the hallway and straight into her bedroom. "But he doesn't need to see what comes next. Also, I don't want any interruptions."

In front of Tristan's unmade bed, she pulled her t-shirt over her head and dropped it on the floor. Removed her panties and stood naked in front of her. With her heart pounding inside her chest, Alys observed her bodyguard watching her. Tristan had bared her soul to her just moments before. Now it was her turn to reciprocate, physically. Alys wanted this moment to feel like a gift, and it was clearly received as such.

"You're so beautiful, Alys."

Tristan managed to turn every look into a tender caress as she slowly took her in. She dispensed tingles in forbidden places, sparkling green eyes softening beautifully as they lingered over her breasts, the curve of her hips, and the soft triangle of dark-blond hair between her legs.

"Your smile right now is the sexiest thing I've ever seen in my life," Alys murmured in reply.

In one quick motion, Tristan got rid of her own t-shirt and boxers. Alys had seen her more than once in the gym with just a bra and shorts on. She'd admired her fighter's body and tight muscles. Now she bit thoughtfully on her bottom lip at the sight of Tristan's secret soft places. She was enticingly strong, and also magnificently female. They each took an easy step toward the other at the same time, and embraced wordlessly. Alys held her tightly. She pressed herself against her and delighted in Tristan's sigh of surrender.

"Is your skin always so hot?" she asked.

"I don't know… Are your nipples always so tight?"

With a laugh, Alys pulled her sideways and they both fell onto the bed. Quickly, she straddled her hips, although she was careful not to settle too low. *Not yet.* She seized Tristan's wrists and brought her hands up to her breasts.

"I don't know either… You tell me."

The sight of Tristan under her made her want to blink and stare. The sensation that she managed to unleash just by rolling her nipples softly in between her thumb and index finger, and fondling her breasts, would make Alys embarrass herself in a hot minute if she were not careful. Tristan Briggs; nude, with her gorgeous mouth half open and her green eyes sparkling with desire, was a thing of ultimate beauty.

"Is this a dream?" Alys whispered.

"Absolutely not."

Eyes flashing harder suddenly, Tristan laced an arm around her waist and briskly switched their positions. With Alys below, now, she lay almost fully on top of her and slid a powerful thigh between her legs. Not careful. Not patient anymore. Just eager. *And so wonderful.*

"Oh, yes..." Alys moaned at the feel of smooth lips closing over her nipples and sucking gently.

She caressed the back of Tristan's neck and went upwards, sinking her fingertips in thick bristle. Tristan had told her once that she kept her hair off like this because it was one less thing for an opponent to grab hold of in combat. It made her stronger then. But now, naked in each other's arms, Alys appreciated her vulnerability. It was sexy to her, precisely because Tristan was so strong.

"Kiss m—"

Tristan obliged, capturing her mouth before she could even finish. She was hot on top of her and prodding deliciously deep with her tongue. Alys relished the weight of heavy muscles, bare skin gliding on skin, the scent of their arousal mixing in a heady perfume. No other woman had ever felt so perfect.

"I've been wanting to kiss you," Tristan whispered against her lips. "To do this with you, Alys. Since Day 1."

"You... Yes?" Alys struggled to find her words.

"Yes." Tristan pushed her leg higher, insistent and precise.

Alys clung to her, fingernails digging into her shoulders.

"You waited a long time."

"Duty." Tristan met her eyes on that word. "Fear."

"You don't have to be afraid anymore, Tris."

"I know."

CHAPTER 29

They found their rhythm quickly and easily. For Alys, the feel of Tristan's heated core pressed against her leg was almost more exciting than the steady push of her knee between her open thighs. Tristan was wet. Swollen. Alys could feel that, and see it in her eyes too. Tristan was holding back but she was ready. Still in control, but her eyes were dark now. Pupils fully dilated, fire reflected in their depths.

"It's okay?" she asked, rocking gently.

"It's perfect. You're close, aren't you?"

"Mm. I could be."

Alys cupped her right breast in her palm and flicked her thumb over a hard nipple, just to see the reaction it may cause. Tristan moaned low in her throat and she dropped her head, forehead pressed against her shoulder.

"Be careful... I—" But Alys did it again, causing Tristan to shudder. A nice, satisfying, full-body shudder. "Fuck."

"It's okay, babe. Don't hold back. Let go, Tristan."

As she spoke, Alys squeezed her breast and she raised her leg a little bit more, intentionally disrupting her careful rhythm.

Tristan's response was instant and stunning. With a possessive growl, she pushed hard into her and took her mouth with equal passion. Okay, no more waiting. For real, this time. Alys gasped when she found her, talented fingers sliding through her swollen folds and almost making her head explode.

"Yes... Yes, yes, keep going," she demanded.

Tristan slipped two fingers inside of her, hitting bullseye on her first try and triggering a wave of the most delicious pleasure to uncoil from the base of her spine. *Oh, God.*

"I'm going to... Ah! I'm going to come," Alys exclaimed. *Or pass out from what she's doing to me. Maybe both...*

Tristan was ahead on the first option. She stopped riding her leg suddenly. Squeezed hard, stopped breathing, convulsed in reaction. With two urgent strokes and her thumb pressed over the tender bud of Alys's clitoris, she sent her skyrocketing into orgasm at the very same time that she erupted.

●●

Tristan never saw sunshine when she woke up in the morning; 04:30 a.m. always guaranteed that she caught her sunrises when out on a run, an early motorbike ride, or some kind of job-related task. But she opened her eyes to a beam of warm sunlight across the bedroom the next morning, and a most welcome sight. Alys was watching her, a faint smile playing on her lips.

"Mm..." Tristan stretched and reached for her, pulling her close. "So, it really wasn't a dream."

"Nope. Or if it is, I don't want to wake up."

"You're looking kinda smug, Ms. Huxley."

"That's because I feel very happy." Alys kissed her softly on the lips. "And that's *'Alys'* to you. Remember?"

"I remember," Tristan murmured. "Every little thing."

Alys snuggled in her arms felt like the missing part that she didn't even know should be there. They fitted together like two pieces of the same puzzle.

"How do you feel?" Alys whispered.

Tristan searched for any hint of discomfort, regret, or guilt. The usual for her. But she could not find any.

"Amazing," she said softly.

"Yeah?" Alys's smile rivaled the sun in its intensity. "Me too."

"What time is it?"

"Just after eight."

"Wow…" Tristan chuckled. "Middle of the day for me."

"I didn't want to wake you. You slept hard, like you needed it. Also, like a woman knocked you out good and proper last night."

"Not just any woman," Tristan smiled. "You. Twice."

Alys had claimed top for the second time: one hand pinning her wrists above her head, the other between her legs, hot mouth feasting on her breasts… Tristan had never come so hard. Now Alys kissed the side of her mouth and slid a hand between them.

"I want you again."

This breathless statement, and the smooth palm of her hand pressed over her, had Tristan immediately wet and wanting.

"Please," she whispered.

Alys licked her lips, kissed an already rock-hard nipple, and moved down the length of her body until she was between her legs, her chin resting on Tristan's abdomen.

"You're so gorgeous."

"You make me feel weak," Tristan chuckled.

"Haven't started yet." Alys grinned. "But that's the plan."

Tristan's cell phone went off with the first tantalizing brush of lips over her tight clitoris.

"Goddammit." She shot out one arm to grab the phone, fumbled for a moment as her fingers refused to grip, and just managed not to drop the stupid thing on the floor. Alys licked her nice and hard, not helping in the least.

"Switch it off," she drawled.

"It's Miller. Just a minute, okay?" Alys groaned in reply but she did pause, resting a hot cheek against the inside of Tristan's thigh. "Yeah. Briggs."

"Hey, how's it going?" Miller asked.

"Going great," Tristan said, noting Alys's ironic smirk at her answer. "What's up, Miller?"

"Bad news, I'm afraid," the detective announced. "We got the guy, but it's not him."

Tristan sat up and put an arm around Alys's shoulders as her lover came up to rest against her side.

"Just got you on speakerphone, Miller. Alys is here."

"Hello, Ms. Huxley." The cop went on in a calm voice that belied her frustration. "We found out the reason for our suspect shutting down his business in Dallas. Turns out he was moving to California to be with a woman he met online. Got hit by a car on arrival and has been in a coma ever since."

"So he can't be responsible for the stalker's recent activity!" Alys exclaimed quickly, in crushing dismay. "It's not him?"

"That's right, it rules him out."

Tristan closed her eyes as tension flooded her body. *Son of a bitch.* This whole time, they'd been looking for the wrong guy?

"But what does that mean?" Alys wondered, blue eyes wide and puzzled. "Don't tell me you're going to have to start your investigation from scratch!"

Tristan imagined that she could hear the detective gritting her teeth in frustration. She could totally sympathize with her, despite her own simmering anger with the circumstances. False leads were never fun. To her credit, Miller did not attempt to hide behind a wall of excuses.

"Yes," she admitted. "I'm afraid we're going to have to start again."

●●

Alys was adamant.

"No, absolutely not! I refuse to stay here any longer than we planned originally. I can't! How am I supposed to work without a studio? How can I prepare for the Australia tour if I am locked up on the other side of the world? I don't want to do it, Tristan. I won't."

So, now the vacation in Maine had turned into being locked up on the other side of the world. Tristan could understand this change in perspective also.

"Okay," she conceded. "That's fine."

Alys picked up her puppy and buried her face into his fur. She stood in front of the large living room window, staring out at the beach in the distance. Tristan noticed her shoulders quiver and she moved to stand up close. She kissed the side of her neck, wrapped her arms around her, and held her close.

"I'm not scared for me," Alys declared after a few seconds, turning to face her. "I've got security at events and you're with me all the time. That idiot would be crazy to try anything."

Tristan remained silent, reflecting that the guy must be, in fact, insane. She also understood that Alys needed to stay defiant in order to face this challenge.

"I told you before; I'm worried that he'll attempt to hurt my people," the singer went on. "If anything happened to my family... To Erik, to Brad, or my little guy." She deposited her wriggling pup onto the floor. "I would never forgive myself."

"I know. But it's not going to happen. And—"

"I worry about you, too," Alys interrupted sharply.

Tristan held her tighter.

"At least you can be at ease on this count. I may not look it when I'm in bed with you, but I'm actually quite dangerous and hardcore. You know? The lethal kind."

She was pleased when the exaggerated statement triggered a genuine smile from her lover.

"I know how skilled and tough you are. In bed, you're very gentle and extremely obedient too. It was a wonderful surprise."

"Please don't tell anyone about the obedience bit," Tristan pretended to moan, although she flushed, hard, for real. "Or I'll never live it down."

Alys kissed her gently on the lips.

"I won't tell a soul. It's only with me, right?"

"Only with you," Tristan murmured. "Absolutely."

Not only was this true, but it also felt like a future promise.

"Good," Alys said, and her blue eyes flashed. "I've never felt with anyone the way that I do with you, Tris. Safe. Inspired. Relaxed."

"Do you trust me?"

"One hundred percent." Alys answered without hesitation, just with an enormous, rather theatrical sigh.

"What was that for?" Tristan grinned.

"You're going to insist that I stay here, aren't you? Just like Miller. Please, Tristan, I cannot put my entire existence on hold indefinitely!"

She was correct... Even though Tristan wished that it were in her power to send her off the planet for a while, in order to fully guarantee her safety.

"The show must go on," she mused. "Right?"

"Yes, the show, life... Same difference, really. I know I said I was going to quit everything recently, but it was just in reaction to the threat against Sex Pistol. If I knew for sure that doing this will guarantee the safety of my loved ones, I would be happy to spend the rest of my life holed up in here. But it won't... Will it?"

"Even if it did, it would be completely irrational."

"There you go, then." Alys sighed again. "I have no choice."

"Yes, you do," Tristan corrected gently. "And I think you're making the right one by deciding to keep going. I would just like to sit down with you and Brad when we get home and review your upcoming schedule."

"Again?" Alys sounded tired. "We did it only last week."

"Yes, but what we agreed on then was on the basis of Miller arresting your stalker soon. With this setback, I'll need to change a few things."

"Brad will have a meltdown."

"Tough," Tristan shrugged.

Frankly, she could not care less. Bradley Wright was good at his job, that had to be said. He'd be fine juggling a few tweaks, no doubt. Alys leaned into her, arms locked tightly around her neck. She brushed her lips over her mouth and smiled.

"I love that you call it a setback, this situation."

"Sure, just a temporary setback. Believe me when I tell you that Miller's going through every shade of pissed-off and furious at the moment. Nothing like this sort of thing to motivate a cop to do better. She won't rest now until she gets our guy."

"Do you trust her?"

"Yes. One hundred percent."

"Okay, then. Can I ask you a favor?"

"Of course you can, Alys." *Or a million, and consider it done.*

Tristan did not commit lightly to anything or anyone. She was either *All in* or *Out*. As for breaking the rules of her chosen profession… She would have said it was less likely to happen than a loss of gravity on Earth. Now, though, Alys Huxley had her all in and even a bit extra. Willingly… Totally. Was this love? Tristan thought it might be. She knew she'd have to watch herself and be even more careful on the job. Being emotionally involved with her client carried the potential to leave her blind in some areas. Their closeness may impair her ability to remain impartial and keep sight of the big picture. But forewarned was forearmed. Tristan knew the risks, so she would simply mitigate them. *No problem.*

"It's about Sex Pistol," Alys explained. "I would feel a lot better if he could go and stay somewhere else until the stalker's arrested."

"Good idea."

"I only know musicians or artists who are on the road a lot. How about you, Tris?"

CHAPTER 30

They flew home a day later. Erik, fresh from his own trip with his buddies, was late to pick them up, which resulted in Alys being mobbed in front of the airport. Tristan had a few choice words for their driver which left him looking pale. Barely twenty minutes after they arrived home, as she headed to her studio for a shower and a change of clothes, Alys called her right back to her apartment. Tristan went flying. She burst into the bedroom, looking around aggressively.

"What's wrong?" Her lover seemed upset.

"Another email. Dammit, Tris! How does he know?"

Tristan turned to the open laptop on her desk, and read the email on the screen:

'How was Maine?'

Three simple words that caused an icy shiver to run down her spine. *Fuck!* How did he know about that, indeed? They'd been extremely careful. Told only Erik and Brad about the trip, and Alys had been posting on her social media about the other location, the fake one that she was supposedly at. Tristan made a mental list of who else was in the know: the pilot of the aircraft;

But he's been with Alys for years. The ex-cop who picked them up; *No way Dagger failed in their vetting process.* Me, Tristan reflected darkly. Alys wanted to go out, in and around Jacques Harbor, and she'd allowed it. Maybe they were spotted during a beach walk. *It's called a safe house for a reason, Tristan!* Sloppy work.

"My fault," she muttered. "We should have stayed inside the house at all times."

"Then it's my fault," Alys retorted. "I insisted we turn this time into a vacation. I'm sorry."

Arguing about it wouldn't help.

"Let's not dwell on this now," Tristan decided. "I need to go speak to Miller at the station."

"Alright. I'll be in my studio."

"Actually… Would you come with me please? We can drop Sex Pistol at his temporary home. I'll make sure no one follows. I just don't want to leave you here alone." *Or anywhere else for that matter. Not anymore.*

Alys pulled her into a tight embrace, prompting Tristan to lace both arms around her waist. This had already turned into a favorite default position.

"Good thing I don't want you to go anywhere without me, eh?"

"Yeah. That's lucky."

"Tris…" Alys held her gaze. "This latest thing is not your fault. Okay?"

"Mmm. It is, but I won't argue."

"You just did, my love, but it's alright."

My love. The words rolled easily off her tongue and beamed a ray of light across Tristan's mind, illuminating dark places she didn't even remember needed healing. Alys kissed her slow and gentle with an aftertaste of heat and desire.

"I need a quick shower," Tristan murmured.

"Me too, let's do it at your place," Alys invited.

Forty minutes and two orgasms later, they climbed into the back of the Rover. Alys's hair was still wet. A spot on Tristan's shoulder ached deliciously where her lover had sunk her teeth as she climaxed only moments earlier. They sat well apart from each other in the car, neither of them keen to broadcast the recent change in their relationship. If only for tactical reasons, it was best not to. Alys added that it was too new and precious to share just yet. Tristan agreed with that as well.

"Where to?" Erik inquired.

Alys, cradling Sex Pistol in her arms, gave him the address of a popular health spa in downtown Lewiston. Tristan caught his eyes on them both in the mirror a couple of times while he drove. Each time their gazes met, he was quick to glance away. She looked at her lover, who had noticed too. Alys just shrugged and flashed her a private smile. Erik spent such a lot of time with her… For sure, he must sense that something was different now. Whether or not he figured it out was not Tristan's problem. Also, none of his business.

"You can go home after dropping us off," she advised him.

"You'll make your own way back?"

"Yes."

"Alright. Whatever."

He'd been subdued since the airport fiasco, when she told him to either get his act together *right now,* or look for another job. For all his muscles and confident attitude, it actually didn't take much to floor the big guy.

"Thanks, man," she added in a warmer tone.

Immediately, he relaxed and smiled back.

"You got it, Briggs."

Tristan led Alys across the lobby of the spa place, through a door marked *Private,* and out via another fire exit into a quiet back street. The getaway vehicle was a black BMW 8 Coupé this time. They were back on the road in less than a minute, and she took the long way around to Old-Lewiston and her ex-partner's house. Nobody followed, she was dead sure of it.

"Thanks for taking him on, Katie," Tristan said to her friend as they watched Alys introduce Sex Pistol to a delighted young Jake.

"No problem, Tris. Jake understands that it's only for a little while, but Mark and I were considering getting him a puppy. So, this'll be a good trial run."

"Sounds like things are still going well with Mark," Tristan remarked.

"Oh, things are great with us!" Katie nodded with a dreamy smile. "I never thought I'd feel this way again… And for sure, it's not the same as with Jake. We do our own thing with Mark. It's different, but just as special and wonderful."

"Well, you deserve to be happy. Jake should have a solid man in his life too."

"The two of them adore each other."

"Awesome."

"Yes, I'm very lucky."

"So is Mark," Tristan pointed out.

Katie nodded toward Alys, currently sprawled on the living room floor with Jake and Sex Pistol.

"This is a bit strange. Before tonight, I'd only ever seen Alys Huxley on TV, performing. She's very different in real life. And I mean it in a good way, of course."

"You only saw the Rock Goddess before." Tristan could not suppress a smile of her own. "This is Alys."

"Yes, indeed... And it's great for you too, Tristan."

Tristan hesitated, but her friend's meaning was pretty clear.

"Wow," she grumbled. "Is it written all over my forehead or something?"

"Something like that, yes," Katie confirmed with a grin. "I think it's in the way you two look at each other. Never thought I'd see the day, Tris... Good for you, darling."

"I wasn't supposed to—" Tristan stopped before the words came out, raw and unfiltered. *Wasn't supposed to fall in love with a client.* She adjusted, choosing the lighter version. "Mix business with the personal."

"Life's full of surprises, I can tell you." Katie fixed her with an urgent stare. "Do you regret it?"

Tristan shook her head as Alys turned, looked at her, and flashed a smile that managed to be both tender and sizzling hot at the same time. The answer to the question was easy.

"No," she said. "Not for a split-second."

••

Alys watched her drive, one hand confidently on the wheel and the other resting on the elbow rest between the two front seats. Tristan seemed relaxed. Alys thought of asking her to pull over somewhere so that she could slide onto her lap and kiss her. She wanted to taste her again. Slow at first, then deep and hard. Like in the shower this morning. She gave a soft sigh, smiling at the memories. Tristan glanced at her with a raised eyebrow.

"You okay?"

"Yes. I'll miss my baby... But at least I won't worry every time I leave the house. He'll be alright with Jake."

"Guaranteed. And it's only temporary."

"That's right." Alys kept her eyes on her as Tristan snaked her way through city traffic toward Lewiston P.D. "Hey, did you share anything with Katie?"

"About the stalker? No."

"I mean, about us."

"Why?"

"Because she hugged me like I was family."

Another glance, a joyful flash of vivid green eyes.

"I'm glad she did. You are. And I didn't have to tell her. She said it was obvious from the way that we look at each other. She likes you too."

"Ah... Sorry, Tris. I wasn't aware of making it obvious."

"Don't be sorry." Tristan squeezed her leg. "As long as I'm good for the job, I don't care who sees, who knows, or what the hell people think about me."

"What about your boss?"

"Same. So long as it doesn't affect my performance and put you at risk, which it won't, she's cool with it. She knows I'm not into one-offs."

"I can't decide if that's a cold-ass way to talk about it or the most romantic thing I've ever heard," Alys stated, amused and genuinely torn between the two.

"Romantic," Tristan said. "Definitely."

"You know, we won't be able to keep this a secret for very long. Even Erik realized, and he's not quick with these things."

"Are you giving me a way out?"

"Sort of."

"I don't want it, Al."

"Wait till the paparazzi get on your case."

"I don't think they'll last long behind a fast Kawasaki. Do you?"

Joking, with a hint of dangerous mixed in. *Very, very sexy.* Alys wrapped her arms around her, needing to hug her and feel close. *I love you.* She wouldn't say it yet, but she was sure. Rose's voice echoed in her mind. *Told you, didn't I?* She smiled.

"You know, I'm not really giving you a way out. It's too late for that."

"Good."

Tristan clasped her hand when they got out of the car at the station and she did not let go as they walked in. The gesture was possessive. Thrilling. *'Mine.'* It proclaimed it loud and clear, and Alys held her the same way. Proudly.

"Hey, Briggs." They bumped into the dark-blonde cop from the other day. "You keep hanging around my station, I'm going to give you a job."

"Sorry, Quinn," Tristan announced. "Already taken."

"Yes, I see." Wesley nodded in approval. "Ms. Huxley. Nice to see you again."

"Hi," Alys smiled. "You too, Quinn."

They spent the next two hours with Miller in a small office which dominant feature was a large board affixed to the wall. It felt strange to Alys to see a picture of herself, and elements of her personal life, displayed on there... Including ex-lovers she had not seen or interacted with in years. *Like a stalking in reverse,* she reflected. The task of identifying the guy behind the threats could easily be compared to looking for a needle in a hay stack, but it was reassuring to observe how hard Miller and her team were working at it, leaving no stone unturned.

"It's not anybody I know," Alys repeated as they went over old ground. "I don't have enemies. Yeah, I'm in show-business: flashy on the outside, for sure. But when you've been doing it for as long as I have, it's pretty tame and boring in the background.

Everyone that I work with, from musicians and dancers to video producers, show organizers, etc., have been with me for years and years. We're a tight community. I trust them. Not because I am naïve but because they've earned it."

Miller helped herself to a cup of coffee from the machine in the corner.

"You know what I'm thinking now, don't you?" she said as she turned back, looking at Tristan.

"What?" Alys prompted when her lover did not reply.

Tristan remained silent. She seemed tense again, watching the board with a dark and reluctant expression in her eyes.

"We need to draw him out somehow, this stalker," Miller offered.

"Somehow?" Alys repeated. "How do you mean?"

Tristan blew air out sharply and she stood up to pace.

"She means using you as bait, Alys."

"Well, Tristan," the detective started to protest. "That's not exactly what I—"

"Yeah, it is." Tristan interrupted, eyes flashing in warning. "It's exactly what you had in mind. And that's a negative. We're not going down that road, putting Alys at risk. Got it?"

"Okay," Miller shrugged. "I got it, Briggs."

The meeting ended frostily and without clear resolution some time after that. Alys was the first to break the silence in the car on the way back home.

"Do you miss it?" she asked. "Being a cop?"

"I don't miss the undercover bit. Too easy to lose yourself in that. But all the rest of it; the work, the people..." Tristan nodded pensively. "Yeah, I guess I do."

"Would your friend really give you a job if you asked her for one? Is she in charge here?"

"Quinn's been promoted to Lieutenant and Assistant-Chief now." Tristan had found that out at dinner the other night. And also that her friend had almost lost her life saving others during a mass shooting event. Tristan had missed it all. *Not been that much of a friend to Quinn, really.* And yet... "Yes. She would like me to join her team."

"Are you tempted?"

"Sometimes."

Sensing her reserve on the matter, Alys held back on any more questions.

"Thanks for telling me," she just said. "And being willing to share."

Tristan looked at her, warmth piercing through a remaining level of tension in her eyes.

"Thanks for being interested. It means a lot."

Back home, Alys proceeded to show her the full extent of her *'Interest'*. Lying in her arms a few hours later, feeling Tristan finally at ease, she brought up the topic again.

"So, about what Miller said..."

CHAPTER 31

Tristan agreed to the plan because they had no other choice, and it also made sense. Miller, pretending to be Alys and using her private email, would enter into conversation with the stalker.

"It'll be fine," the detective stated. "If we can get him to talk back, to engage... A- we're re-taking control. And B- we run a much better chance that he'll reveal some clue that will lead us to him eventually."

The Lewiston P.D. Hostage Rescue negotiator approved of the idea, convinced that it would be the best course of action to bring the case to an end. Quinn was consulted, and agreed with the plan. Miller could not wait to get cracking and Tristan was cautiously optimistic. Of course, this was no longer just 'A case' for her. She trusted the team and understood that it was the best way to bring about resolution, but it was a dangerous game to play, and she was only too aware of where it might lead. Miller would push for the stalker to reveal himself. If it meant using Alys as bait later on, she would not hesitate to do what she had to. And Tristan knew that her lover, as brave and determined as she was, would be the first to volunteer for a dangerous mission.

"We won't put her at risk, Briggs," Miller assured.

All Tristan could do was focus on doing her own job the best way she could. And as it was, the first email that Miller sent, drafted with the help of the negotiator, remained unanswered. A week passed. Alys carried on with her engagements, albeit on a reduced schedule and no Live shows. She was, not surprisingly, furious about this particular point.

"Lives are my oxygen, goddammit! I have a special relationship with my fans. A genuine bond, you understand? If I can't be out there connecting with them, my career may as well be over! You need to do something, and fast."

She directed this tirade at Miller, in full rock-goddess mode. *'Lighting my ass on fire'*, as the detective would describe it later. Very accurate, and Tristan had to laugh. Only two nights later, Miller called. Tristan was still up at just after one a.m., going through case data on her laptop. Alys was asleep with her head resting on her thigh. Sex Pistol curled up on the other side, snoring faintly.

"I need you both to come to the station, Briggs."

"What's going on?"

"I'll tell you when you get there."

It was a fifteen-minute ride on the Kawasaki, and the night-duty officer directed them straight to Miller's office when they arrived. She was not alone.

"Joan!" Alys blurted out in surprise and consternation. "Oh, darling... What happened to you?"

Tristan recognized Joan Beck, the video director who was on set with Alys on that first day. She remembered the woman's brisk manner and powerful voice as she rounded everyone up for the shoot. Now, her lively brown eyes were dull with shock. A painful-looking bruise marred the flawless skin along her jaw.

Her face was ashen, and it was obvious that she'd been crying. Alys threw her arms around her, holding her close as her friend also clung to her.

"Alys," Joan whispered intently. "Are you okay?"

"Of course I am!"

"I was so scared you wouldn't be..."

Alys knelt in front of the chair she sat on, holding tightly onto her hands.

"I'm fine, Joanie. Tell me what happened."

"I got home late after a meeting. About ten-thirty/eleven." Beck searched for Tristan's gaze, as if making sure that she was there, and listening. Tristan had never been more attentive. "He grabbed me at the door, just as I was getting in. Tall guy. Strong. There was nothing I could do. He slammed me into the wall, said he had a message for you."

Tristan glanced at Miller, noticed her furious expression. *So, I'm not the only one feeling it...* Joan continued, holding on to Alys as if she were afraid that she might disappear if she let go. She looked scared. The real deal, not just a bit shook-up. With what she said next, Tristan could understand why.

"*'Tell Alys that I don't want to chat to her – I want to hurt her, and the ones that she loves.'*" Joan swallowed hard a couple times, compulsively. "Then he punched me in the face. Gosh, it hurt! I think I passed out for a moment. As soon as I recovered, I called the police."

"Oh, Joan," Alys murmured. "I'm so sorry."

The look that she turned to give her, in equal parts fury and desperation, made Tristan want to punch something in return. She hated feeling so damn helpless. As Alys continued to hold her friend, and comfort her, Miller pulled her aside.

"Anything?" Tristan asked. "Anything at all?"

"He's on the door-cam for two seconds before knocking it out of alignment."

"Show me."

The footage did not amount to much. A shadowy figure in jeans and a hoody, wearing gloves. Just a flash before the camera went off-line.

"Tall one," Tristan said.

"Over six foot. Bulky with it too."

"Mmm... Can you send me that footage?"

"Sure, I will."

"This guy's the kind of vindictive that makes me think it's personal for him," Tristan added. "I know what Alys says about being on good terms with everyone that she works with, but this behavior hints at someone close to her. And pissed-off. I'll speak to her manager again, get Wright to think of anyone who may be holding a grudge. He handles a lot behind the scenes that Alys may not necessarily always know about."

"Okay," Miller nodded. "We've got an arrogant personality here too. Wanted to let us know that the email we sent him is way off the mark."

"Yeah. Doesn't want to be misunderstood. Maybe he was in the past... We may be looking for someone who was abused or ignored as a child."

"Lack of emotional care is abuse."

"Yes, you're right. Maybe Alys reminds him of something he never had. Or he hates successful women. Definitely, jealousy feels like a factor."

"So, we look into it."

"We do," Tristan approved. "Hell, yeah. I'll help."

"You know, this feels like a real break. We got a lot on this guy tonight. He gave it to us, really."

"You prodded and he reacted. He's angry, for sure."

"We can prod some more." Miller sounded wired. "We can push him to make a mistake."

Tristan looked back to where Joan Beck rested in her lover's arms. Even in the few minutes they'd been talking, the bruise on the side of her face had darkened. She looked exhausted and extremely vulnerable.

"There's a lot at stake, Miller," Tristan murmured.

"Yes, there is," the detective simply replied.

Stay focused. Tristan took a deep breath and inquired about the light patches of color on Joan's blue-jeans and red t-shirt that she was wearing. It looked like paint.

"It is," Miller supplied. "She's redecorating at home and it was still fresh on the walls in the lobby where he pushed her."

"Alright. Stay sharp, Miller."

"You too, Briggs."

●●

Tristan spent the following day pouring over case data, reading profiles, and researching motive, until her eyes felt gritty from the laptop screen and a headache threatened behind her eyes. Alys stayed in her music studio, alone, working on new songs. Both anchoring and seeking solace in doing what they did best. At least until the evening. Then, Alys cooked: fresh tuna steaks on the grill with a basil marinade, coconut rice, and vanilla ice-cream, also home-made, for dessert.

"I don't mind if you drink wine in front of me, you know?" Tristan said, noting that she wasn't.

"Ah, okay. I wasn't sure... Do you miss it?"

"No. I don't need it anymore."

"Good." Alys nodded with thoughtful eyes. "I don't need it either, to be honest."

She led her to the couch at the other end of the tiled patio and lay snuggled against her side with one hand pressed over her chest. Silence grew and the shadows lengthened. The first stars appeared overhead, and still, Alys was silent.

"How are you doing?" Tristan murmured.

"Okay." Alys shrugged. "Ish."

"Did you speak to Joan?"

"Yes. She's going to stay with her brother and his wife, in Vegas, until the situation here is cleared up."

"It won't be long," Tristan promised, and ran her fingers idly through her hair. "On another topic: you are a fantastic chef, Ms. Huxley."

"Thanks. I enjoyed cooking for you tonight." Alys brushed her lips across her mouth, smiling softly. "I really like kissing you, too."

"Oh, yeah?"

"Yeah. And making love to you."

"Keep doing it all and you'll make me want to stay."

"Uh…" Alys pulled back, both eyebrows raised in pretend outrage. "You mean you don't already want to?"

"Maybe." Tristan teased, grinning.

"You know, it's not too late for me to fire you."

"As your bodyguard, perhaps. But as your lover? I think it's too late for that. You're already addicted to me."

"Pretty sure of yourself, aren't you?" Smirking, Alys traced a hot finger around her lips.

"I think I've earned the right to be, Ms. Huxley."

"Wrong, Briggs," her lover laughed. "I'm a tough boss."

"I've noticed that."

"So, get to work," Alys instructed. "Convince me."

"Yes, Boss. With pleasure."

In one swift move, Tristan jumped off the couch and pulled her up too. She caught Alys's delighted chuckle in a kiss which started off light and playful and soon turned deep, hot. Bumping into walls, stopping to pull items of clothing off each other, they finally made it to the bedroom. Still not in the clear. Trying to get rid of her jeans and keep a kiss going at the same time made Tristan trip. She ended up on both knees on the plush carpet, in front of her laughing partner.

"Mmm…" Alys purred in satisfaction. "Good idea. You can worship your queen now."

Tristan had to pause. Alys stood looking down at her with a teasing smile over her gorgeous lips. Her blue eyes sparkled full of joy and a hint of challenge. As she reached a gentle hand to caress her cheek, Tristan took her wrist and kissed the palm of her hand. She rested in that simple touch for an instant, with her eyes closed. Then she looked up and met her lover's smile with one of her own.

"Gladly," she murmured.

As Alys leaned against the bedpost, Tristan had fun teasing her Chanel thong down the length of her slender legs. Slowly, infinitely slowly, enjoying every single one of Alys's involuntary twitches. Feeling her trembling harder, she circled a strong arm around her knees.

"I've got you, Al. Relax."

She pressed her lips against her lower abdomen, registering the instant unconscious lift of Alys's hips. Tristan felt her heat. She reveled in the clean scent of her arousal.

"Please," Alys whispered. "Touch me."

Tristan brushed her mouth over her clitoris.

"Oh... Yes..."

Tightening her grip around her thighs to keep her steady, Tristan indulged her own desire. She sucked, licked, and stroked her lover with her tongue. With her free hand, she caressed her legs, tickled the back of her knees, and massaged tight buttocks. When she reached upwards, Alys captured her fingers and laid them over her own burning breast.

"Oh, Tristan," she murmured. "I won't... I... I'm close!"

So am I. Tristan did not stop to say it in words. She twisted a nipple, enjoyed the mix of a moan and laughter that it provoked. As Alys gripped the post for better balance, she licked lower, found her way deeper, slipped inside for a tantalizing second before retreating. Alys cried out this time.

"Do that again. Please!"

"Not yet," Tristan whispered.

Her lover was tight, swollen, deliciously hot. Tristan felt her fingers on the back of her head and grinned. No doubt if there had been something to grab hold of there, Alys would have done it. Tristan obeyed the silent command. *More.* She wrapped her lips around her clitoris, took her completely, pushed her tongue over her. She sensed the first tremor and was not surprised to feel an echo of it at the base of her own spine. One more suck, which elicited a full body shudder from Alys.

"Tristan," she moaned. "Now, now, please darling!"

Tristan was more than ready. She was sweating, her heart pounding with need. Even without direct stimulation, she knew she might go off just from pleasuring her partner this way. She pushed her tongue deep inside her. Once. Twice... Alys stopped breathing on three. Her body went rigid and her hand at the back of Tristan's neck gripped her almost hard enough to hurt. But it was all pleasure.

"Tristan!"

Alys surrendered with a sharp cry, flooding her mouth with sweet juices.

NATALIE DEBRABANDERE

CHAPTER 32

Sleep eluded her, despite every muscle in her body singing in satisfaction. Alys fell hard into slumber some time after treating her to a sensual massage, but Tristan remained awake for a long time afterwards. She was calm. Just staring at the ceiling as faces and statements, and pieces of Miller's wall board, flashed across her mind.

Jealous. Arrogant. Obsessed.

These three words would not go away. When she was a cop too, she would often lie awake at night, unable to put aside the details of a case. Not that she wanted to, now. It was always personal for her, and this time, even more so. Tristan slid away from her sleeping partner, got dressed, and headed downstairs. It was hot tonight, the air muggy and close, with not a breath of wind coming in from the ocean. She went on a slow walk around the grounds, thinking about the stalker. *'I want to hurt her and the ones that she loves'.* The message worried Tristan a lot more than she let on. Who would be next? How to keep everyone safe? The answer to this one was rather obvious: Tristan could not. Alys had been forced to warn her people and members of her family.

A disturbed individual was on the loose, and decompensating fast. From random emails sent to a website, then to her private address... Escalating to a tangible symbol of death, the dead rat mailed to Alys's home address. And now, a physical assault on a person in her circle. Tristan hated to think what the guy's next step would be if they were not able to stop him.

"Evening, Briggs."

She came upon Erik, sitting by the side of the pool.

"Hey, buddy." Tristan nodded at the acoustic guitar in his lap. "Didn't know you played that."

"Yep. Not good enough to make the band, but it impresses the girls." He performed a sexy blues riff which sounded pretty good to Tristan, even if she was no expert.

"I'm impressed."

"Thanks. You sing?"

"Gosh, no," she muttered.

He laughed, gave a philosophical shrug, and took a drag of his cigarette. Funny that, she thought as he finger-picked a slow tune. She thought he was a health nut.

"Alys in bed?"

Ah. Okay, then. His tone of voice, and his expression, were less than subtle. She got the message. Clearly, what he wanted to know was if they were done fucking for the night.

"Yeah," she replied, and left it at that.

"I see." He sneered. "You two got it on, uh?"

Tristan gave a nonchalant shrug, hoping he'd realize that it was none of his business, and drop it. But he insisted.

"Were you going to tell me, or what?"

Now he sounded like a petulant child, and she resisted the impulse to put him in his place with a resounding, *'No!'*. And perhaps a quick friendly *'Fuck off'*, to make sure he got the point.

She already knew that he resented being left out of the picture a lot when Alys made decisions. According to his own self, Erik was always the last to know about anything. As far as Tristan was concerned, he should just shut up and be grateful. Not only was he paid over the odds to perform an easy job, but his hard-working cousin allowed him to live in her house, free of charge. Why he seemed to think that he was entitled to know about her private life, Tristan had no idea. *Entitled,* she thought. *Arrogant. Jealous.* Her skin prickled.

"We weren't going to make a big deal of it, Erik."

"No." He shrugged, flashed a mirthless smile. "I guess not, uh."

He went back to his instrument, humming under his breath as he played and dragging on his cigarette. Tristan recalled their first day of sparring in the gym, and being surprised at his skills. He was as good as some cops she knew who trained to compete. She hadn't known he played the guitar. Had no idea he smoked. The guy was full of surprises.

"Hey, Erik?" she prompted.

"Huh?" He raised an eyebrow, still bent over his guitar and refusing to meet her eyes.

"Are we good?"

"Of course." He did look at her, briefly. "'Night, Briggs."

She headed back to the house, her mind throbbing from the encounter. *Erik.* Goofy Erik. Not too bright, but loveable Erik. He was alone in the Rover when the stalker allegedly approached to deliver the note that said *I'M WATCHING YOU.* He was on his own at the house again, when the dead rat came in a package. Of course, he knew Alys's private email address. And he was aware that to threaten her puppy would send her into full panic mode. *He was one of the few who knew about the trip to Maine...*

"Fucking crazy." Tristan hissed under her breath. Her head was pounding. "He's got no motive!"

Not good enough to make the band... Had Erik tried and failed? Low self-esteem fitted a narcissistic personality and the desire to control. Did he love his cousin? Or silently despise her because she made him feel inferior? Tristan raced back into the house only to stop in front of the stairs leading up to Alys's apartment. The door to Erik's place was closed. She locked the front to make sure that she would hear him come back when he did. She was prepared to break into his private rooms if she had to, but all she had to do was turn the knob. She almost laughed.

"You're losing it, Tristan."

Of course she was. This was ridiculous. No criminal would leave their door unlocked like that. And Erik was no criminal. *No way.* Still... Her cop instinct had been triggered. She reflected it wouldn't hurt to have a look.

••

Back at Lewiston P.D., Cody Miller helped herself to a cold slice of veggie pizza from the open box on her desk. That, and a full-fat Coke, would be dinner. Another long day, but she was used to them. A five-year veteran on the force, she was still relatively new in years, but not in experience. Before moving to Lewiston, she'd worked the streets of New York for two years, then joined the investigative division. She was smart, tough, and currently very pissed off with the lack of results on this case. Tonight, she was going back to square one, starting with the less obvious: close family and friends who had been eliminated from her non-existent list of suspects. Murder was often extremely personal. So was stalking, if not more so. She picked up the first folder;

Bradley Wright. Huxley's manager. And started reading through it one more time. In light of the new profiling info that they now had on the stalker, a revealing clue might pop up which she and others had not noticed before.

"Still at it, Miller?"

Cody looked up to see Quinn leaning in the open doorway, in jeans and a t-shirt, backpack slung over one shoulder. Looking like she may be on her way home.

"Yeah, I'm feeling lucky."

"Need any help with it?"

There were faint shadows under her bright blue eyes, traces of fatigue not usually so apparent. Quinn also spent more hours on the job than most in the department, Cody knew. And she was married now. At eleven o'clock on a Sunday night, she must be wanting to be someplace else.

"I've got it, thanks," Cody nodded. "Just a bit more reading and then I'll call it a night."

Glancing at the files scattered over her desk, Quinn seemed reluctant to leave.

"You sure?"

"Totally."

"Okay. Yeah." As if convincing herself. "I should go home, really. Haven't seen Lia much this week."

She flashed a brilliant smile at the mention of her wife, and Cody experienced a tiny tug of longing. Why, she had no idea. She adored her job and relished her independence, dinners of cold pizza at her desk included.

"No worries, Chief," she said. "Have a good 'un."

"You too. Call me if anything gives."

Cody searched in her drawer for a sachet of mayonnaise in the collection of sauces she'd accumulated from previous meals.

271

She dumped it on the cold pizza, along with chili flakes from her improvised kitchen drawer, took a bite, and nodded. *Yep, not bad at all.* She resumed her reading, still on the illustrious Bradley Wright and his accomplishments. The man had a magnificent resume. He'd worked for Huxley and a number of very famous stars before going exclusive with her. Cody was intrigued to discover a four-week gap in the chronological list of jobs and clients he'd handled. It was around the same time that Huxley took a break from her own career, before re-emerging as a full-fledged rock goddess. Just a coincidence? The gap was marked as *'Sabbatical'* for Wright. It was fair enough... *But not enough.* Cody flicked impatiently through the file pages until she found what she was looking for.

"Well, well..."

She scanned the info, heart racing at the discovery of what the man had been up to during his four-week break. Was Briggs even aware of this information? Cody immediately dialed her number. No answer. She tried again a minute later and got the same result. Alys Huxley was also unreachable at this time, on both her home and cell phones. Without hesitation, Cody called Quinn, who answered before the end of the second ring.

"Wesley."

"Hey. I just found out that Huxley's manager, Wright, spent four weeks at a psychiatric hospital a few years back."

"What for?"

"According to the file, he was in for a bout of depression. I know he's on our list of Cleared, but—"

"You ran this past Tristan?" Quinn interrupted.

"She's not answering her phone, nor is Huxley. I'm going to drop by the house now to check on them both."

"Meet you there," Quinn said tightly.

••

Erik's place was painfully clean and tidy, beyond fashionable minimalism and into sterile territory. It was yet another thing which Tristan had not expected, and in contradiction with his casual behavior. She made an additional interesting discovery in the top drawer of his impeccably organized dresser, in the form of an S&M play kit. He had a flogger, a pair of handcuffs, leather restraints, a bunch of toys... Oh, well. This was not against the law, and she already knew that he enjoyed girls and sex. So, he liked it spicy. So what? So did she, sometimes, though perhaps not to the point of wanting to put a partner in steel cuffs. These were police issue, not designed for easy wear. Maybe comfort was not the point... Not her thing. Tristan did not linger. She moved through the rest of the apartment quickly and silently, taking in the spotless kitchen, which looked more like an unused science lab than a cheerful space, and an equally impersonal bathroom. *Something's not right here...* She could feel it now, and it was nothing to do with the decor. *But what, exactly?* It was a disconnect, she figured. A chasm starting to form between the idea that she'd formed of Erik, with the cool-dude image that he always projected, and what she was seeing of his private space. *Get out of there, Tristan, before he comes back.* Her time undercover had served to sharpen an already keen sixth sense. But the same intuition also whispered that there was more for her to find here. Something else, relevant. On impulse, she drifted back toward the kitchen. Trash can to the left of the open door. She stepped on the pedal, the lid lifted, and she froze in reaction. *Ah, fuck!* She'd seen Erik wearing the pair of Nikes that were stuffed in there. Right on the side of the left shoe, there was a light stain.

273

Cream-colored. Tristan picked it up and had a sniff to confirm, but she already knew. It was paint. The same color she'd seen on Joan Beck's clothes at the station.

"You shouldn't be here."

Her weapon was in her hand, and she spun around before the last word even fully registered across her mind. Impeccable reflexes, but it was still too late. Tristan did not have time to see what happened next. She heard a clean *woosh*, felt the air move in front of her face. Something heavy and hard struck the side of her head. Pain exploded between her eyes. She went down, out cold before she even hit the floor.

CHAPTER 33

Alys awoke with a lingering smile, her skin still tingling from Tristan's caresses. Her only disappointment was to find her gone from bed, although it was no longer such a surprise. She knew by now that her lover rarely slept through the night, and that she liked to roam. Especially when she was mulling over a problem. Alys just pulled on a pair of shorts, Tristan's t-shirt that she liked to wear, and went in search of her. When she reached the stairs, she was surprised to find Erik racing up toward her. His face was livid.

"Al!" he yelled. "Alys, are you okay?"

"What? Of course, I am." She frowned as he grabbed her by the arms, frantic blue eyes searching her face to ensure that she really was. "What are you—"

"We've got to go. Gotta go right now!"

She had never seen him look or sound so scared.

"Go where?" she insisted, confused. "Why? Where's Tris?"

"It's not safe here, we have to leave," he repeated as he led her quickly down the stairs. "Tristan is down. She's hurt. I think the stalker's here, Al!"

Alys barely registered the last part of that sentence. But her blood turned to ice, and she stumbled, at the mention of Tristan being hurt.

"Where is she?" she shouted at him. "Where, Erik?"

"In my apartment. Look, we have to get you out of here and to a safe—"

"Let me go!"

Shaking herself loose from his grasp, Alys raced down the hallway and rushed into the apartment. She found Tristan on the kitchen floor, lying on her side, unconscious. *Jesus Christ!* Alys dropped to her knees in front of her.

"Tristan."

Her lover's face was ashen. Her lips had lost all their color. She moaned softly when Alys slid a hand under her neck. If not, Alys might have believed that she was already dead.

"Ambulance," she tossed over her shoulder. "Call 911 right now!"

As gently as possible, she moved Tristan's head to bring her to rest on her thigh. Warm blood coated her fingers when she cradled the side of her head. More of it was in evidence on the corner of the marble counter. Imagining the sickening force of the impact that would cause the two-inch laceration in her skull made Alys's stomach turn. And what about the dark bruise on the other side of her head? She'd been struck by something, it was obvious. Hit full-on in the face, and she must have clipped the counter as she fell back. Who could have done this? Was he still lurking inside the house, as Erik feared? Or prowling on the outside? Alys struggled to think as her lover continued to bleed, though she added another directive to her cousin.

"Call detective Miller! Her number's in my phone, passcode 1029."

She did not turn to check that Erik was getting on with the task. Tristan was her sole and only focus. *I can't believe he wanted me to leave without her!*

"It's okay, my love," she assured her when Tristan jerked in her arms. "I've got you. An ambulance will be here soon. Just lie still, okay?"

Tristan briefly opened her eyes at the sound of her voice but Alys was not sure that she recognized or even saw her. She was cold and shivering, her eyes glassy and unfocused. Alys held her gently as blood continued to seep through her fingers, over her bare leg and onto the floor. She had to bite on her lip not to start crying. Inside, she was scared and close to panic… But she could not let Tristan hear that, and risk that it would make her worse in her current state.

"I'm with you, Tris," she repeated softly. "Any second now, the ambulance will be here. I know you can hear me, babe. Ssh, it's okay…"

And then, she heard him laugh. Startled, Alys looked up to find that Erik had moved to stand in front of them. And he was laughing. His reaction, so blatantly wrong, baffled her at first. She was left speechless. Was the stress getting to him, or what? Before she could ask, she was shocked to notice a change in his appearance as well. This was Erik… And yet it no longer was. His usually clear blue eyes were darker. The lines of his face seemed harder too, which made him look older and almost like a stranger. His laughter sounded cold and threatening. *No,* Alys reflected. This was not the Erik that she knew.

"Very sweet, Al," he mocked. "Like a scene out of Romeo and Juliet."

Slowly, as if in a dream, she watched him pull Tristan's gun from the waistband of his jeans.

"What are you doing?" She was feeling faint and the words came out the same.

"What's the matter, Alys?" he growled aggressively. "Is the legendary rock goddess losing her voice? Scared I'm gonna hurt your useless bodyguard some more?"

He laughed again as she instinctively placed a protective hand over Tristan's face. *Jesus...* With a sinking feeling, Alys understood that this was no joke. No one was in the house but Erik. And he had done this to Tristan, struck her so hard that he could have killed her. She swallowed hard, fighting a wave of nausea at the realization of what this meant. Erik must be behind all the rest of it as well. The emails, the threats... Every fiber of her being rebelled at the idea of him being the stalker. Why? What had she ever done to him, other than put a roof over his head and give him a cushy job?

"Please, call an ambulance for her. Please, Erik!"

He snorted. Shrugged. Still with that eerie expression in his eyes.

"Are you on drugs?" she snapped.

"Shut the fuck up!"

He raised his fist, sniggered when she recoiled, and did not carry through. Her reaction just seemed to please him.

●●

Tristan heard all this as if from a great distance. For a while, she was detached. Floating. Drifting. The urge to sink deeper, and let the darkness and silence take over, was felt. Only one thing kept her fighting not to give in. One thought. *Alys.* In the end, she was actually grateful for the ice-cold water that Erik threw in her face to wake her up. Regrets flashed in her mind as she came back.

Should have gone to Alys first. Should have called Miller. Damn, he's got my gun! This pissed her off, you bet. She noticed a touch of regret in Alys's eyes as well, but most of all, it was love. The look hit Tristan harder than Erik's cowardly blow. It settled her and re-energized her, all in one lingering and loaded glance... Made her forget the pain in her cracked skull, the pounding headache, the stabbing sensation in her eyes. A solid wall of concentration fell over her.

"Let's go. Move!" he shouted at them both. "To the Rover, now!"

It was easy to make him think that she was struggling, and less of a threat. The world spun wildly in front of her eyes as she got to her feet. Tristan might have dropped if Alys had not been holding on to her so tightly. *Breathe. Keep your focus.* It was easier outside in the fresh air.

"I love you," Alys murmured against her ear.

"Love you too," Tristan replied through gritted teeth.

Did Alys think that they would not survive this night? *No fucking way.*

"Stop," Erik instructed in front of the car. He took out a pair of handcuffs, probably the ones she'd seen before, and waved the gun in her direction. Tristan winced inside at the gesture. He had no idea how sensitive her weapon was. "You. Hands on the car. You know the drill, I'm sure."

Alys held her tighter, refusing to let her go.

"No. Leave her alone," she hissed. "Why are you doing this, Erik? Please, stop! Put that gun down. We can talk, okay? Just let us—"

"Even now, you think that you can order me?" he cut her.

His pupils were dark, his voice hollow. Whoever used to be inside his head was no longer in charge. Was this schizophrenia?

279

Drugs? For sure, some kind of devastating mental breakdown. It must have been deteriorating for a while. *And no one noticed. I did not see it.* Tristan fumed. She knew Erik might not react very well if Alys insisted on trying to reason with him.

"All my life, I've had to fall in line," he went on, spitting on the edge of fury. "You always came first. Always mattered more. It's time for you to learn your place."

"Erik—"

In the blink of an eye, he charged forward. Grabbed Alys by the throat, wrenched her out of Tristan's arms, and slammed her against the Rover.

"You move, she's dead," Erik snarled in warning.

He said that but pointed the Glock at her own head. Tristan raised her open hands in a pacifying gesture.

"I won't do anything," she promised. At the same time, she was calculating how best to remove him from Alys. "Hey, man. What's going on with you? The Erik I know wouldn't be doing this."

"That's just it. You don't know me."

"Put the gun down then. Let's talk."

As Alys audibly choked, struggling for breath, he sent her to the ground with a vicious slap across the face. Tristan forced herself not to react. *Better,* she thought. A little bit more distance between the two now. *Just not far enough away yet.*

"Get here," Erik barked, repeating his earlier order. "Hands on the car now."

Tristan glanced at Alys still on the ground. He'd cut her lip open. *The bastard.* Still, her lover's eyes were unusually bright and clear. She was watching her too. Attentive and alert. *Ready.* Tristan nodded. *I love you.* In spite of everything, she smiled. Of course, he did not like it.

"Don't make me tell you again, Briggs. Here, now."

Tristan knew she'd only have one chance. She moved to the back of the vehicle to lure him further away from Alys. When he got to her side and she was sure that he would not see her do it, she mouthed one word to her. *RUN.* She saw Alys tighten and purse her lips in reaction. Fear and reluctance flashed across her eyes. Tristan nodded imperceptibly before she forced herself to look away. She had a job to do now.

"Don't you dare fucking move," Erik warned as he placed himself behind her.

"You know, I'm kinda beat," she replied. He was nervous. Didn't trust her. *Excellent.*

"Not as good as you thought, uh?"

She dropped her head in pretend surrender. He'd need both hands to cuff her. She was so wired that she heard the sound of the fabric against the gun as he slid it back into his jeans. She did not resist when he pulled her left arm behind her back. He was not agile with the cuffs and fumbled a bit. She felt the cold metal around her wrist. Sure enough, he was using both hands. It was now or never.

"RUN!" she screamed, and jerked her head back violently.

Her skull was already killing so she figured one more hit would not make much of a difference. Tristan was pleased at the sound of crunching bone that followed; his nose, she knew. She spun around, did not linger on the sight of blood running down his face. *Join the club.* So long as he was still standing, she was not done. She swung a hard right, which he managed to block, but not the clever kick that followed. As the air whooshed out of his lungs, he staggered back one step. Still not done, Tristan did not pause to think or even breathe. Moving forward as well, she grabbed him by the shoulders and lifted her knee into his face.

Another good smash, although he gripped her hips and swiped her legs out from under her. He fell on top. Heavy son of a bitch! Her vision blurred. She could not avoid another fist in the face. *Fuck!* She reminded herself that he was good in training, but she was still better. Faster, too. Of course, she was not weak from blood loss and a concussion when they were sparring in the gym. *Don't you dare give up. Do it for Alys.* Tristan thought of her. And Jake. Rage would keep her going when her body would let her down.

"Fucking bitch," Erik barked.

He looked more animal than human, with crazy eyes and foaming at the mouth. As he tried to wrap both hands around her throat, she sank her teeth into the fleshy part between his thumb and index finger. That got him howling, and she seized the opportunity to plant both feet over his chest. She pushed him off. The gun fell from his jeans and slid under the car. They both lunged for it at the same time.

CHAPTER 34

Alys did run when Tristan pounced, but only to the garden shed to grab herself anything that may be used as a weapon to defend her. Armed with a shovel, she spotted Miller and Quinn Wesley approaching on foot from the front gate. *Oh, thank you God...* She screamed, and they came running.

"It's Erik!" Alys panted. "They're fighting! Tristan—"

A single gunshot exploded across the night, making them all jump. Alys faltered, legs feeling like cotton suddenly, mind blank, her startled eyes hooked on Miller's. *Tristan. No. Please no!* Miller did not wait. Quick as lightning, the detective took off at a dead run, weapon drawn. Quinn caught her by the wrist before Alys could follow.

"Stay behind me," she ordered, eyes flashing. "Let's go!"

Tristan and Erik were still on the ground. Still thrashing for advantage. So tangled in each other that it was impossible to see at a distance who was doing what, or in possession of the gun.

"Miller," Quinn barked, still running.

"Gotcha," Miller answered, and she yelled. "Police! Freeze! Drop your weapon!"

From the sideline, heart in her mouth, Alys watched Quinn jump onto her cousin's back and punch him twice in the head. Hard.

"Let go, you asshole!"

A third punch did the trick, and she rolled him off Tristan.

"Don't move!" From the front, Miller pointed her gun at his flushed and snarling face. "Stay still or I won't hesitate to shoot you."

Straddling his body, Quinn yanked his arms back without any regard for his protests. Unlike Erik, she knew how to secure someone in handcuffs the right way. In the blink of an eye, she had him restrained and neutralized.

"Stay down." She patted his shoulder. "Good boy."

He shot her a murderous glance as she stood up.

"She assaulted me. Briggs. She—"

"Shut up," Miller instructed. "Erik Huxley, you are under arrest. You have the right to remain silent. Anything you say can and will be used against you in a court of law…"

"Bitch!" Erik spat.

Alys could barely recognize him. Miller calmly continued to inform him of his rights, without paying the slightest attention to his insults.

"Alys! Al!"

He called to her, of course, but Alys did not stop. Later, she would. She would talk to him and attempt to make sense of this nightmare. But later. Right now, only one person in the world mattered to her. She raced ahead of Quinn to Tristan, who was on her hands and knees in front of the Rover, struggling to get back on her feet.

"Tristan!" Alys grabbed hold of her and peered frantically into her face. "Are you okay? Tris?"

Just behind her, Quinn was issuing rapid orders to someone on her phone. Something about backup and medical assistance. It was all a faint buzz on a background of racing heart and rapid breathing; her own, Alys realized. And it was all fear. *There was a shot fired...*

"Tristan," she repeated. Her lover had blood on her face, on the side of her neck. She couldn't tell where it came from. "Baby, are you—"

"I'm fine," Tristan answered roughly. Eyes burning fierce, she reached for her with two strong hands. "It's okay, Alys. Are you alright?"

"Yes, yes!"

"Are you sure?"

"Yes, don't worry about me."

"Erik?" Tristan glanced at Quinn.

"We've got him, Briggs. You can stand down."

"Where's my gun?"

"Got it too." Quinn released the mag and racked the slide on it as she spoke.

As Tristan met her gaze again, green eyes almost black from tension, Alys could feel it coursing violently through her body. Tristan was vibrating with it still, adrenalin pouring out of her in waves.

"It's over," she whispered gently to her, her eyes swimming with tears of relief. "It's over."

"Kiss me," Tristan groaned.

Alys would have, whether she asked for it or not. With both hands framing her face, she pressed her lips over her mouth to reassure them both of the reality of the other's presence. Tristan pulled back first. She stared into her eyes, as if to double-check that she was fine, and touched a soft finger to her busted lip.

"Does this hurt?"

"Not when I kiss you."

"Good."

As sirens echoed into the distance, Tristan breathed in deep and released a stronger exhale. Now that she was calming down, Alys suspected that the pain would kick in.

"Where's that ambulance?" she asked when she noticed her eyes glazing over. "Sit down, Tris. I've got you."

"Coming right up," Quinn confirmed. "One minute."

"S'okay," Tristan said thickly. "It just grazed me."

"What, babe?"

"The bullet," Tristan replied with a bit more difficulty. "Just took a slice off."

There was a shot fired... Alys glanced down with another jolt of apprehension. For the first time, she noticed an additional tear on Tristan's t-shirt, just under her left breast, and a dark circle of blood spreading quickly around the material.

"Oh my God... Tris!"

"It's nothing," Tristan insisted.

But *'nothing'* did not bleed like that... Alys lifted her t-shirt and immediately felt sick to her stomach at the sight of another fresh wound. Her lover's beautiful flesh was marred by a gaping gash that oozed blood with every shuddering breath that Tristan took.

"He shot you!" she exclaimed, eyes wide in horror.

"Grazed," Tristan maintained. "Fought him for the gun... I won. Don't worry..."

I'm not worried, Alys wanted to scream, *I'm fucking terrified!*

"The medics are here, Ms. Huxley," Quinn announced, and she squeezed her shoulder in reassurance. "Tristan's right, this is just a flesh wound. She's going to be okay."

"Trust her," Tristan chuckled weakly. "The woman knows."

Damn if Wesley didn't laugh at that, causing Alys to stare in disbelief. Was that cop's humor? If it was, she wasn't sure that she liked it. She stayed close as two EMTs carrying trauma kit bags arrived on scene and busied themselves around Tristan. It was confirmed that the gunshot wound was a *'bleeder'*, but not life-threatening. The head injury was a bit trickier to assess and would require a CT scan, but the medics were optimistic that pain killers and rest would lead to a prompt recovery. Catching her anxious gaze, Tristan flashed her a drunken grin that made Alys's heart swell.

"Told you," she slurred. "Iss' all good... I love you."

••

Angie looked up from her frothy Latte at the familiar rumble of Tristan's bike. She watched her pull into the parking lot of their usual meeting place. Same café, same motorbike, same woman. But there was a new sparkle in Tristan's eyes. She looked rested for a change, instead of like a woman who simply ran on nerves and regrets, and she was quick to smile when she took off her helmet and joined her on the terrace.

"You are looking extremely well for somebody who just got shot," Angie remarked in satisfaction.

"Hey, that was three months ago, Ange." Tristan grabbed a seat, raked fingers through her growing black hair, and flashed her a teasing wink. "I've been to Australia since then, remember? And New Zealand. Keep up."

"Yes, indeed," Angie chuckled. "My apologies. How was it all for you?"

"10/10. Surfers Paradise lived up to its name."

"Great. And how is your client?"

Tristan appeared momentarily confused before nodding.

"Oh. Alys."

"Mm-mmm," Angie smiled knowingly.

"She's great. Fine. She's very fine."

"Think you can blush any harder?"

"Nope," Tristan grinned, but of course, she did exactly that. Signaling to a passing waiter for a diversion, she ordered herself a fresh mango and kiwi juice and crossed a blue-jeaned leg at the ankle. "So. I need to tell you something."

"Yes?" Angie encouraged.

"I got fired."

She delivered the news with another luminous smile which prompted her former boss to laugh at her obvious delight.

"You mean promoted?" she queried. "From security officer to regular partner?"

"You got it."

"That's awesome, Tristan. Really great for you and Alys. I guess it was worth taking a risk in the end, uh? And breaking a few rules along the way."

"A million times. I'm still on the job, of course." A familiar layer of seriousness swept over Tristan's tanned features. "Only this time it's unofficially, and there's no longer a specific threat."

"More great news. How is Erik Huxley doing?"

"Well... Struggling. Not so good. I know the man shot me, but I do feel sorry for him."

"Really?"

"Yeah, sure." Tristan shrugged. "Turns out he's mentally ill, not evil. Some weird mental thing got a hold of him. That's sad. I just wish I'd figured it out a lot sooner, you know? Spared Alys some trauma."

"I see… But you're okay with this, yes?"

Tristan caught her cautious glance and she shook her head.

"Yes, I'm fine." She paused briefly. "I got the job done."

There was no, *'I didn't fuck up this time'*. No mention of the mistake that she thought she had made with Jake, and the guilt that almost destroyed her. No reference to the past at all, in fact. She was healing, finally, and Angie could not have been more pleased.

"Yes, you got the job done," she repeated, and squeezed her arm. "Totally."

"Miller was beating herself up for getting it wrong twice," Tristan added. "And for pursuing false leads. She thought that Wright may be our stalker, but he checked out clear. Which, by the way, is a huge relief."

"Miller's a good cop."

"Yes, she is. It was a hard one to figure out, that's all."

"And is Alys still not pressing any charges? Are you?"

"No, we won't be doing that." Tristan smiled again, eyes sparkling with pride and affection. "No matter what happens, Alys does take care of her people. She's got Erik a place at a top mental institution, with very good doctors. Miller went through his laptop after he was arrested and turned up some useful stuff. Six months ago, he started googling topics like split personality disorder and schizophrenia. He must have realized something was wrong…"

"And no one suspected anything? Not even Alys?"

"In retrospect, she and a few others said that they thought Erik acted strange at times. But it wasn't consistent, so they just forgot about it. Whatever he suffers from did get the best of him in the end. His father struggled with bipolar disorder. He killed himself when Erik was three. It could be genetic."

"I hope the doctors manage to figure it out for him."

"Yes, me too. Erik has a good guy side to him. I saw that, I know for sure that he wasn't pretending all the time. I hope that with enough care and the right therapy, he'll recover that part of himself."

"Do you think he'll ever be well enough to be released?"

"It's hard to say… But again, I do hope so. In the meantime, Alys will make sure that he has all the support he needs."

"The woman sounds pretty awesome."

"Yeah…"

Angie nodded in approval and amusement when all Tristan could manage was that one word, and the goofiest smile she had ever seen on her handsome face. Head over heels in love did not even begin to describe it.

"I think you'll be pleased to know that I've received several requests to provide security for some of Huxley's friends in the showbiz world," she added. "This sort of endorsement is exactly what Dagger Inc. needed at this time."

"Ah, perfect. Alys said she'd spread the word that she had a superior experience with Dagger."

"Superior, eh? Fancy that."

"Apparently so." Tristan smirked. "In every way."

"Well, thank you for going above and beyond and being such a wonderful ambassador."

"My pleasure."

"Yeah, I'll bet."

"Do I still get bonus pay?"

"Nope, but I can buy you a muffin if you like?"

"Blueberry with sugar glaze on top?"

"I guess I could push to that."

"Alright! Deal."

They both laughed.

"So, what's the plan for you two next?" Angie inquired.

"You know what…" Tristan smiled, green eyes sparkling in joyful anticipation. "I think that we'll just go with the flow for a while."

EPILOGUE

They took the Coast Road, riding south, chasing the warmth and the sunshine.

"I want to get feral with you, Tristan," Alys had declared a few days after the successful Australian tour, much to the horror of her manager, who happened to be present at the time. "Let's take a week off and have an adventure!"

Tristan was all for it. On the first night, they found a remote stretch of beach to camp at, out of the way of other would-be adventurers or prying eyes. Dinner consisted of two Wayfarer meals rehydrated in steel mugs on the Jet-Boil, and fresh fruit that they picked up at a small market along the way. When it grew dark, they snuggled inside their joined-up sleeping bags to admire the stars over the ocean.

"Ah..." Alys sighed. "This is the life!"

"Better than a luxury hotel on the Australian Gold Coast?" Tristan teased.

"Different, but I like both."

"You might change your mind when I begin to stink."

"I don't think so." Alys arched a mischievous eyebrow and looked at her with twinkling eyes. "It'll just be an excuse to book a room and get you nude in the shower."

"Oh, yeah," Tristan chuckled. "There is that. Good point."

Alys lingered, clear eyes shifting to cool blue. Tristan stole a light-hearted kiss from her lips.

"What's on your mind, Ms. Huxley?"

Alys asked her point-blank.

"You took a bullet for me, Tris. Didn't you?"

Tristan let out a careful breath. They had not discussed how she'd come to be injured since the night of the shooting. Not in any detail, anyway. And she'd kind of assumed that Alys would forget about it. Foolish assumption, obviously.

"Not exactly," she started to explain. To lie, really. "I—"

"No, don't say it," Alys whispered. She kissed her deep and hard, possessively, before pulling back to translate the message into words. "Thank you for keeping me safe. And don't ever do it again. I love you so much!"

"I love you too, Alys."

"You'll be careful, won't you? When you go back to being a cop?"

Now, then... Although Tristan had never tried to keep this a secret, it was apparently no longer just a quiet consideration in her own head.

"How do you know I was thinking about that?"

Alys lifted an ironic eyebrow, rock-goddess style, as if again Tristan should know better.

"You and Quinn spent a long time whispering to each other during the barbecue at Katie's house last weekend. Like two kids planning forbidden stuff. So, is it just thinking about it for now?"

"Yes. Quinn is very keen, but I—"

"I think you should do it."

A charge of naked excitement rippled through Tristan, but she ignored it.

"I already have a job, Ms. Huxley."

"You got fired, beautiful."

"Alys," Tristan frowned. "You know you need security."

"And I'm sure your friend Angie will get me someone else we'll both approve of. But you," Alys went on, locking a snug arm around her neck, "are way too good to carry on working as my bodyguard."

Tristan allowed a little bit of excitement to trickle back.

"Quinn has gathered a great crew of people," she reflected. "They handle all major crime cases in Lewiston and the greater area. Homicide, fraud…"

"Such fun," Alys deadpanned.

"Well." Tristan grinned. "Just to say that they're making a real difference out there."

"And she wants you on the team."

"Yes, she does."

"Clever woman. No undercover stuff?"

"No, I won't be doing that again."

"Then go for it, babe. You know you're a cop through and through. Always were. Don't waste your time and skills hanging backstage waiting for me."

The thought of getting back her shield and the job that she had always loved brought tears to Tristan's eyes. She thought of Jake, and what he might have to say about this. His smiling face floated across her mind. *Damn, Briggs! Finally!* Tristan wrapped her arms around her lover. She kissed the side of her neck, her jaw, cheeks, eyelids.

"Are you sure?"

"Hundred percent. Take the job, Tristan."

"I'll talk to Angie about a replacement for you as soon as we get back."

"Alright."

"Promise me you'll let them do their job and protect you the way that they see fit."

"If you promise to be careful on the streets of Lewiston and stay away from flying bullets."

"I promise."

"Me too."

"Damn." Tristan chuckled. "I'm so happy, I'm shaking!"

"I like it," Alys reflected with a dazzling smile. "Very sexy. One more thing, though, before I drag you inside the tent and make you shake a whole lot more."

"Can't wait. What's the thing?"

Alys fixed her with fierce and tender eyes.

"Marry me, Tristan. Let's do it this week."

"On the road? A feral wedding?"

"Oh, yeah! Great!" Alys laughed. "Perfect title for a song, this. I'm going to write one about us."

"I hope so, Ms. Huxley." Tristan smiled, trembling again for all the right reasons. "You'll always be my easiest *Yes*."

DID YOU ENJOY THIS?

CHECK OUT MORE TITLES!
www.nataliedebrabandere.com

Thank You
for
Reading and Reviewing!

Printed in Great Britain
by Amazon

34886805R00169